Blood Bound

Blood Bound

BERRING COLLEGE
BOOK TWO

KAYLA BROOKS

For Dad, Dadoo, The Father. I bet you never expected to have a gay vampire romance dedicated to you as a birthday present, but here it is. Thanks for always loving and supporting the wacky daughter you got instead of trying to make me into someone else. Love. Always.

A Note About Content

A NOTE ABOUT CONTENT

Dear reader,

Blood Bound contains adult themes and events that are not suitable for all readers. You can find a full list of content warnings here: https://kaylabrooksauthor.com/content-warnings

Please be aware of your own needs and take care of yourself as you see fit. I promise, if some aspect of this book is just not for you, or not healthy for you to read at the moment, I will not be hurt by you taking care of yourself and giving it a pass. Life is hard enough without us forcing ourselves to read things that make us unhappy.

I want to note that one of the characters in this story partakes in behavior akin to disordered eating. There is no discussion of food or diet as it pertains to size or weight, but there is discussion of food restriction in the context of self-harm.

If you believe I've missed something, please let me know directly through email at Kayla@kaylabrooksauthor.com so I can fix it. I will always want to know what I can do to make your experience with my books better!

Sincerely,
Kayla Brooks

Chapter One

DEVON - PRESENT

"I put all of your hats right on top of the dresser so they'll be easy to find without looking." Mom wrings her hands while she talks, her eyes already searching for something else to do.

"Yep. I can see them." I work hard to not roll my eyes, but I can't help the annoyance that creeps into my voice.

She's too busy worrying—panicking, more like—to notice it, though. "And you're going to remember them, right? Every single time. No exceptions and no excuses."

I bring her in for a hug. I know she means well, and it's coming from a place of love and all that, but I am just about out of patience and going to say something we'll all regret if she doesn't let up soon.

Dad saves me with a heavy pat on the back.

"We should probably give him some air, honey. We don't want his new roommates walking in on us getting all mushy and then teasing him all year, right?"

Trust Dad to make it seem like I'm a little kid in danger of being bullied rather than an eighteen-year-old moving into a college dorm.

"Oh, you're probably right." My mom's voice is suspiciously watery as she pulls back from the hug. "But you promise you'll wear your hats? And call if you need anything at all? We are not too far away to come and get you if you need us."

I grind my teeth behind a smile. "I promise to wear the hats. I've got your number. I know where you live. I love you. I'm going to be okay."

The thing is, I get where they're coming from. Mom wasn't always like this, but then I made her into the mess of tears and anxiety currently standing before me. This is all my own damn fault, so I just need to suck it up and deal with the consequences of my actions. But at the same time, this is probably the worst part of becoming a vampire. Sure, the sun sensitivity and inability to taste most of the food I used to love are pretty sucky, but the extra grey hairs I've noticed on my dad's head and the worry in my mom's eyes—and the way they both tend to treat me like some terribly fragile, already broken thing—are way worse than the physical changes.

"Okay, okay. We'll go away and let you get started with unpacking. Just one more hug to get me through the next few weeks."

I oblige without argument, though I do send up a silent prayer that they manage to stay away for more than my first three weeks of college.

Then Dad is pulling me in for a hug that would squeeze all the air out of me if that was still an issue. "I snuck a box of condoms into your sock drawer so you can stay safe," he whispers gruffly in my ear before breaking away and leading Mom away.

Good thing my blood doesn't work the same way it did

when I was human, or I would be blushing firetruck red right now.

And, just like that, I'm on my own to start putting things away and get settled in my dorm.

In the past few months, I came out, became a vampire, and moved away to college.

This will be just like all of the other changes in my life, I remind myself. It will take some adjustment, but I'll survive it.

MARCUS - PRESENT

I clamp my fingers down on my knee to keep from fidgeting, or tapping, or giving away any of the everything that I'm feeling right now. "So, I guess this is it," I say to the empty space between my mother and me.

"It's not too late to change your mind," she tells me without shifting from her position, perched on the edge of her seat and staring straight ahead. Like a royal expecting the paparazzi to spring out at any moment and try to catch her doing something improper.

As if they could see her at all through the tinted windows of our car.

I guess that's what her non-life has done to her. It's turned her into this frozen, perfect thing. I've never known her as anything other than ice-cold and hard as glass, but sometimes I try to imagine what she was like before she became the queen of ice. By definition, she was softer and warmer as a human, but I've never been able to picture her as anything other than vampiric perfection. This has been her since I was born.

I give up on waiting for some kind of loving response from her—I should know better by now that she just doesn't have that kind of emotion to throw around—and reach for the door.

"Wait," she calls me back with just one small sound. "Don't forget your hat."

I jam the cap down over my eyes and escape the car before I can let myself be hurt any more.

* * *

I hurry into the building before the sun can become an issue, not looking back to check if the movers my mom hired are following or not. They'll figure it out one way or another. And I need to worry about myself, not them.

I find the correct line to check in and settle in to wait, but a timid tap on my shoulder reveals a nervous-looking vampire. Probably within a few years of my age, I decide, since he doesn't have the musty smell that vampires sometimes develop after half a century or so.

"Mr. Levine?"

His nervous blinking grates my nerves, but what good will it do to let him know that?

"Yeah, that's me."

"I've got you checked in already, if you'll just follow me. I can show you to your room."

Just what I need, someone acting like a servant and leading me to where I'm going to be living. Definitely the best way to make the right impression. Well, that's probably exactly what my father had in mind, come to think of it. He lost the battle about sending me directly to the family frat, but he can still try to control me in these other little ways.

"That won't be necessary," I tell him. "If you'll just give me the keys and the room number?"

His relief is almost embarrassing as he shoves a manila envelope in my hands and mutters a hurried, "Good luck with college," before he makes his escape.

And this is the kind of loyalty and pride that my father's brand of leadership invokes. At least I'm free to go to my dorm alone now.

My fingers shake a little as I unlock my door, but I tell myself it's okay because there's no one here to see. It's understandable to feel some nerves in a situation like this, right? Not that my father or any of his minions would accept that kind of excuse if they were here to see me.

I work to clamp down on my self-control. That's part of what this is all about, after all. I don't think he would have let me do this at all if he thought I was actually ready to start following in his footsteps. My stomach flips at just the thought of that.

Four years, I remind myself. I've got four years to get this figured out so I can do my duty.

The shared living room of the suite is already furnished with someone's belongings in the process of being unpacked. A huge TV sits unplugged in front of the couch. A coffeepot, also unplugged, sits on top of the tiny counter space that supposedly serves as a kitchen.

"Hey! Roommate!" a guy shouts cheerfully as he steps out of a bedroom.

My mouth dries up like a desert when I see him.

Almost my height. Maybe an inch or two shorter. And bright red hair and a face full of freckles that make him look more alive than any vampire has a right to. But the clincher is his wide grin and sparkling eyes. Topaz, I think. No, tiger's eye.

Shit.

I catch the direction my thoughts are taking and bite down hard on my tongue to bring myself back to reality.

I don't live a life that allows me to notice guys' eyes or freckles or anything else. I need to shut this down fast.

And that's when I realize I'm just standing there awkwardly and biting my tongue almost to the point of bleeding and not speaking, and his smile is slipping and . . .

"Right. Um. Yes. Roommate." *Come on*, I beg myself. *Get it together.* "Marcus. That's me, I mean."

His smile returns full force, and I'm able to loosen some of the tension in my shoulders.

"I'm Devon. I hope it's alright that I started unloading some stuff out here. I figured, since I got here first, I'd set up my TV and stuff out here. But if someone else wants their TV out here, that's no big deal. I can move mine into my room. Same thing with the coffeepot. And gaming consoles. I mean, if any of the roommates don't want them out here for some reason. I'm easy. Or . . . Shit, I'm kind of babbling, aren't I?"

The babbling was good, from my standpoint. It meant he wasn't expecting me to contribute anything. Now, we're back to me doing the awkward, silent staring thing again.

"It's fine with me," I finally choke out from my dust-dry mouth. "I like coffee."

Right then—oh joy—is when the door opens, and my movers start bringing in boxes.

"Mr. Levine?" The oldest, baldest of the movers addresses me. "Which room are these headed to?"

"I . . . ummm . . ." I avoid looking Devon in the eyes, but I also need to get over my embarrassment at being the guy who hires movers to move into a dorm. "Does it matter which room I take?"

Devon shrugs like this is normal—for which I am eternally grateful—and points toward his door. "I'm in there. As far as I know, none of the other rooms are claimed. I say choose whichever room you want."

Wanting this whole thing over with as soon as possible, I point to the door next to Devon's. "That one's fine. Everything can go in there."

* * *

DEVON - PRESENT

Things I've learned about roommate number one:

He's hot. Like in a dark fantasy where the vampire king lures unsuspecting innocents to his dungeon and has his way with them type hot. Like too beautiful to be true paired with brooding eyes that just might be hiding a painful secret past type hot. Like I'm going to be taking cold showers all year to keep myself from doing something incredibly stupid type hot.

Also, he's rich. Unless having minions to move all of his stuff for him is some kind of show he's putting on, he's way wealthier than me. I have no idea why a hot, rich vampire is rooming with me instead of with the other hot, rich vampires, but you won't catch me complaining.

Things I already know about myself:

Hooking up with my roommate is a terrible idea.

I get myself into trouble when I think with my dick.

This seems like a risk I'm willing to take.

Shit. No. Bad. Think with your brain, dumbass.

"Want to help me get all of this set up?" I ask, waving at the mess of TV, gaming consoles, and wires I had started pulling from boxes before he showed up.

Marcus jerks a nod of agreement and sits on the floor to get started.

If he's hoping to put me off with the man-of-few-words thing, he's going to be disappointed. My mouth practically waters from thinking up ways to get him talking.

And reminding myself again that hooking up with my roommate would be a terrible idea doesn't put the slightest damper on those thoughts.

"Are you from around here?" I try to kick off some normal conversation.

"No," he answers with a grunt and then continues silently sorting out electronics.

Be still my dead, barely beating heart. He must know I like a challenge.

"Oh? Did you have a long drive, then?"

"Just from the airport."

I almost pump my fist in the air. Four words and some actual information.

"Nice. So you flew in?"

And so the conversation continues. Me carrying most of the actual speaking parts. Him averting his eyes and answering my questions in five syllables or less. Both of us ignoring his minions as they move what seems like an apartment's worth of stuff into what I know is a smaller-than-average-sized bedroom. Once the entertainment center is set up, we move on to the kitchen.

"I hope I'm not the only coffee drinker," I babble, needing a break from trying to think up questions for a little while. "It's one of the few things I feel like I can still taste since, well, you know."

Marcus's head jerks up in surprise. "You mean you're newly turned?"

Oh shit. In my attempt to make conversation, I've gone more intimate than most people are comfortable with on a first meeting. "Uh. Yeah. Less than a year ago, actually. There's still a lot I'm kind of figuring out as I go. You?" I've been told countless times that it isn't really polite to ask, but he brought it up first, right?

"No," he mumbles, back to looking anywhere but at me. "I mean, I'm not . . . I wasn't turned."

"Oh. Right. I shouldn't have assumed anything."

So that's another thing I've learned about my roommate. He's hereditary, born as a vampire, so he won't have any memories of being human. He won't have any experience of what it's like to transition from living to dead.

And now, shit is awkward between us, which is a good

reminder of why vampires tend to steer clear of these kinds of conversations whenever possible.

Marcus is the one to break the silence, for the first time since he came into the dorm. "You're definitely not the only coffee drinker, though," he assures me. "I pretty much can't function without at least one cup, so . . . you won't be alone in that . . . I guess."

An image of the two of us, naked and snuggled together in bed, both with a coffee in hand, flashes through my mind.

Nope, I tell myself. *That is a terrible, bad, dangerous thought to have.*

Telling myself that doesn't stop the fantasy from playing on repeat for the rest of the day.

Chapter Two

MARCUS - EIGHT YEARS AGO

"Let's see how long it takes for daddy to find you in here," Vincent's voice sneers before I find myself shoved into the storage room.

I jump back to slam against the door as soon as they let me go, but it's too late. The door is already locked, my tormentors snickering as they escape to the hallway. I pound my frustration against the closed door, but I know there's no point. No one is coming back to this room until morning classes. Just in case, I test the light switch. Dead. Of course. I sink to the floor and settle in to wait for morning. It's not the first time I've been caught like this. It won't be the last.

The night passes as slowly as I expect it to. I manage to sleep, curled up on the hard floor, for a few minutes at a time, but the rustling of rats and roaches in the walls keeps me awake most of the night. When I hear movement on the other side of the door and pound to get their attention, Mr. Hopwell opens the door with a pitying rather than surprised look.

"Better get cleaned up before anyone can miss you at breakfast" is all he says.

* * *

My appearance at breakfast is met with studious avoidance from most of my classmates and wicked snickers from Vincent and his friends that shoved me in the closet.

I stand as tall as I can to make the trek across the mess hall to pick up my blood bag and a cup of coffee for breakfast. Supposedly, it wasn't that long ago that a host of live human blood donors lived on campus to feed the students. That wouldn't exactly work with modern public relations, though. Vampires have been trying to improve their public perception, so sterile blood bags have replaced live blood supply pretty much everywhere.

"Levine!" The headmaster's voice rings out over the breakfast sounds, and I duck my head instinctively before realizing he's glaring right at me.

I stand slowly and face him. "Yes, sir?"

"Visitor for you." He turns and walks away without further explanation, assuming I'll follow.

Of course I follow. The bullies in my class can make my life miserable, but the headmaster can destroy me. He plays poker with my father more often than I see the man.

The first thing I see is a giant hat taking up about half of the headmaster's office. I have no idea who it could be. My father never visits. Mother visits on the prescheduled visitors' days.

"Darling!"

I've never seen the woman who's beaming at me from under her gigantic hat in my life, but I'm not going to let that slip until I know where I stand with her.

"I know it's short notice, but I'm in town just for today,

and there is not a chance in the world I'm going to miss taking my little brother out when I have the chance!"

Headmaster's face looks more pinched with every word she says.

"Really, Miss Levine," he says the moment she gives him space to speak. "The boys here benefit from the high amount of structure in their schedules. I don't think it's wise to take—"

She silences him with a wave of her hand and a look, cementing her place as my current favorite person in the world. If she says I'm her brother, fine, I'll take it. I know that I have siblings, but no one wants me to meet them. Maybe this is why.

"I'm sorry, Headmaster, I simply can't take no for an answer today. I'll be taking Marcus with me, unless he doesn't want to go, and you really can't stop me."

She turns to me expectantly, and my mind whirs, trying to figure out what she's waiting for.

"Oh, um, yes," I finally say. "I'd like to go." Anything to get away from this school and my horrible classmates and the villainous headmaster, even if just for a few hours. Hell, I'd take a few minutes reprieve, I'm that desperate.

"Perfect! We'll be off, then!"

The headmaster puffs up like he's about to argue, then deflates just as quickly, maybe realizing that I'm not worth his attention. "Curfew is eight o'clock, strictly enforced," he grumbles at his desk but makes no move to stop us as she sweeps us out of the room.

I wait until we're riding away from the school in a car with darkened windows before I ask any questions.

"Are you really my sister?"

She turns in her seat to grin at me before focusing back on the road. "I am. Your oldest sister, actually. You can call me Pris."

"Oh." I wish I could think of something clever or cool to say, since she seems like the epitome of clever and cool, but nothing is coming to mind.

"Thirty-seven," she says before I can think of any conversation starters.

"Thirty . . . huh?"

"I'm thirty-seven. Ten years older than your mother. And the oldest child of Magnus Levine–not that he advertises my connection with his name–who currently walks the Earth. Yes, this is my very own car that I'm driving. No, I don't have access to any of the Levine family money. Yes, I have a job. No, I don't keep in touch with our father. Um, let's see . . . what else is there . . ."

"Where are you taking me?"

"Oh!" She snaps her fingers in excitement. "We're going out so you can see how the other half lives."

"Other half?"

Pris–my sister, and that thought sends an excited lurch through my stomach–gives me another wide grin. "Maybe it's more accurate to say 'the other ninety-nine percent.' I'm guessing you haven't spent much time around humans or people who aren't paid by your father. Well, I think you're old enough now. My sisterly training officially begins today."

I feel like a whirlwind has blown through the car and I'm doing my best to hang onto it so I don't get tossed out on the pavement.

"I don't think I understand."

"Look. I've been keeping an eye on you since your mother's pregnancy was first announced. I thought, if you were a girl, you would need someone to look out for you. And if you were a boy, well, you would need someone to keep Magnus from completely destroying you in his quest to create the perfect heir."

I still don't really know where she's going with this, but

she seems to have a point she's trying to make, so I sit back and do my best to understand.

"You turned out to be a boy, and the presumptive heir to the Levine," she waves her hand carelessly, "blah blah blah, so I knew you would need some guidance if you're going to be worthy of taking on the mantle. So here I am, ready to show you what you've been missing."

Just getting me away from my oppressive life at school for a day is enough to get me on her side. If she says I've been missing something, I believe her. And if she's going to keep getting me out of school, I'll do just about anything for her.

Chapter Three

MARCUS - PRESENT

I am hiding. I should be way too old for this shit, but apparently not, because I'm closed off in my new bedroom while my new roommates sound like they're having a blast playing video games less than twenty feet from me.

It's not like they're missing me out there. I definitely wouldn't be adding to the fun. Jeff—so human and friendly I have no idea how to act around him—turned up about five minutes after Devon and I got the coffee maker organized. He took all of half an hour to carry a few boxes and suitcases into his room and declare himself moved in and ready to start in on the video games.

I managed a few rounds. Long enough to meet the final roommate, a blond wolf shifter named Jimmy, who turned up with a single backpack and a large duffle bag slung over his shoulder and absolutely nothing else. How does anyone live like that? But by then, I had officially run out of energy for being social.

The problem is, I don't have anywhere else to be or anything else to do. Hence, hiding in my room while my roommates play some kind of bunny death match game.

"Suck it, losers!" one of them shouts.

Probably over something video game related. That doesn't stop my brain from zooming to somewhere completely unrelated to the killer bunny video game.

Is there really any harm in indulging? I start to ask myself but thankfully catch myself in time before I have to work too hard to bring myself back. How could I forget what's at stake for even a moment?

I'm weak as fuck, that's how.

Needing to remind myself of how important this is, I grab my phone and call the second most used contact in my contacts list.

"You better have dialed my number by accident because it's too soon for you to be calling me on purpose," Priscilla answers with a lazy drawl.

"I know," I mumble into my phone. "I am completely worthless and pathetic, and I need you."

"Well, shit." I can hear movement over the phone and imagine her sitting up so she can actually pay attention to me. "What's up, kiddo?"

"I wish you'd stop calling me that."

"Tough. Even your mom is younger than me. You are and always will be a baby in my eyes and therefore will always be 'kiddo' to me. What's going on?"

I scowl at her, knowing that she can't see it, and am thankful for that fact. "What am I doing here again? I already don't fit in and I feel like I'm just going to fuck everything up anyway and it won't do any good and I'm going to end up—"

"Like me?" she cuts in.

"No, not like—" I think it through for a moment. Pris has had to fight for every single good thing in her life. She didn't have anyone to pay for her education, or provide her with easy blood, or put in a good word for her first job. "Well, actually, yes. No offense?"

Pris chuckles. "Believe it or not, little brother, I really get where you're coming from. I probably wouldn't want to have ended up like me if I'd had any other option. So, do you want the pep talk about how you do have options and should do what it takes to take advantage of them or the pep talk about how it isn't actually that bad to be the biggest loser of all the vampires?"

I groan. "That first one, please." I can't even think all the way about what would happen if I changed course at this point. It wouldn't be pretty.

I'm not that worried about what would happen to me. At least, I like to think I could survive without everything my father provides. My mother, though, would be in for more suffering than I'm willing to cause her.

"Okay then. One pep talk coming right up. You are smart and rich and powerful and born into a world of privilege that most people can't even begin to imagine. And if you fuck all of that up and lose everything because it's hard to make friends at college, I will hunt you down and decapitate you in your sleep. So don't fuck this up."

"Thanks, Pris," I sigh. Maybe it's not the most conventional sibling relationship, but she does get me, and she's always willing to help. That's a lot more than I can say about any of my other siblings.

* * *

I wake up to so many sounds of life outside my door. And coffee smells. And a few hours of sleep have apparently erased my half sister's lecture from my memory because I want to go out there and hang with the guys more than anything else in the world.

It's just a little bit of socialization. With people I'm already living with, no less. Surely, there's no harm in me leaving my room and getting to know the guys I'm sharing a dorm with.

I gulp down a bag of blood from the minifridge beside my bed so my roommates don't have to witness me eating. And also so they don't have to experience me being hangry. It's too early in the year for the warmbloods to be introduced to the darker side of their vampire roommates.

"Marcus! Grab a controller!" Jeff shouts as soon as I leave my room.

I recoil internally at the thought of embarrassing myself with how terrible I am at video games. "No, thanks," I tell him. "You go ahead." *Great job, Marcus. You're already doing a great job of making friends and winning people over.* And while I'm thinking of it, why did I get fully dressed in slacks and a button-up shirt? Looking around, my roommates are all in some form of pajamas, underwear, or bathrobes. Not only am I overdressed, but I'm the only one who's actually dressed.

My stomach gives an uncomfortable flip. Maybe I should have just stayed in my room after all. Too late to turn back now, so I settle in to watch and try not to make too much of a fool of myself. It's awkward at first, but the fist of anxiety in my chest starts to unclench, one finger at a time. Our collective switch from coffee to beer plays a part. Eventually, the guys even convince me to play a bit. I'm terrible, but it's nice to be a part of things.

"Were you all planning to eat any food with all this beer?" I ask them once I've loosened up enough to join in the festivities.

The guys share a confused look around the room. "Do we even have food here?"

I snap to attention. This is actually an area I can add value to the dorm. Learning how to cook was one of my earliest rebellions. I can't actually eat the food I make, but I like the process of putting ingredients together. And it would make my father furious if he knew about it. Low stakes, but it makes me feel good to know that I'm rebelling. While my roommates are still debating ordering pizza, I'm assessing the options. There aren't a whole lot, but that just makes it an interesting challenge. There's a giant package of instant ramen that I set aside as having potential, and one of these guys apparently owns a hot plate, though they don't seem to remember it right now. That will come in handy. I won't have to go searching for a stove. Cooking is a bit like chemistry class. As long as you understand some basic principles, you can do just about anything. Moreover, anyone who doesn't understand those principles will think you've worked magic.

"I don't understand," Jeff says between shoveling stir-fry ramen into his mouth. "How did you manage to do this?"

I shrug and try to play it cool, but I'm pretty fucking pleased with myself. "You know. Salt, carbs, fat. Put them together, and it makes the human brain happy."

"Yeah, I mean, no. That's not what I'm talking about. How are you such an amazing cook? I thought vampires didn't, you know . . . eat this stuff." Jeff waves his fork at me. "Look at you. You're not even eating any of it. How do you know what it's supposed to taste like? How do you know what it actually tastes like? I can't wrap my head around you being able to put this together."

In some circles, saying that to a vampire would lead to that vampire literally taking your head off. I'm trying to get away from that type of vampire society, though, so I clamp down the snarky reply that springs to mind first. Jeff doesn't mean anything by it. I know he's not trying to be rude.

Devon surprises me by coming to my rescue. "Why would we eat human food? It tastes like shit to us, not to mention the stomachache it'll give you." He sniffs at Jeff's plate, then pulls a disgusted face.

"But," Jimmy gives a perplexed look between Devon and me, "if you can't eat any of this stuff, why do you know how to cook it?"

Okay, maybe I am running a little low on patience. "Do farmers not know how to feed their cows?" I ask in a flat voice, then immediately wish I could take it back. What's not a good way to make friends with my roommates? Compare them to cattle and imply I'm thinking of eating them is probably at the top of the list.

After a long moment of silence in which I beg the floor to swallow me whole, Jeff bursts out laughing, followed by everyone else.

"Good point!" he gasps through his laughter. "Maybe I should learn to cook too. I wouldn't want my future girlfriend to get hungry either!"

Jimmy grins around a mouthful of noodles. His face is so stuffed with food that his cheeks are puffed out like a chipmunk's. "Dude, I am not complaining. Whatever you did here, I'll be happy anytime you decide to do it again." He falls silent again, the better to noisily slurp up more noodles from his plate.

My dead heart gives a heavy attempt at a heartbeat. Maybe, just maybe, this is something I can have. Something for myself that my father can't ruin. I hardly dare to hope, but maybe if I'm careful, if I follow my father's other rules, if I don't get caught with any more guys–if I stay away from Devon–I can still have these friends, and it will all be okay.

Chapter Four

"Are you seriously not doing anything for your birthday?" Eli almost knocks me over as he pounces on my back while I stare blankly into my locker.

I snap back to attention and put on my Friend Face for him. "Dude, I'm turning eighteen. Isn't that a little old for me to have a birthday party?"

What I don't tell him is that I'm pretty sure none of my friends want to do the same things I want to do for my birthday. I've been planning this for weeks now, and there's no way in hell I'm letting any of my friends in on my plans. It's not that I think they would be disgusted with me or anything like that if they knew I've been questioning my sexuality. It's more like, this is something personal. I have to figure this out for myself, and what's the point of telling someone that I might feel attracted to guys if I've never even tested it? Okay, maybe "test" is the wrong way to think about this. I mean, I realized a long time ago that I have some kind of same-sex attraction.

I've come to grips with that. But I can't settle on how far that attraction goes. What if all this was ever meant to be was my dick perking up occasionally at the sight of an athletic guy doing athletic things? What if I try kissing a man and find it revolting? There's no point making a big fuss about this if it turns out I'm mostly straight and don't even belong in the queer community.

No. This is something I'm going to figure out on my own, and then, if there's anything to tell, I'll come out to people once I've figured it out.

"Devon? Earth to Devon." Eli snaps his fingers in front of my face. Shit. I guess I let the Friend Face slip while I was wallowing in my inner turmoil.

"Sorry. I'm here. I'm paying attention. But I'm not throwing a birthday party. It feels too juvenile."

He heaves a sigh and turns me to walk toward our next class. "Fine. I guess there will be other chances to party."

"Probably true."

"But I'm having a birthday party when my birthday comes, and you'd better not pull this shit about it being too juvenile. You'll come, and you'll like it."

My lips twitch, wanting to make the obvious joke about coming, but that might also be seen as juvenile.

* * *

I quadruple-checked that this club has an eighteen-and-over night every Thursday, but I'm still a nervous wreck as I wait to get in. I keep running through scenarios in my head. I get to the door and realize I've lost my wallet. I get to the door, and the bouncer tells me they're not letting anyone else in. I get to the door, and the bouncer gives my T-shirt and jeans one disgusted look before tossing me into the street. The thoughts spiral around and around until I'm finally standing at the door for real, where the bouncer gives my ID a cursory glance before waving me in.

Okay. Step one, check. I am in an honest-to-gods gay club, complete with the pulsing music and rainbow lighting to prove it.

What next?

Oh, right. Step two. I need to try and meet a guy.

With my heart pounding twice as fast as the music, I scan the room for candidates. Some are easy to discard. I don't want someone twice my age, nor do I want someone in an outfit made entirely out of leather straps and complicated buckles. I'm trying to dip my toes in tonight, not dive in head-first. No one jumps out at me right away, so I decide to get out on the dance floor and see what happens. Worst-case scenario, I don't find anyone to dance with, right?

It's easier to loosen up once I'm out there, surrounded by moving bodies. I might even be enjoying myself. About when I've lost my nerves and self-consciousness to the pounding beat, I feel a pair of strong, slender hands slide down my ribs and land on my hips. My body responds with a shiver of excitement. So, step two and step three are officially successful. Met a guy. Enjoyed being touched by him.

"What's your name?" His voice rumbling in my ear sends another shiver through me.

The evidence is definitely piling up. I spin to face him without breaking contact with his hands and am met by an absolute perfect specimen of a man. Definitely not a kid, his ice-grey eyes look like he probably knows secrets about things that I've never even imagined. Dark hair is perfectly styled to frame a pale, full-lipped face with just enough stubble that I catch myself wondering what it would feel like scraping against my inner thigh. There is an undeniable attraction here. On to step four.

"I'm Devon. Do you want to go somewhere we can talk a little easier?"

He answers by smiling and tangling our fingers together to lead me away to a quieter corner of the club. It is easier to talk here, and it's easy to talk to him. When he traces my arm with his fingertips, that feels easy too. Then, he's leaning in, and I'm leaning in, and our lips meet, and that's easy too.

Step four is a big fucking success, as far as I'm concerned. I'm not only attracted to him, but I feel like my body is lighting up under his touch. Seriously, fireworks wherever his fingers connect.

"We could go somewhere more private," he murmurs between neck kisses that leave me shaking.

"Yeah, sounds good." Again, easy.

He maneuvers me through a door, and I find my back pressed against a brick wall. His thigh pressing between my legs rubs against my hardening cock, and I groan into his mouth with need. We've blown past all of my wildest dreams of what might happen tonight, and he doesn't seem to be slowing down at all.

"I can't wait to hear the noises you make when I'm inside of you."

I've lost the ability to speak, so I just groan again. I wanted to see if being close to a man would be as good in real life as in my head, but I can't believe I'm about to find out. This is actually happening. I feel clumsy as I start to undo my fly, and I guess I'm too slow for him because he does it for me before turning me around and pressing me flat against the wall with his body.

My dick is hard enough now that I could probably break this brick wall with it if I wanted to.

"You want this, baby?" he whispers into my ear.

I whimper a yes. Because I do. I know I should be asking about protection. Having the adult conversation before I do this adult thing. But what if that makes him stop? I don't want him to stop.

Then he's pushing my jeans down and sliding a finger down my crack, and then he's inside of me, and it's all still so stupidly easy.

I don't realize there's anything wrong until he tears into my neck. I go from being consumed by feelings of pleasure and excitement to having my world narrow down to a dark tunnel of pain and fear. I'm distantly aware of my fingers scrambling against brick, trying to find purchase, and my feet trying to kick out but having nowhere to go with the powerful body pinning me to the wall. The light from the nearest street-lamp seems to hum in and out of existence, and I'm slumping to the ground, and there's come cooling and dripping down my leg and blood cooling and dripping down my neck, and I can't hear anything over the insect buzz that's started up in my ears.

Then, something disgusting is filling my mouth, gooey and metallic-tasting and lukewarm, and I hear his voice saying, "This was fun. We should do it again sometime," and the world drops away around me, leaving black and empty and pain.

* * *

Sound returns first, throbbing back into my brain with a sickening hum. Then light knifes into my skull with a sharp enough pain to make me cry out. Immediately, caressing hands are on me, offering comfort.

The sound coalesces into speech, but it takes me a while to parse through what's being said. Or who's speaking.

"Mom?" I croak out when I recognize her voice as part of the noise.

"Yes, sweetheart. I'm right here."

She sounds so worried. Like I've never heard her before. "Where am I?"

The comforting hands slow on my body, then redouble their work of smoothing away all of my pains and fears.

"I need you to stay calm, sweetheart. Your father went out to get the doctor. He'll explain everything better than we can."

"Doctor?"

She looks ten years older than when I saw her last. "The doctor will explain it better."

The door opens, stopping me from asking her any more questions, and my dad holds the door open while a man in a white coat strides in.

"Devon, it's good to see you awake," he says without actually looking up at me. He looks at a chart at the foot of the bed, then some kind of monitor beside me, but he doesn't seem interested in the person in the bed at all.

"This is Dr. Wilkins," my mom supplies. I manage some kind of grunt in response, which I'm pleased with, considering how overwhelmed I am and the splitting headache that's making me want to peel my own skull in half to get it out of my head. "He'll explain everything."

I look expectantly at Dr. Wilkins, but he's still checking whatever monitor is hooked up to me. Heart? It's not beeping like a heart monitor in a TV show, but TV heart monitors are the extent of my medical knowledge, so who knows.

Finally, the doctor turns to look at me. "Alright, Devon. First of all, how much do you remember from the other night?"

"I remember . . ." My eyes flick to my parents. Oh boy, this is going to be awkward. I guess I could ask them to leave, but it takes me about two seconds to realize that they've probably already heard the gory details of where I was and how I got there. My shame is already complete. Why try to hide it? "I met this guy . . . and we seemed to . . . um . . . hit it off." I almost can't feel the embarrassment through my headache. Almost.

The doctor saves me from having to say the rest. "Devon, a vampire—probably the guy you met at the club, but we can't be sure—drank your blood and exchanged enough bodily fluids with you to turn you into a vampire. You are currently still undergoing the change, which may take up to two more days before it is complete. We're monitoring you closely, but everything seems to be going as expected. That said, we do need to keep an eye on you in case of complications."

My mind is reeling. Yes, I remember the pain of the bite on my neck, and I definitely remember bodily fluids being exchanged, but I'm still playing catch-up trying to put all the pieces together.

Thankfully, my dad speaks up, because I have no idea what to say right now, but I'm pretty sure something needs to be said.

"What are the potential complications we're worried about?"

"The main concern is that we fuel the change with suffi-cient blood," the doctor answers, all business, like this is a totally normal conversation he has on a daily basis. "In the days before bagged blood and blood monitors, new vampires might rampage across the country in a feeding frenzy. These days, we have a better way of doing this." He taps the monitor beside me with a knowing smile. "This machine monitors your blood replacement levels, and this, of course, is where the blood is being replaced." He points to the hanging bag with a long tube attached to an IV in my arm. "Now that you're awake, we need to start having you feed normally, though."

"Feed . . . normally?" My voice comes out in a rasp, I'm so uncomfortable at the mere thought of what he's asking me to do.

Instead of answering, he unlocks a cabinet in the wall I

hadn't noticed before and pulls out a plastic bag, almost exactly like the one dripping into my IV, but this one has a nozzle almost like on a water bottle. He holds it up like a display for me and my parents to see. "From this point on, you need to think of blood as not just sustenance but medicine as well. Blood is life, quite literally, and going without can be extremely dangerous for you. Here." He hands me the bag. "It's designed so you can either open the nozzle and drink from there, or you can simply bite through the plastic and drink that way. In an emergency, you won't want to bother with the nozzle. Just do whatever's expedient to get the medicine into your body. For now, let's give the nozzle a try."

His smile is encouraging, so I follow his instructions. A slight twist opens it, and I bring the bag tentatively to my lips. I try not to think too hard about what I'm actually putting up to my lips. Blood. Real, human blood. Taken from someone who willingly gave it at a blood bank, I'm sure, but still.

The first mouthful hits my tongue, along with a surge of memories. The pleasure of being fucked, followed by the far worse pain of being bitten. The horror as I realized I was going to die in a dirty alley with a stranger's come dripping down my legs. My remorse at knowing that would be the last thing my parents would know about me, that I let myself get fucked, then killed in a dirty alley.

I immediately gag and spew the blood out of my mouth. The doctor doesn't seem surprised. In fact, he managed to get a bed pan under my chin in time to catch everything. This must happen a lot.

"Sometimes it takes a few tries to get the hang of it," he says. "I want you to give it another go now that you know what to expect."

I glance over to my parents. My dad has his eyes fixed on me. One of his hands is white-knuckled, gripping his knee, while the other is twisted through my mom's fingers. My mom has her other hand pressed against her mouth, and her eyes are shining with tears she's working hard to hold back. They both look so old, so frail, right now. I did this. I'm the one who fucked up, and they have to sit there looking old and sad and frail in a hospital room.

Determined to not put them through any more pain, I take the bag in my mouth again and force myself to swallow the vile contents past my gag reflex. I want to spit it out. I want to throw it up. I want to throw a tantrum and tear this fucking hospital room apart. But I manage to finish the bag because my parents don't need to have one more reason to worry about me.

"Good job, Devon." The doctor takes the bag and drops it into a biohazard trashcan. "I think you should try to sleep some more now. If you feel any hunger, press the call button, and we'll have you feed. If you don't press the button, we'll put you on an hourly feeding schedule whether you feel hunger or not. It will help to get you used to taking the blood bag. I'll be back to check on you in a bit."

Oh joy. I sink back in the hospital bed. I can't meet my parents' eyes, but I can't seem to close my eyes and rest, and there aren't that many things to look at in this little room.

"I guess . . . you want to know what I was doing there?" I finally ask, cautious, embarrassed, walking on eggshells because I don't want to cause them any more pain and I don't want to talk about it and I don't want them getting the wrong ideas. Not that there are any really "right" ideas for them to get.

"The doctor said you should try and rest," my dad says, barely above a whisper.

I don't want to rest. I don't think I can rest. Not with this conversation hanging over me.

I swallow and steel myself to just say it. My fingers are picking reflexively at the blanket that's on top of me. "I think

I'm bi," I blurt out. "I went there to, I don't know, test it out, I guess? I wanted to see if being with a guy was . . . the same . . . and I don't know any guys at school I could . . ." My throat is closing up, and it's harder to speak, but I have to get through this. "There was no one at school I could ask to try it out, so I went to that club, and I guess I got that answered, at least."

"Oh, Devon." I look up just in time to see my mom's face crumple into tears.

Dad puts an arm around her but looks torn between comforting her and saying something to me.

"I'm sorry." My voice cracks, and I swipe at the tears that are suddenly tracking down my cheeks. "It was so stupid, and I'm so sorry. It was just supposed to be one stupid night out. I'm so sorry."

Arms come around me, and a weight settles on the mattress beside me.

"Shhh," my dad whispers into my hair. "It's going to be okay. You rest now."

Mom settles on my other side, and her tears get my hospital gown wet while she and my dad rock me between them and let me cry it out. I know, down to my very soul, that nothing is ever going to be the same again. Maybe it will be okay, though. Eventually.

Chapter Five

MARCUS - PRESENT

I double check that only a blank wall is visible behind me from my computer's camera. The dorm is thankfully quiet. Not an accident, as I chose a time I thought all of my roommates would be in class. It's just easier if I don't have to ask them to be quiet. It's easier if I don't have to explain anything to them.

After tossing one last desperate prayer out to the universe, I square my shoulders and click the button to call my father.

He makes me wait, of course, and when his face does appear on my screen, his expression conveys that same mix of anger, disgust, and disappointment he always holds for me.

"My sources tell me you haven't moved to pledge yet."

Great. We're getting right into the reporting part of the meeting without any kind of preamble. I can't say I expected anything different.

"I'm still getting used to college life," I say, trying to keep my voice calm. "The brotherhood has been there for two hundred years. It's not like they're going anywhere."

His eyebrows lower slightly. "They're not going anywhere, but you have a limited window of opportunity in which to prove yourself. You understood this part of the agreement when we negotiated it. I am being patient while you . . . sow your wild oats. I need to see proof that you aren't wasting the opportunities I've given you."

"I know. I know I agreed to go to the brotherhood. And I will. I'm just still finding my footing is all."

"What you're doing is making a joke of our family name. I don't want to be embarrassed by more stories about you and the other fruity boys at school. Whether you like it or not, you are in the public eye and you will represent our family appropriately."

I force myself to stay sitting tall and look him in the eye as he tears me down.

He shifts tactics. "Your mother is moved into the new house. She seems to like it there."

Right. Because we can't get through a single conversation without at least one reminder of which strings he can pull.

"Good," I say. Saying anything else will spring his trap around me.

"She's comfortable there. And safe."

As safe as someone can be when they're living under the roof of a narcissistic sociopath who controls every aspect of their life. Perfectly safe.

"Good," I say again.

My father shows his shark-toothed smile. "I'm tired of waiting for you to do your duty, son. I would hate to have to demonstrate any of the negative consequences, should you continue to delay. You may be a plane ride away from me, but your mother is very easy for me to reach."

"Yes, sir."

I want to crawl through my computer screen and punch him in the face. But even if I were right there in the room with him, I couldn't do anything. He would still have all the power, and I would have to bow and beg and hope he doesn't decide to destroy my life, or my mother's life, just to teach me a lesson.

"So you'll visit the fraternity, then." He doesn't bother voicing it as a question. We both know it's an order and a threat.

"As soon as I get the chance," I promise and hope he doesn't try to pin down a specific deadline.

"In that case, I think we're done here."

With one last threatening smile, he ends the call and leaves me staring at my computer with cold sweat drenching my shirt. Unfortunately, that call went exactly how I expected.

DEVON - PRESENT

Marcus is avoiding me. Or maybe he's avoiding all of us—our other two roommates have been easy and friendly and fun to be around—but I can't help but take it a little personally.

Jeff and Jimmy have been a blast, though, and make me think this whole college thing will be alright.

I was a little worried when I realized one of my roommates was human. Partly worried that he would be afraid of me and partly worried he should be afraid of me. But so far, it's been fine. He hasn't asked too many uncomfortable questions about my eating habits or anything like that, and I can admit to having a few moments of jealousy without descending entirely into wallowing in self-pity, so there's that. I've mostly managed to steer clear of the wallowing in the past few months since I was changed. I know it won't do any good, so I suck it up and put on a cheerful face and keep on moving.

But then something happens, like seeing a group of guys playing soccer out on the lawn in front of the dorm, and of course, they're all shirtless and gorgeous and glistening, and I'm swathed in layer after layer of SPF clothing. Not that I think I would actually get anywhere with any of them if I could whip my shirt off and join their game, but it's awfully lonely some days. All I ever get to do is watch other people living. There's so much I don't get to join in on anymore.

Shit. Now I really do seem to be wallowing.

"You want to get out of here for a while?" I ask but really beg Jeff since he's the only one around at the moment. Jimmy is—from what I can tell, at least—off stalking some girl he met the day we all moved in. I make a mental note to do something to stop that if it seems like he's getting creepy about it. Marcus has successfully avoided being in the same room as me for three of the last four days, which I think is impressive considering we share most of our living space.

Jeff looks up from the notebook he's been scribbling in for the past hour. "Huh?"

"I said, do you want to get out of here for a while? I feel like the walls are closing in, and I'm about to start panicking if I don't get away from this room, like, three hours ago."

"Sorry." He waves his notebook at me by way of explanation. "I've got an art class that is already kicking my ass, and I've only been once. Next time?"

"Yeah. Next time."

I scratch at the back of my head, at a loss for what to do now.

I mean, I suppose I could just go out on my own and look for some fun. But the last time I did that, I ended up in agony, bleeding out on a dirty sidewalk. It's possible I'm a little gun-shy.

It's also possible I need to get back on that horse.

I swaddle myself according to my mom's repeated instructions and finish the ensemble with one of the caps she picked out for me. It has the mascot of a gas station chain from back home on it, and I hate it as much as it is possible to hate an item of clothing. But it's no worse than any of the other terrible caps, and it will keep me from frying to death on my walk across campus.

* * *

I don't really have a goal in mind. It's not like midday is a great time to go clubbing. I take note of a rainbow flag hanging in front of a small brick building and think about stopping to investigate, but every potential scenario I run just seems embarrassing and awkward.

Hello, I imagine myself saying to a random stranger. *I couldn't help but notice your rainbow flag. Is it possible that you aren't straight? If so, are you possibly in the market for some not-straight friends?*

Ugh. This is why people go to gay clubs.

But going to a gay club is what got me into trouble to begin with. I just wanted to test the bounds of my sexuality, maybe see if I enjoyed kissing a guy as much as I'd enjoyed kissing girls in the past. The beginning of that experiment went pretty well, as I remember. I felt . . . well, everything I'd ever imagined I might feel in that sort of situation. And then it all went sour when the guy's teeth sank into my neck. Everything after that moment I only remember vaguely through a haze of pain and fear. There is truly nothing that can prepare you for the experience of having your life sucked out of you.

But, somehow, I survived. Somehow, the worst thing that could ever happen to me did happen, and it didn't kill me. Not all the way, at least.

I'm starting to feel the first warning signs of sun sickness before I make it halfway across campus.

Shit. I guess I need to pause my little adventure away from the dorm.

I duck into the closest building and half walk, half stumble to a bench near a coffee kiosk. I probably look like a mess. Cold sweat is pouring down my face and drenching all my protective clothes. I'm gasping for breath, even though I don't actually need the oxygen anymore. My brain senses danger and automatically tries everything it used to do to keep me safe, and that translates to a racing heart that's struggling to pump my sludge like blood through my atrophied veins and shriveled lungs struggling to fill with air that has nowhere to go.

Shit. Shit. Shit. If I die for real because I was careless, my mom is never going to get over it.

Suddenly, I'm yanked to my feet and dragged . . . somewhere. I'm too far gone to understand what's happening right now, but I end up somewhere cool and dark, so that's an improvement. Something is in my mouth. Fingers? Skin and the salt of sweat are two of the things I can still taste, and that's what I'm tasting now. Then something clamps my jaws closed, and my mouth is filled with a lifesaving gush of blood. I swallow reflexively, beginning to come back to myself almost immediately.

"What the fuck did you think you were doing?" Marcus shouts at me.

When did Marcus get here? My thoughts come slowly, like they're traveling from far away.

"Do you even have any blood capsules in case you get stuck like that? Do you have any idea how close of a call you just had?"

"Marcus?" My voice is even slower than my brain right now, but it's finally starting to catch up.

"Did you *want* to die today? Was that your plan, going out this time of day without any emergency blood?"

"Plan?"

Marcus stands up and takes an angry lap around the room before kneeling in front of me again. "Devon, do you understand what happened?"

I shake my head. I still haven't figured out where we are or how Marcus is here. "I felt a little off. Figured I'd been outside too long."

He rakes his fingers through his hair and glares at me. "Once you're back to normal, we need to have a serious talk about some things. For now, though, let's just focus on you surviving the next few minutes. Do you have any blood capsules?"

I make a face. "Hate them."

His scowl deepens. "Too bad." He reaches into a jacket pocket and produces one. "You need at least one more before I'm letting you try to stand up."

I groan, realizing that's what he put in my mouth before. My stomach reminds me with a lurch how much I hate even the idea of taking these things. Drinking blood bags is bad enough. Vampire hunger and instincts take over, so my human sensibilities aren't bothered when I feed. The blood capsules are too small and gooey for my vampiric aspect to recognize them as food, so I'm stuck focusing on how gross they are.

"I'll puke if I take one now," I warn him.

"Quit being a baby about it, or we'll be here all day," he counters. "If your body wants to survive, it won't let you puke it up."

He's probably right. I'll just want to puke. Lovely. "Give me a minute?"

Marcus shrugs. "Sure, but the longer you wait, the longer you have to build it up in your mind."

"Fine." I hold out my hand and pop the disgusting thing in my mouth before I can think about it anymore.

Blech. I'd rather eat glue. Or possibly bugs. But the capsule does its job. My heartbeat is back to its normal almost nonexistent pace. My lungs stop fighting against my rib cage.

"Do you think you can walk again?"

I stretch my legs and test them out, gathering them under me slowly and keeping a hand out in case I fall right back down. "I think so," I say.

He puts an arm around my waist and loops my arm over my shoulder. "We'll go underground wherever we can. You'd better be thinking over your mistakes on the way back because I won't always be around to save you like this."

It's only then that it hits me how close I just came to really fucking up. I could have died because I went for a walk without planning ahead. As much as I hate it, I'm going to have to admit to Mom that she was right.

* * *

MARCUS - PRESENT

I know I should go easy on Devon. I know he didn't mean to get caught out like that, and he's still getting used to things that I've taken for granted my entire life. I also know that seeing him fading out on a random bench when I was leaving class scared me shitless.

"Did you even think about avoiding the sun when you left the dorm today?" I grumble as I support him down one of the many tunnels connecting the campus buildings.

"I didn't think that far ahead," he says, sounding annoyed that he has to explain himself. Which is too damn bad because he does have to explain himself.

"How far ahead do you have to think to take the tunnels instead of walking in the midday sun?"

Devon looks around like he's just now noticed our surroundings. "Tunnels?"

I stop in my tracks and almost let him fall from walking without me.

"You didn't know about the tunnels?"

He shrugs uncomfortably. "I guess I missed that part of the campus tour. I take it there's tunnels connecting everything?"

I shut my eyes and try to find my calm. How could no one have told him about taking the tunnels whenever possible? How has he gotten by to this point without knowing about the tunnels or carrying blood capsules? "Yes," I whisper because I'm not in control of my voice right now, and I'm worried I'll start shouting again if I'm not careful. "There are tunnels connecting everything on campus. You can probably manage going above ground in the early morning or late after-noon, but at midday, you should always try to take the tunnels. And while we're talking about basic precautions, it doesn't matter how much you hate them, you should always carry a few blood capsules in case of emergencies. At least you have a hat, but a ball cap like this is never going to protect you for more than a few minutes in full sunlight. It's best to avoid the sun at all costs."

"Thanks, Mom," he grumbles and starts walking again. "This lecture is exactly what I needed today."

"Apparently!"

He turns on me. "Look, maybe you don't get this because you've never had to deal with it, but the blood capsules make me sick. They remind me of everything I can't taste anymore and how far I am from being human. My mom picked out all of my clothes after I was changed, and she chose all of them to be protective, and all of them make me look absolutely ridiculous. Maybe someone mentioned the tunnels when I visited Berring a year ago, but I wasn't a vampire at the time, so the information wasn't exactly relevant. Now, would you please just get off my fucking back? I'm doing the best I can right now."

Shit. My guilt cuts through my rage, and now I don't know what to feel.

"Right. Fine. I will try to get off your back. But can you also try not to die while we're roommates, at least?"

Devon snorts in what might be amusement and starts walking again. I'm pleased to see he's already looking steadier on his feet. "I'm not great at not dying," he tells me. "I wasn't trying to die the first time, and I did anyway. I wasn't trying to die today, but I probably would have if you hadn't come along. I can try not to die, but I can't promise any results."

Frustration powers my legs as I lengthen my stride to catch up with him. I'm relieved he doesn't actually have a death wish, but holy fuck, did he have a close call today. I never expected to spend my freshman year babysitting a fresh-turned vampire with no idea of how to keep himself safe.

* * *

When we get back to the dorm, I get an eye roll for reminding him to feed before doing anything else and decide a tactical retreat to my bedroom is my best current plan of action.

I pull out my phone and stare at it for a long time before actually opening my messages.

Me: You got a minute? I think I fucked up again.

Priscilla answers almost immediately.

Pris: I'm shocked. Better tell me everything.

Me: My roommate is fresh turned and apparently didn't even know to stay underground and he nearly died today.

I hesitate, trying to decide how much she should know and how to present it.

Me: And I was the one who found him and saved him. Even though I've been trying to keep my distance.

Pris: What else?

Of course Pris can see through me even over text.

Me: I think he might need someone to help him out.

Pris: And?

Me: And I happen to think he's cute.

I finally admit it, hating myself. I can practically hear Priscilla's laughter filling the space before her next message.

Pris: Okay, little brother, which pep talk do you want this time?

I bang my phone against my forehead a few times before I can answer. There's only one acceptable answer. I know this. Toe the line. Stay on my father's good side. Protect my mother and myself and prepare to inherit the legacy that's rightfully mine.

Me: The one about duty and achieving my potential, please.

I have to grit my teeth as I type the words, but I know it's the only real option. No matter how much I might want to find an excuse to spend more time with a certain freckled vampire. No matter how well he fit by my side with my arm around his waist. We're not going there. I can't go there.

* * *

Pricilla's pep-talk-turned-lecture is still ringing in my ears when I leave my bedroom a few hours later. If it were an option, I would have never left my room again for the rest of the semester. It's the only way of guaranteeing that I stay away from Devon.

Sure enough, all of my roommates, plus a couple guys I've never met before, are gathered around the TV, squeezed together on the sofa and chairs, when I come out.

Perfect.

"Marcus!" Jeff is way too excited for my current mood, but my only options are to turn around and hide in my room again or paste on a friendly face and try to be polite until I can escape without being rude. "This is Taylor," He says and points to a vampire big enough that he barely fits in an armchair, "and this is Gabe," he points to a human who seems the epitome of average next to his giant friend.

"Hi. Nice to meet you." I search for an excuse to leave, but my mind is blank.

While I'm still doing my silent and awkward act, Devon grabs a beer and holds it out for me. "Why don't you hang out for a while?" He asks like I didn't have to scrape him off a bench and force-feed him blood just a few hours ago.

"I . . . probably shouldn't . . ." I hedge.

"It's not going to kill you, is it?" He waggles the beer in my face with a grin.

What is it about this guy? Nothing seems to bring him down for long. Meanwhile, I'm pretty sure I've been down my entire life. Against all of my best intentions, I feel a smile tugging at my lips. Before I can think too hard about it, I snatch the beer from his hand and take a long swallow.

Is it a terrible idea? Probably. But my father isn't here to see me, and it's not like he can retaliate against me for drinking a few beers in my own dorm. Even he would have to realize that it's unreasonable to expect me to never cut loose. And, like Devon said, it's not going to kill me.

* * *

It takes one beer and two shots of tequila to convince me to have another go at the killer bunny video game my roommates love so much. I'm at least as bad at it drunk as I was sober, but it feels good to have people around me—some of them with blood pumping so fast I can hear each beat of it—and cheering me on and heckling me and acting like I'm an average dude who happens to be bad at video games.

In the midst of one of the bunny battles, Jeff gets distracted by his phone and tells everyone to gather for a dorm meeting. There are groans and eye rolls all around the room, but we all agree to stop the game so we can listen.

Jeff holds his hands up like some kind of high priest initiating a religious rite. "Alright, who has ideas for where to take some ladies in need of entertainment?"

Ah. So almost as important as a religious rite.

I have to ask. "Are you taking two girls on a date at once? Because I feel like I should warn you, that's never going to work like in the movies."

He laughs it off. "No, asshole, it's not a date. I'm just trying to think of a friendly way to get to know them better."

Consensus around the dorm is that it's too early in the year and too much of a Monday night for any good parties. But then I realize, I actually do know of a party. It may not be a good party. In fact, it will probably be a horrible party. But I also want my roommates to see that I'm useful. And if I show my face at the fraternity, that might help to appease my father.

"Actually, I do know of something," I hear myself say and don't allow myself to think too hard about it. "It's probably going to be boring and embarrassing and not at all what you're looking for, but there is this vampire fraternity that will be hosting an event tonight."

Jimmy is the most resistant. I can't blame him, really. A lot of vampires really are terrible people who would happily feed and kill indiscriminately if there weren't rules against it. I hate how Devon looks a little more downtrodden with every bigoted comment Jimmy makes, though. I try to remind myself that Jimmy just doesn't know any better. Obviously, this is how he was raised. If I'm going to change his view of vampires, it's not going to happen all at once, nor will it happen because I shout at him. He's hurting Devon with his comments, though, and I kind of want to walk across the room and slap him.

"Look," Jimmy says. "It's not that I don't think I can trust you–"

I interrupt him, because it doesn't matter whether he can trust me or not.

"Don't worry about it. If I have to go to this thing, I'd honestly rather not show up with anyone who might draw extra attention. How about I tell you the code to get in, but then I let you go in on your own," I finally suggest, mostly in an attempt to keep the peace. His agreement means it will also be easier for me to pretend I'm only there to make my father happy. No one will believe I'm thinking of officially joining if I show up with multiple shifters and humans in tow. "I'll check party details and let you know," I say, trying to play Mr. Cool, even though I'm certain this is the first time in my life that I've been within touching distance of "cool."

Jimmy leans in to fist-bump me. "I knew I liked you," he

says with a grin. "I just had this feeling about you the first time we met."

"Right. I'm sure you figured out in that first interaction that I was the guy who could get you into all the good vampire parties." I give a look to make sure he's catching on to my sarcasm. "I am, after all, known as the guy to go to for access to vampire parties."

"Okay," he admits, "I definitely didn't peg you as the party guy when we first met, but that doesn't mean I didn't have a good feeling about you."

I cave under his earnest stare. "Alright. I accept your supposed good feeling."

"And I accept the invitation that you've so far forgotten to extend to me to this party you're taking Jimmy to," Devon cuts in.

"Oh. Um. You want to come too?"

"Yes, thank you!" He grins and kisses me on the cheek like it's nothing.

The conversation moves on without me, and all I can do is sit there staring blankly at the wall and feeling my cheek burn where his lips touched me.

Chapter Six

DEVON - TWO YEARS AGO

"**W**here are you taking me tonight?"

Allie's question isn't exactly unwelcome. I guess I'm not in the right mindset for it right now. Following the dating pattern our friend group has gone through the past couple of years, Allie is up next for me. Or maybe I'm up next for her. I tend to date whoever's broken up with Dan two or three weeks before, but Allie seems to cycle through all of the guys alphabetically. Dan, then me, then Elliot. This will be my third time dating her, and that's fine. I suppose. Why mess with the system that's been working so well for us for two of our three high school years.

I put on a bright face for her. "I'm taking you somewhere tonight?"

She toys with the fabric of my shirt and smiles up at me. "Well, it's Friday, and I'm single, and you're single. Is there a reason you shouldn't take me somewhere tonight?"

Just that I'm pretty sure I've been there and done that, but if she's up for another round, shouldn't I go along with it? If nothing else, it'll keep the peace. "No reason." Just that I think maybe, if I haven't felt anything earth-shattering for her before, it doesn't seem like it's going to happen. "Where do you want to go? Movie? Dinner? Dinner, then a movie?"

"Or we drive up the hill and find a private place to park the car?"

"Cutting out all the unnecessary steps, I see." Not that I'm complaining. Allie's been a fun time every time I've been with her.

She grins. "You and I are good together. I say we get straight to what makes us good together."

Again, the suggestion isn't unwelcome, just . . . boring. "Absolutely," I tell her. "Let's go out to the woods tonight so you can use me for my body."

She presses a quick kiss to my lips and disappears down the hall. The first time we dated, or hooked up, or whatever this is called, I was infatuated with Allie. I would hang on her every word and physically hang on to her body as much as I could. Then she was done with me about a month later, and I learned that what we had wasn't that special after all. And now we're juniors, and I still like her fine, but I keep thinking there has to be something more. Right? Shouldn't it feel like this means something if it, you know, means something?

Or maybe I'm wrong, and the physical part is enough. On the other hand, even if the physical part is all there is to it, there are so many people in the world that I haven't even tried the physical part with. There are entire genders that I haven't tried the physical part with. Who knows? Maybe there's someone out there that I'll really feel something with. If I don't keep settling for just the physical parts with the same girls I see every day at school.

Chapter Seven

DEVON - PRESENT

Marcus is staring at the wall like he expects a swirling vortex to open and suck him in. I'm thinking that means I shouldn't have kissed him.

I mean, it was just a peck on the cheek, right? But some guys get weird about stuff like that. Something that's just a sign of friendly affection to me can be a Big Deal to someone else. Yet again, I act before I think, and now, Marcus is probably back to hating me.

I can't win with him!

After staring at the wall for a full ten minutes, he abruptly stands and walks back to his room without a word or a backward glance.

* * *

I'm still thinking about Marcus staring into the void after that kiss when I find myself standing in front of an imposing stone mansion—who am I kidding? It's a castle—dressed like I'm going clubbing and twisting nervously at each finger because this will be my first time interacting with a crowd of mostly vampires like this.

But I did invite myself along, so I guess I'd better follow through. Besides, standing around outside the party seems like a lot less fun than going in to be a part of it. I almost wish I'd gone along with Jimmy and Jeff and everyone else, but I'd had this vision of someone letting all of them in and kicking me out for being . . . who knows. Not straight enough? Not vampire enough? If I'm about to be humiliated, I'd rather it be in front of strangers instead of friends. I walk up to the front door, trying to exude confidence, like I actually belong here. Like I didn't have to ask Jimmy for the party details because I was worried Marcus wouldn't want me to actually show up. Like I'm a guy who has every right to kiss his room-mates and show up to frat parties and hang out with people who grew up as vampires and didn't have to learn how to do it at seventeen.

"What brings an outsider to our door tonight?" the vampire at the door asks me.

It takes me by surprise. Am I really an outsider, even though I'm a vampire and he's a vampire and this whole house is for vampires? I shake it off. Maybe I'm an outsider now, but that's the point of coming tonight, right? Tonight, I stop being an outsider. Or, at least, I become less of one.

"I come as one curious, with open mind and open heart. I come to see and not to judge." I repeat the phrase Jimmy taught me.

The guy at the door breaks his over-the-top solemnity by bursting out laughing at me.

"Ummm . . . did I say it wrong?"

He doesn't bother to answer, just keeps laughing.

"What the fuck? What's so funny?"

He finally gets control of himself but keeps chuckling as

he shoos me away. "It's cute and all, but it's time for the baby vampires to go home."

"The . . . what?" My skin is prickling with embarrassment, and I don't even know what I'm supposed to be embarrassed about.

"For real." He shoos me again, still laughing at the joke I'm not privy to. "Go home, little baby. This party isn't for you."

"Quit being an ass," a voice comes from behind me.

Marcus. I tense up, not sure if he's talking to me or the guy at the door. I don't think it's me that's being an ass, but I've been wrong before.

"He's with me," Marcus tells the doorman, who suddenly seems a lot more serious. "And let me remind you that you never know who is watching and listening to you. You ought to be more careful with how you speak to people."

"Yes, sir." The guy nods, keeping his face serious and his eyes trained on the ground.

"Come on in, Devon." Marcus waves me forward.

I'll be damned if I've ever been more turned on than this in my life.

I gape after him for a moment before remembering what I'm supposed to be doing. "Did you . . . did you just save me from a bully?" I ask.

Marcus scowls around the too-loud, too-full of partiers room we've just entered, then takes me by the elbow and steers me down a hallway to a slightly quieter corner.

"Why didn't you just ask me for the right code to get in?" I can't tell if he looks more angry or annoyed. He isn't happy, that's for sure, and the confusion obvious on my face doesn't seem to be lightening his mood at all.

"What are you talking about?"

"The lines you're supposed to say to get in. I told Jimmy what he should say, but he's not a vampire, so he's got different things to say than us. If you'd asked me, I could have told you."

I catch myself, yet again, staring at him like an idiot. "You mean, he was being an ass because I said the non-vampire line instead of the vampire line?" I finally say.

"Yeah. Why didn't you ask me instead of Jimmy?"

Why indeed. It couldn't have anything to do with the fact that I was sure I'd fucked everything up by kissing him. Not a chance of that. I hunch my shoulders. "I thought you might not want to tell me, and Jimmy was right there, so why not ask him?"

Now, he looks confused. "Why wouldn't I want to tell you? I said you were invited, didn't I?"

"Yeah, you did. I know. But that was . . . you know . . . before I trampled all over your boundaries and kissed you?"

He looks even more lost. "You thought . . ." He rubs a knuckle into one of his eyebrows, like maybe he's trying to rub away the headache I'm giving him. "You thought I was upset about you kissing me?"

"What was I supposed to think?" I shrug helplessly. "I thought I just gave you an innocent peck on the cheek, but then you totally shut down and disappeared, and I haven't seen you since. What other conclusion could I come to?"

Marcus glares into my eyes, and it's all I can do not to break eye contact. He's a cobra, and I'm the mouse he's set his sights on. "I know it was just a peck on the cheek," he says slowly, "but you did it so casually. Like, it was nothing to kiss me. No one has ever given me a casual kiss of any kind, and you did it without even thinking about it."

"You weren't mad?"

He shakes his head.

"Disturbed?"

He shakes his head again, still staring straight into my soul.

"Disgusted?" Okay, now I'm sounding breathless and pathetic and—

He wraps a hand around the back of my neck and pulls me in before I can register what's happening.

"Do I look disgusted?" His pupils are so wide I can't tell what color his eyes are anymore.

I shake my head slightly, not hard enough to dislodge his hand or give him the idea that I want him to let go. "No, you don't look disgusted," I whisper, practically saying the words into his mouth.

He nods. Starts to pull away. But, no, that's not going to work for me. Before he can back off, I grab a fistful of his shirt in each hand and close the distance between us.

This kiss is not casual. Nor is it innocent. In an instant, I'm tasting him, running the tip of my tongue over his top lip, nipping at his bottom lip, trying to swallow any breath he might have stored in his body. He stiffens for a moment, then sets out to retaliate with his own kisses. Our tongues battle each other while our hands explore. He's slightly taller than me, with the same carved-from-stone muscles that seem to go along with being a vampire. He whimpers when I press him up against the wall and moans when I trail kisses down his neck. This is the fastest my blood has moved since I became a vampire, and I can feel it thundering through me, an echo of the rushing pulse I can hear in his veins.

"This is a terrible idea," he gasps at me.

"Yes, terrible," I murmur, rocking my hard cock against his leg.

"We really shouldn't—"

"I do things I shouldn't do all the time," I cut him off.

"Fuuuuck," he groans when my fingers find his nipple and give it a hard tweak. "Okay, let's find a room."

Chapter Eight

MARCUS - FIFTEEN YEARS AGO

When you're three, everything seems big, but my father's house takes that to a different level entirely. It's imposingly large, but there's more to it than that. There's a row of fluted columns out front and an echoing cathedral of an entryway. It's all ancient hardwood and white marble and gilt edges, every inch specially designed to intimidate.

My mother's hand grips my shoulder in a frozen claw. Even though she's coached me and coached me on what to say and how to behave, she doesn't trust me to remember, and her fear rolls off her in waves, like fog over the ocean. It only takes a few years for that fog of fear to be replaced by impenetrable ice, but back then, I guess she was still learning the ropes.

I try not to stare at the too-large furniture around me—she hammered it into me that I can't let myself look out of place—but I can't help the feeling that everything here was built for giants, not just adults.

And there *he* is. Sitting in a chair that could swallow him whole, I think, if he allowed it to. Like his chair and his desk combine to make a gaping shark's mouth, and he's sitting between the teeth without a worry in the world. He commands this shark. Why would he fear it?

"This is him?" His question is direct, without even a welcome or an invitation to sit.

The claw at my shoulder clamps down and presses me forward. "Yes, sir. This is your son."

It will be years before I recognize that most mothers don't call their child's father "sir," but all I'd known until then was our quiet, cold family.

"Good afternoon, sir," I echo my coaching. "My name is Marcus Levine, I am three years old, and I am pleased to make your acquaintance."

I hold out my hand to shake, as I was instructed, but he glances at it for a split second before disregarding it and appraising me from head to toe.

"At least you've taught this one to speak properly," he finally says. "It's a nice touch that you can see the resemblance." I don't understand exactly what that means, but I hold myself a little taller at the perceived compliment. "I suppose he'll do," he finally pronounces.

"Thank you, sir," my mother murmurs.

My father shifts the papers on his desk in some incomprehensible way for my three-year-old mind before taking out a pen and holding it poised to write. "So, what do you want? A bigger house? More staff?"

I can't help a glance over my shoulder to gauge how my mother will respond. What does she want?

"He'll be starting his formal education soon." She speaks over my head, her hand on my shoulder a cold reminder that the adults are speaking and I should stay quiet. "The cost of tuition, plus tutors, and an allowance for school uniforms and other miscellaneous items."

It's the first I've heard of any of that, and I want to ask her what she's talking about. What is formal education? Will I have to go away for it? Can I stay with her?

My father has no interest in my concerns, though.

"Fine." He waves a dismissive hand. "I'll tell the lawyers to sort out the details with you. Unless there's something else?"

"No, sir. Thank you." And then she's bustling me out the door and out of the house entirely.

Chapter Nine

MARCUS - PRESENT

This is the worst idea in the world. This is the worst idea in all of history. It is not possible for me to have a worse idea than this.

And I can't seem to stop. I can't seem to remember why I need to stop.

The third door we try opens to an unoccupied bedroom, and Devon pushes me toward the bed and locks the door behind him.

Each kiss leaves a brand on my skin. How does his skin feel so hot against mine when I know that we're both the exact same temperature?

"Why does your shirt have so many fucking buttons?" he mutters against my neck as he works through each one.

I don't bother to answer, just set to work on my own job of pulling his too-tight shirt over his head. With a forceful shove that has me hard enough to practically tear through my fly, Devon lands me on my back in the center of the bed. He doesn't waste time, I'll give him that.

"Is this okay?" he asks as he trails kisses and licks and bites down my chest and stomach.

Fuck yes is the resounding reply from my cock. *Fuck no* is my brain's faint reply. All I manage to say is a tortured moan.

Then, before I realize it's coming, Devon slides my pants down to my knees and is kneeling between my legs.

"Are you sure . . ." I don't finish the question because I'm not sure at all, but I know I don't want him to stop.

"Yeah, I'm sure," Devon tells me, then swallows half my cock while still keeping eye contact.

My hips buck off the bed, and I let out an embarrassingly desperate groan.

I haven't had that many blow jobs in my life. And most of them were mediocre at best, some girl trying to curry favor with the higher-ups who didn't realize that I'm not really into it. There have been a few guys, all fast and secret and resulting in immediate fear and regret. But Devon feels different already. We haven't talked about sexuality, so he can't have come after me just because of that, and we haven't talked about family, so I'm inclined to believe he's not in it for that either. The way he looks at me is so . . . hungry . . . like the only reason he exists is to make a meal of me.

Fuck, it turns me on.

I'm about to warn him that I'm on the verge of coming, in case he wants to avoid a mouthful of my jizz, when he pops his mouth off my dick and climbs up my body.

"I really want to fuck you. Is that alright?" he asks so earnestly that I almost can't figure out what he's saying.

"Um. Yeah. Sure. Of course." Fuck. Awkward response of the year award goes to me.

He pulls a small bottle of lube out of his pocket and drips a generous amount on his fingers. I nearly climb right out of my skin when he presses those fingers against my hole and circles my entrance.

"Still okay?" he asks.

"Ungh. I mean, yes," I answer with the help of my two still-functioning brain cells. Every other brain cell has shorted out.

His fingers circle again, and then one slips inside the ring of muscle, making me gasp and twitch. This is something I've experienced even less than blow jobs. My mind is flying in every direction between pleasure and panic, but need wins out.

"More," I beg, and his one finger is quickly joined by two, then three, all with his eyes intent on me for any signal to stop or continue.

"More," I beg again. Devon's eyes smolder above me. I might just burst into flame from having him watch me like this.

I can't help the disappointed moan that escapes me when he takes his fingers out, but his eyes are still on me, so I know he's not stopping entirely.

I give a confused look between him and the condom he pulls from his pocket. "You know you can't get me pregnant, right?" Shit. That's probably not the right thing to say in this situation. If my brain was working right now, I would know the right thing to say, but that wasn't it. I blame it on all of my slow-pumping blood being currently gathered in my cock instead of my brain.

"Yeah. I know that, but . . . what about STDs?"

I huff out a laugh. "The only thing vampires can pass through blood is vampirism," I promise him. "Now, would you just fuck me already?"

He slides the unopened condom back into his pocket and starts slicking lube over his—rather delectable-looking, if I may say so—erection.

"Ready?" He hesitates at my entrance, looking worried.

I don't have time for worry or second thoughts or any of

that. This is my one night. It has to be my only night. "Yes. Fuck me," I beg.

The instant he slides in, it feels right. Like a piece of me has clicked back into place. Like I just came home from a long trip and clicked the lock on my front door.

Devon lets out a long groan as he settles inside of me, holding his body completely still above me with his eyes closed in concentration.

"I-is this okay?" he whispers.

I answer by wrapping my legs around his torso and rocking my hips up toward him. This is more than okay. This is the stars aligning. This is what home is supposed to feel like. This is the rumble of my world shattering around me.

He takes my nonverbal answer and responds with a tentative thrust of his hips. When I groan encouragement, he does it again, then again, picking up speed until we find the perfect rhythm together. The press of his thighs against mine, the nip of his teeth against my neck, the mind-blowing thought that this—*this*—is actually happening right now, all combine to set my senses alight.

"Devon, I'm—"

"Good," he grunts, continuing his rhythmic fucking. "Want you to come for me."

I capture one of his hands and wrap it around my cock, showing him the rhythm I want him to stroke it with. It only takes a few seconds before I'm spurting out stream after stream of hot come between us. It's hotter than our body temperature, so it practically burns against my stomach. I can't focus on it for long, though, because suddenly I feel Devon jerk inside of me, feel the heat of his release filling me up.

He rides it out until each of us finally stops moving and twitching through the aftershocks, then gently pulls himself free and flops down on the bed beside me.

"Fuck," he groans. "I'm going to want to do that every day from now on."

And, of course, those are the words that bring sense crashing back into my head.

DEVON - PRESENT

About one minute. That's what I get. About one minute to hold Marcus in my arms and think about how fucking amazing that was. One minute to start thinking maybe this wasn't the worst mistake ever and to start making plans that involve at least ten repetitions of what we just did.

And then Marcus remembers . . . everything, I guess.

"Fuck, fuck, fuck!" He disentangles himself from my arms and scrambles for his clothes. I can see his hands shaking as he gets dressed, and he won't meet my eyes at all.

"Marcus? What's wrong? Can you slow down for a second?"

No. Apparently, he can't.

"What the fuck was I thinking? I knew I couldn't do this. Why the fuck did I think I could do this?"

He's not talking to me, and he's not slowing his own panicked mutterings enough for me to talk to him.

"Marcus!" I stand up and catch him by the shoulders. "Would you please just fucking pause for a moment?"

The clench of his jaw and glaring eyes say no.

"This was a mistake," he finally says. "We both know it. Let's just, you know, put it behind us before there can be any more repercussions from it."

"Repercussions? What the fuck are you talking about?"

Marcus goes back to jerking his clothes back on. "How can you possibly not know what I'm talking about?"

"Because I don't! I guess the same way I didn't bring any blood capsules on my walk the other day! You and I obviously have very different life experiences, but I thought whatever this was"—I wave a hand between the two of us—"could just be something enjoyable and not complicated. I guess I got that wrong. My fucking bad!"

I grab my own clothes and start getting dressed.

"Fucking bully for you that you can have something like that and have it be enjoyable and not complicated! Not all of us have that luxury!" He pats himself down to make sure his clothes are presentable. "Here's what we're going to do. We're never going to admit to anyone else that this happened. We're never going to talk about this with each other again. If possible, we're never going to talk to each other again. Dorm conversations are going to go like, 'Did you make coffee?' 'Not yet.' 'Okay, I'll make some.' Do you get that?"

Well, fuck my life. This is up there on my bad hookups list with the time I went clubbing and got turned into a vampire.

"Whatever, Marcus." I can't keep the bitterness out of my voice. "I won't embarrass you by letting anyone know we hooked up. Just . . . stay the fuck away from me, and it won't be an issue."

Maybe I should feel good at the flash of hurt I see in his eyes, but it just mirrors my own and amplifies it so all I can feel is hurt. How is it that every time I try connecting with someone, I just end up with this god-awful hurt?

* * *

"Did you make coffee?" Marcus asks it with a straight face. No sense of the irony showing through whatsoever.

"Not. Yet." I bite the words out, and if our roommates decide to make something out of it, that's not my issue. Jeff and Jimmy follow our conversation with wide eyes and closed mouths but are thankfully both smart enough not to comment.

Marcus doesn't answer, just slams around the tiny kitchen area making coffee like the coffee pot wronged him. I grind my teeth and try my hardest to ignore him.

At least Jeff catches on to how badly I want to move past this. "So what's the latest with Gloria?" he asks, reaching for a video game controller. This is what we do. We play video games and try to help Jimmy with his love life. It's funny. I have no idea who Jeff is attracted to or if he's even attracted to anyone at all. He always deflects to talking about someone else's love life, it seems. And since he's astute enough to pick up on the tension between Marcus and me, the ongoing Jimmy and Gloria drama is really the only safe topic these days.

"I think I can get her to agree to be my partner for our big history project," Jimmy says. "That will be progress, right?"

"Sure," Jeff agrees, but his voice isn't particularly convincing. "Today, you're study buddies, tomorrow, you'll probably be married. It is the natural next step, or so I've heard."

I snort out a laugh but manage to get it under control before Jimmy catches on to the sarcasm in Jeff's voice.

"God, I hope so," he says fervently.

"Coffee's ready," Marcus growls at us before stomping back to his room with his mug.

I guess it's good that he's following his own mandate. He hasn't stayed in the same room as me for more than five minutes since our hookup, and each time, he's spoken five words or less.

I vaguely remember thinking on move-in day that it would be a terrible idea to hook up with one of my roommates. Why oh fucking why didn't I follow my own advice?

* * *

The next week passes just like that, with all of us busy settling into classes, Jeff minding Jimmy's business and giving me space and Marcus never spending more than five minutes in the same room as me. I'm even beginning to feel comfortable with this new setup when Jeff catches me alone in the dorm.

"So . . . do you want to talk about it?" he asks in an overly casual voice that makes me wonder if he's been rehearsing this conversation.

"No," I grunt and make a point of turning back toward my math homework.

But he continues. "Because you and Marcus seemed pretty cozy at that party we went to, but since then, you seem to have stopped talking to each other entirely. It feels like, you know, our whole suite could probably benefit from some clearing of the air?"

I keep my eyes on my math, but I can't see a single number clearly anymore. All I can see is the replay—first glorious, then painful—of that night at the frat house. Shit. What he just said sinks in. He saw us at that party, but we sure as hell didn't see him. The realization of what he probably saw doesn't bother me in the slightest, but judging by Marcus's postcoital panic attack, he's going to lose his shit if and when he learns that someone knows we hooked up.

"I don't know what you're talking about," I mumble toward my textbook.

Jeff huffs. "Oh, come on. Is it really that big of a deal? Guys hook up. Jimmy and I are both fine with it. Jimmy and I are both rooting for the two of you. Whatever went wrong between you can probably be fixed if you just talk about it."

I run my shaking hands through my hair while I try to gather my thoughts. Unlikely, but a guy has to try something.

"Jeff, whatever you saw or think you saw, promise me you're not going to bring it up to Marcus, okay? It isn't your business. Stay out of it."

He makes an argumentative sound in his throat, but I glare him down before he can say anything.

"I'm serious about this. You're only going to make things worse if you try having this conversation with Marcus. Please don't make things any worse."

Jeff looks like a fucking toddler, crossing his arms and

hunching his shoulders as he scowls and puffs out an angry breath.

"Promise me," I press him for a response.

"Fine." He throws up his hands in defeat. "I won't talk to him about it, but it's going to be a fucking miserable year for all of us if the two of you keep going like this. Would you let me know what's going on at least, so I know why we're all being miserable?"

I scrub a hand over my face. I guess it's been a couple of weeks since I've had anyone get in my face and try to keep me accountable. It's not the same when my parents try to do it over the phone, and they're the only people in the world who try to do it at all these days.

"Fine," I agree. "I will share the parts that I'm allowed to share, and once I'm done telling you, you aren't allowed to ask any questions or try to get any more details about it."

"Absolutely." He holds up a hand like he's being sworn in in a courtroom. "Whatever we say here never leaves this room."

Guarantee he's going to be talking about this later. But I need to talk to someone. "Okay, fine. Marcus and I did hook up at that party."

Jeff interrupts to let out a loud cheer. "I knew it! Yes!"

I give him a look to remind him that this is the only time I'm going to talk about this.

"Right. Sorry. Go on." He has the grace to look chagrined as he motions for me to keep talking.

"I thought that I'd completely messed things up between us by being too . . . I don't know, too touchy, too over-the-top, too whatever I am, but when I confronted him about it, it turned out that he actually already felt something for me. So . . . he kind of kissed me to prove that I hadn't turned him off, I guess, and that kiss escalated, and—" I break off in embarrassment. "You don't want to hear this."

"Oh, yes I do," Jeff insists.

Great. My roommate is voyeuristic on top of being just regular old nosy. "Oh my god. You don't get any details. Just, it happened, and it was really good. Right up until Marcus realized what happened and freaked out on me and told me to pretend it had never happened."

"Ouch."

"Yeah. Ouch. And he hasn't said more than five words in a row to me since. The end."

Jeff gets a faraway look in his eyes. "Okay, but here's what I don't understand. This isn't the same world of, like, fifty years ago or whatever when guys couldn't openly be in relationships. What's the problem?"

"It's more complicated than that. The fact is, there are still reasons for people to stay in the closet. That's Marcus's choice. He knows his own situation better than anyone else, and he gets to decide if or when he comes out. I hate it, but I have to respect it."

"Well, for what it's worth, I hate it for you too."

I shrug. "I just need to move past it. There will be someone else who doesn't make me hate myself."

Chapter Ten

MARCUS - PRESENT

Pris: Haven't heard from you for a while. How are you doing?

I ignore Priscilla's text. The library I'm studying in isn't conducive to chatting.

That's what I'm telling myself, at least.

Pris: Assuming you're either really busy with school work OR really busy getting laid.

I roll my eyes at the message but ignore it again.

Pris: Okay, that second one is just way too ridiculous. I was giving you the benefit of the doubt, but now I realize there's absolutely no chance.

I give up and take my phone out to the library entrance, where I can talk without getting death glares from the student working the resource desk.

"What's ridiculous?" I ask first when she answers my video call. I have to grit my teeth together to make sure no secrets get out.

Pris puts on a mock surprised expression. "Oh, wow! You are still alive! I thought for sure you were dead because I know there's no chance you would just be ignoring me."

"Not ignoring you, just busy," I assure her.

"Busy with school or busy with a guy?"

I do a panicked sweep of the room to make sure no one could have heard that. "Would you keep your voice down? You don't know who might be listening in."

Priscilla rolls her eyes. "Right. You are the paragon of secrecy and discretion. No one will ever realize who you're attracted to unless the spies on your phone hear me talking about it."

"I know you think you're funny," I tell her with a flat look, "but you're really not."

"Okay, fine. I'm the soul of discretion. My lips are sealed. They'll have to torture the truth out of me. Now, what's up, and why have you gotten paranoid since the last time we talked?"

I hunch down on the nearest bench, wishing I hadn't called her. Maybe a text would have been enough, and I wouldn't have to deal with this conversation.

Who am I kidding? Priscilla has never been put off the scent by a simple text, and it's not going to magically start happening today.

"Holy. Shit." She sits forward to lean closer into her phone screen. "Something really did happen, didn't it?"

"I'm not talking about this with you. Goodb—"

"Don't you dare!" she shouts loud enough that I really hope there's no one nearby to hear her. "I'm the only person you can talk to about this, so you're fucking going to talk to me about this. Out with it. Now."

I groan and hunch down even lower, but she doesn't take pity on me. "If I don't say it, it never happened."

"Sadly, not true. Now, tell me."

"I . . . kind of slipped up with my roommate," I admit and am surprised and a bit horrified to realize my eyes are wet. Whatever happened, a mistake like this is not worth crying over. I'm certain of that.

Pris sits still and quiet for a moment. "What kind of a slipup are we talking about here?"

"Like, the kind of slipup that would be worthy of punishment if our father hears about it."

"Hmmm. Sadly, we both know that doesn't narrow it down enough. You can give me the details now, or I can squeeze them out of you in some less pleasant way."

I squeeze my eyelids shut to avoid seeing her expression when I tell her. "The kind of slipup that requires lube and a bed," I whisper.

Silence stretches between us until I can't handle it anymore and peek at her through slitted eyelids.

"Okay. Wow. I really thought I was joking before, but I guess not. So . . . how likely is it that our father hears about it?"

Letting all of the unnecessary air out of my lungs doesn't help calm me down. Scrubbing a hand over my face doesn't help either. "It was . . . not the best choice of places. It was at a party . . ."

"A party where?"

"The frat house," I tell her in a tortured whisper.

"What?" She's back to shouting, and I really, really hope there's no one within hearing range because she goes off. She calls me every kind of idiot, reminds me of every reason I can't have what I want, calls me an idiot again, and finishes with, "I thought you were at least smart enough to keep it discreet, Marcus. I'm all for you living your truth and all that, but waving it around under your father's nose is the worst way to do it. I thought you had things under control."

"I thought I had things under control too," I say, "and then I didn't anymore."

It's her turn to rake her fingers through her hair. "Okay. The fact that he hasn't come out with some kind of punishment yet is probably a good sign. I'm assuming—probably wrongly, I know, but a girl can hope—that you've been keeping your distance from the roommate since then? Please tell me it was only the one time."

"Just the once," I confirm. She doesn't have to know that I've thought about it every minute of every day since. The only relevant facts are the ones my father can trace.

"Okay. Just the once. Even if he does find out, if you can prove that it's just one lapse and you're playing by his rules again, you should be okay."

"I know I'll be okay," I mutter, unable to meet her eye. "What about mother, though? She's the one right there. Dealing with him."

Priscilla sighs. "Your mother is and has been in a precarious position for years now." *Ever since my father sired a second son.* We're both thinking it, but neither of us says it out loud. "She knew the dangers when she let you leave for college. She'll have to take care of herself for the time being."

"I hate that I was so careless. I hate that I put her at risk like this."

Pris shrugs her helplessness. "At some point, you have to be a little bit human, kiddo. Try not to do it where he might see, though, okay? You can't be half in and half out with him."

I know it. I've known it my whole life, and here I am, still making the same mistakes.

"It won't happen again," I promise. "I know that it can't happen again. I told him—the roommate, I mean—not to let anyone know. I've been more careful about keeping my distance. I won't let it happen again."

Another long silence stretches between us. When I look

up at her again, I can't stand the pity in her eyes and immediately drop my gaze to my knees.

"Don't forget that you can call me anytime, okay?" she finally says. "Day or night or whatever. I will happily drop whatever I'm doing and come to your rescue. You just have to ask."

I nod my understanding because I'm going to choke on any words I try to speak out loud.

With that, she makes kissy noises into her phone and signs off. My super in-control and mature way of handling the situation is to scream and possibly cry into my pillow for half an hour after I get back to my room.

* * *

I can't sleep. I feel like I'll never sleep again. Every time I close my eyes, I see Devon. Sometimes even smell him, taste him, feel him on my skin. He's a phantom that follows everywhere I go, especially when I'm trying to get more distance from him.

So I turn to the only thing I know that quiets my thoughts at all.

Thank every higher being, no one else is awake, because I can't deal with anyone else right now as I sneak out of my room and start pulling out baking ingredients without turning on any lights. I know the contents of this little kitchen by touch and smell by now, even if my vampire eyes couldn't see in close to pitch dark. It didn't take long to get things set up as a real kitchen, and none of my roommates are complaining that I've claimed the space as my own. Two of them, plus any living friends they bring over, are happy to sample whatever I produce with my makeshift setup of hotplates, kettles, and toaster oven. Technically, I'm not allowed to have most of this stuff in the dorms, but Berring isn't likely to complain much about the son of one of their biggest donors, and it's not like my roommates are ratting me out to the RA or anything. So I get to keep my little hobby, and father doesn't have to know about it, and maybe my roommates will have a reason to like me, even when I'm too uptight and grumpy and awkward to really fit in with the group.

The cooking itself is easy. I let myself sink into it until a combination of intuition and experience guides my movements. It's been a long time since I had to measure ingredients or set timers. I just know. Sometimes by smell. Often just by . . . well, someone outside of my bubble of intuition might call it magic. Even when I first snuck into the almost unused kitchen in my childhood home and started messing around with whatever food I found there–I learned later it was food the human staff who lived on the estate kept for themselves–it just made sense to me how things should go together and what would happen if I added this or that ingredient. After a few months of those experiments, which felt so dangerous and subversive to me at the time, one of the maids turned up in the middle and started giving me some more formal instruction.

That was the highlight of my life for years. Every time I came home for a school holiday, I looked forward to my late night cooking lessons. Always quiet, except for the sounds of oil popping in a hot pan or a spatula scraping along the bottom of a skillet. Always with an adult human I wasn't supposed to speak to, whose name I didn't even know.

And now I'm doing it alone. Late at night with no one to tell me I'm doing something right or wrong.

"Whoa." Devon's voice wrenches me out of my memories. "I guess this is why our dorm keeps waking up to fresh baked goods in the morning."

I force myself to keep my movements steady. One tray of cinnamon rolls comes out of the tiny oven and the next goes in. They can only be baked in small batches because the oven is so small.

It's easier to talk while I'm working. It's always been easier to exist in general while I'm working, so I keep my hands busy with the next task and talk over my shoulder.

"I figure someone has to make sure they're eating."

Devon snorts out a half-laugh. "I guess you're just taking care of all of us, then."

"It would be better if everyone could take care of themselves, but yeah. I guess I'm the one taking care of all of you."

I brave a glance at him and catch him staring at me with a look I can't read. Maybe wistful? Or maybe he's just trying to figure me out the same way I'm trying to figure him out.

"Did you need something? Or . . . sorry if I woke you up. I tried to be quiet."

Devon shakes himself. "No. You didn't. I mean. I couldn't sleep, so I thought I'd come out here. But I'll leave you to it."

He starts backing away. "It's okay if you want to be out here. It's your dorm too." Even if he's a complete distraction and having him this close is destroying the zen state I'd found from my baking spree. He has a right to be here.

He looks at me for a long moment. "I'll just grab a glass of water then get out of your way."

I brace myself on the counter as he reaches past me to get a glass, then stands almost touching me as he fills it up.

Doesn't he feel how I'm about to catch fire just from nearly touching him? Doesn't he notice the way every muscle in my body is pulled taut right now, like a bowstring waiting to launch?

I could grab him right now. I could pull him close and kiss him and it would be such a relief to have his skin against mine and to let him push me back against this counter and–

"You should try to get some sleep, too, you know," he says,

walking back to his room and holding his glass up in a salute. "You also need to take care of yourself."

I'm so off-kilter, I almost forget the cinnamon rolls still baking. I don't sleep, though. I'm still wide awake, wondering if I really might combust if I caved and kissed Devon, by the time I need to leave for class.

Chapter Eleven

DEVON - PRESENT

I tap my eraser in time to the professor's voice and try—fuck, I try so hard—to focus on right triangles.

"Now turn to example five. What information do they give?"

I stare at the example and just see dancing squiggles. And I see Marcus' hands, forming dough into rounds, segmenting those rounds expertly without pause, transferring trays of cinnamon rolls in and out of a tiny oven without so much as a glance down to check what he's doing.

"Because the right angle is given, along with the hypotenuse . . ."

The triangle in front of me rearranges into the triangle of Marcus' shoulder to his elbow to his hip, and my fingers almost ache with wanting to fit my fingers right there, on the spot where his shirt meets his pants. I wonder if I could distract him when he's so intent on something like that, so intense and focused that he didn't even notice me standing there and watching him cook. What would he have done if I'd come up behind him and slid my arms around his waist while he worked? Maybe he would have been angry. He might have thrown me off and woken everyone up to kick me out of the dorm. Or maybe his guard was down, and he would have leaned into me and kept working. Maybe he would have stayed focused on his cooking even if I'd planted a trail of kisses from the nape of his neck and down between his shoulder blades and down the length of his spine. What if I'd let my hands wander while I was at it? Would he lose his focus if I untucked that forever tucked in shirt?

"Now, you can see that the most important information in this example is the length of this side."

Shit. The professor has moved on to a new example and I still haven't made a single useful note about anything. I need to focus.

Like how Marcus focused on me when he was forcing blood capsules down my throat.

Like how Marcus focused on me when his hand wrapped around the back of my neck and he brought me in for that blazing first kiss.

Like how Marcus focused on me when I was coming inside of him.

Fuck. I almost bang my head on my desk to try and get rid of these Marcus thoughts, but I definitely don't need to draw more attention to myself in the class that I haven't been paying attention to.

I turn pages until I find the example that matches what the professor is showing at the front and force myself to make sense of the numbers and symbols in front of me. Technically, it's all stuff I should know. In reality, it's stuff I should have learned last year, when I spent the last few months of school missing more classes than I actually went to.

And the numbers aren't cooperating, because now the black lines on my paper are reforming into Marcus' black eyelashes, which frame his criminally beautiful brown–almost black–eyes, and all of these triangles are dancing across the page again to make the angles of his face now. The obtuse angle of his cupid's bow and the acute angles where his lips meet in the corners. The symmetrical perfection of his jaw and his chin and his hair–perfectly controlled, of course–and the perfect asymmetry of his left eye, which is slightly bigger than his right.

I close my eyes and press my palms against them. Letting this imaginary Marcus run wild in my mind isn't helping me in any possible way. Why can't I stop this?

* * *

I know that Jeff is persistent as fuck. I realized that him swearing to let it go wouldn't actually lead to him letting it go. Did I think it would take a bit longer for him to jump back into it? Yeah. I did. I can't decide if I like that about him or absolutely hate it.

Right at this moment, I think it's the second one.

"Come on! It'll be fun! Soccer is fun. Watching people play sports is fun. Therefore, it will be fun to go out and watch people play soccer."

Except it's two in the afternoon, which means enough direct sunlight to lay me out entirely, and I really don't want to have to explain that to him.

"You can go without me," I grumble.

"Yeah, but if I go without you, it completely defeats the purpose of it because I won't accomplish the secret ulterior motive of the trip."

I level a laser-eyed warning look at him, which he completely ignores.

"The what now?"

Jeff turns his full grin on me, and damn him to hell with

his straight teeth and flashing dimples. I can already feel myself wanting to say yes to whatever bullshit he's cooking up.

"The secret ulterior motive of the trip."

"Which is . . ."

He leans forward conspiratorially. "For me to figure out which guys you're into so I can set you up and get you to move past that thing we're not talking about."

I spring to my feet. "For fuck's sake, Jeff! Why do you assume I want to be set up with anyone at all?"

"Isn't it obvious?" He stands up so he can face off with me.

I give a clueless shake of my head.

"Because everyone around you can tell that you're absolutely miserable and lonely! If it's not going to work out with you and . . ." Jeff waves his hand to indicate that we both know damn well who he's talking about, even if he won't name Marcus out loud, "then you might as well find someone else and get it out of your system, right?"

"First of all, I thought I told you to mind your own business. Second of all, I don't really think banging one out with some random guy is going to get anything out of my system. Third of all, even if this plan of yours made any sense to begin with—which it doesn't—why is it a soccer game of all possible scenarios that you think will give you this information?"

"Because . . . soccer players . . . wearing soccer shorts . . ." He gives a confused shrug. "I don't understand the problem."

I pinch the bridge of my nose and wonder if drinking blood or drinking alcohol will help more with the headache forming there. "How about you go and check out the soccer players for yourself and see for yourself which one you want to try and pick up and bang out of your system? That way, you'll have fun, and you'll manage to stay out of my business for a few hours."

"Okay." Jeff draws the word out so long it stretches to the

point of losing all meaning. "So what I'm getting is that soccer players don't do it for you."

I flop back down to the couch with a sigh. "I didn't say soccer players don't do it for me. Actually, I think I started to figure out when I was ten that soccer players do it for me in a way they don't for most of my friends. That doesn't mean I want to go watch soccer players with you or right now."

"But you might later?"

I hate it, but honesty wins out. "I'm a vampire. Try to think about what happens to vampires who go out in the afternoon to watch outdoor sports."

It only takes him a moment. "Oh, shit. I'm sorry. I can't believe I didn't think that through. Shit. I'm the worst friend ever, aren't I?"

I wave him off, relieved that I don't have to explain it to him anymore. "You're not the worst friend. Just . . . try not to tempt me with things I can't have anymore, okay?"

"Yeah. For sure. No more afternoon soccer game suggestions. Done." He gives his fingernails a serious look before looking back up at me. "Is there . . . is there anything else? Because I don't want to put my foot in my mouth like this again."

It's kind of too exhausting to think up a response to this. At the same time, I'd rather avoid a repeat of this conversation.

"I don't know. How about, assume I'd rather not be reminded of any fun summer-specific activities? And food is kind of . . . a touchy subject, I guess."

"Right. Okay. No pool parties and barbecues. Maybe basketball instead? And beer?"

I can't help myself. I let out a chuckle at his desperate scrambling for safe topics. "Sure. Basketball and beer. And maybe indoor swimming pools."

"And . . . as far as checking out guys is concerned?"

"Be honest. Are you just talking about checking out guys because you think that's what I want?"

Jeff looks supremely uncomfortable. "I'm a helper. I help people. I hate seeing you struggle, and you've obviously been struggling. I just keep thinking, if I can help you get over . . . him . . . order will be restored to the universe again. You know?"

I shake my head, bemused. "Marcus isn't the love of my life or something. He was a mistake. One that I will get over with a little time. And if you want to help me out by checking out guys—or girls—with me, then I won't say no."

He throws his arms up in a victory pose. "Yes! I knew I would wear you down eventually!"

"Yeah, yeah." I roll my eyes at him. "Let's go to a coffee shop and check people out so I stop making you sad with my existence."

He gives the air a couple of victorious punches for good measure. "So. Guys and girls. So I guess that makes you—"

"Bisexual. I'm super bi. Bisexual as the day is long."

"Oh." Awkward hesitation. "I'm honestly a little surprised you just came out with it like that. I kind of assumed you were closeted after refusing to talk about the hookup with Marcus and all that."

"Nope," I assure him. "I realized pretty quickly after my parents found out that I'll probably have to keep coming out forever, so I might as well do it whenever I get the chance. Life is too short to let people think I'm something other than what I am."

"Huh. Okay then. I guess I'd never thought about it that way."

"Don't worry about it. So . . . checking out asses at the coffee shop?"

"Checking out asses at the coffee shop," Jeff agrees.

* * *

"Okay, what about him?" Jeff tips his coffee not at all discreetly in the direction of a lanky blond guy hunched over a laptop in the corner of the coffee shop.

I fight my urge to roll my eyes. "What about his body language says that he's interested in someone trying to pick him up right now? The dude is obviously panic-cramming for a test, not trying to hook up with anyone."

"What? It's not possible to study and also want to get laid? Two things can be true, you know."

This time, I do roll my eyes at him. "Yes, oh king of multi-tasking. I'm sure you're the expert on simultaneously dating and studying. I'm in awe of your abilities. But that guy over there? He is very clearly not open to being approached by strangers. Moving on."

We scan the room in silence for a few minutes.

"How about her?" I tilt my chin toward a voluptuous redhead with her bright orange curls piled on top of her head in a sculpture that probably took hours though it's meant to look messy and carefree.

"For you or for me?" Jeff asks after staring at her for a moment.

"For you. Redheads aren't allowed to date each other."

Jeff gives me a long, quizzical look, probably trying to figure out how serious I am. He decides to humor me. "And why aren't redheads allowed to date each other?"

"Think about the genetics. With all of these recessive genes, we're obviously all too closely related. It would practically be incest."

"Okay." He draws it out to let me know he's not taking me seriously. "Well, she looks way too sweet for me."

"What do you mean, too sweet? You're the nicest guy I know. You'd be perfect together."

He holds up an admonishing finger. "That's something people get wrong. You can't have two sweet people in the relationship. It's too much sweetness. It's like putting caramel in a milkshake. You'll get sick." I try to point out that plenty of people mix caramel and ice cream in a variety of ways, but he keeps talking. "What you need is french fries with your milkshake. Then it balances out."

"So, you're looking for someone greasy to balance your sweetness?"

Jeff flips me off with a grin. "I'm looking for someone nice and salty. And I've already found her, I'm just still figuring out how to reel her in."

"Oh, gods, you're talking about the RA again, aren't you?" I drag my hand down my face. "You were serious about liking her because she was mean to you?" I sound judgy, but I get it. If Marcus walked in this minute and ordered me back to the dorm, I'd probably do as he said. I guess whatever's wrong with Jeff is equally wrong with me too.

Jeff just keeps grinning. "Actually, I've just had a brilliant idea. The next vaguely eligible person you see, you're asking them to join us for the dorm mixer on Friday. It'll be the perfect opportunity for you to move on from . . . you know, that other guy, and it'll be the perfect opportunity for me to get closer to the perfectly salty Lacey."

"I thought we agreed that I'm not really feeling like a hookup right now," I groan.

Jeff looks thoughtful. "No, I don't remember agreeing to that. Come on. It will be good for both of us. So, is it going to be the tall guy in the corner, the curvy redhead who I'm sure you're not actually related to, or the next person to walk through the door?"

I turn toward the door and silently pray that this doesn't end up biting me in the ass.

Chapter Twelve

MARCUS - PRESENT

ill me now, I beg the universe when I step out of the tunnel to find that the "dorm mixer" I'd been planning on avoiding is in full swing already.

Berring's attempt at calming the party school reputation is to host parties in the dorms, supposedly without any drugs or alcohol or any of those things that might get freshmen in trouble at a party. Not that anyone is actually stopping partiers from getting wasted in their dorm rooms before coming out to join the main party in the common rooms.

Whatever. It's not my business. I'm keeping my head down and avoiding notice and not making any more mistakes.

Just as long as I can get up to my room without getting sucked in, I can close my door and shut all of this out, and it will be fine.

That's what I'm telling myself when I spot Devon at the opposite end of our dorm lobby. Of course, he looks amazing, and of course, he's dancing. With someone. With some guy in a mesh crop top and shiny pants that might actually be painted on.

This doesn't change anything. This can't change anything. I still need to duck my head and thread my way through the crowd to the stairwell to make the climb up to my room.

I know this is the only viable option.

My feet are rooted in place, and my eyes are glued on Devon and shiny pants.

Who the fuck is that guy? And where did they meet? Is that the type of guy Devon usually goes for? My shoulders twitch in uncomfortable awareness of how out of place I look here, wearing slacks and a button-up shirt while everyone else is dressed for the club.

Devon is smiling. My stomach ties itself into a knot when shiny pants laughs at something Devon said. I suddenly realize that my hands are clenched so tight around the strap of my bag that I can feel it cutting into my skin.

Fuck. I need to get a grip.

It takes a monumental effort, but I force myself to take one step, then a second and a third, toward the stairwell.

Too bad moving toward the stairs also has me moving closer to Devon and shiny pants.

Come on, Marcus. Get it together and get to the stairs. Devon won't even notice you.

In slow motion, I see Devon's hand glide up to brush a stray lock of hair out of shiny pants's eyes, and then his hand comes down to land on shiny pants's pec. The two of them laugh together about something, and a haze of red mists comes down around me.

Okay, maybe not literally, but it might as well be. I can't see anything else besides Devon's fingers rubbing against that stupid mesh shirt. I can't hear anything other than Devon's laugh.

Probably laughing about me, a supremely unhelpful voice

in my head chimes in. *Probably laughing about how lucky he was to get away from me.*

I can't stand it anymore. I'm not in control right now. Without thinking about it, I'm across the room and standing beside him.

Oh, shit. Not just standing beside him. My hand is reaching up and pulling Devon's hand away, and now I'm pulling Devon away, and I'm not sure where I'm taking him, but I know I can't stand seeing him *here* and with *him* for another second.

"Marcus, what the f—"

I cut him off with a rough kiss, then turn and start walking again, pulling him along behind me.

There. The door to the stairs. My feet knew where we were heading, even if my brain is only catching up to the plan now.

There's no one in the stairwell, so I don't waste any time. I press Devon's back to the door we just came through and kiss him, hard and rough and hungry like he's my last meal. Or maybe my first.

With a moan, he opens to me, letting my tongue tangle with his. He rocks his hips, trying to find friction against me, and I can feel his swelling arousal to match mine.

I need to stop this. I need to have never started this. I'm past the point of turning back and pretending nothing happened.

Pleasure zings through me as I rub against him, my slacks whispering against his stiff jeans, a meeting of silky and rough that makes me shiver.

And Devon is kissing me back. Oh, gods, it's good to have him kissing me back. He tangles one hand in the hair at my nape and slides his other hand between us to grip my shaft through my pants.

"Devon," I grit out. "Fuck, that feels good."

His moan, his tongue, his sliding hand all tell me he's feeling the same.

Then he stops. Freezes in a moment like someone's just shot him with a stun gun.

I press my lips back to his, thinking maybe I can bring him back, but he pushes me away with an angry grunt.

Reality crashes in around me. What the fuck am I doing? What was I thinking?

I rake my fingers through my hair and take a step back away from him. His face is a mask of disbelieving anger.

"I'm so—" I start to apologize, but he cuts me off with a glare.

"You can't just drag me off like a caveman when you get jealous," he tells me in a too-careful voice. Emotion heaves beneath the surface, but he doesn't let it loose. "Especially not when we both know you're going to turn chickenshit the moment you realize what we've done."

"I'm sorry," I try again.

He lets out a rough laugh. It's a mean, sarcastic sound that I don't like associating with him. Devon, normally easygoing and upbeat, is making mean, sarcastic noises, and he's making them at me because of something I did.

"You were the one who set the rules. We don't talk to each other unless it's about coffee. We act like we don't know each other outside of our own dorm. We don't spend time together. If you make rules like that, you don't get to decide to break them on a whim. Follow your own rules and leave me the fuck alone, okay?"

He doesn't wait for an answer before escaping back out to the party and leaving me to climb the steps feeling both broken and disgusted with myself.

Chapter Thirteen

I am not prepared for my phone to start ringing before eight in the morning.

"Mrmph?" I ask into it as soon as I find the button to answer.

"We'll be there for lunch, so start thinking about where you want us to take you!"

"Ermph?"

"Did we wake you up or something? I said where do you want to go for lunch?" The voice pounding into my ear rearranges to match my mom's voice.

I sit up with a groan. "What time is it?"

"Devon, we're heading out soon. Make sure the place is presentable, okay? And think about where to go for lunch."

"Lunch?"

"Yeah! We're taking you out. We realized there was a football game tonight and figured we could take a little day trip to visit you. Lunch, then you can show us the sights, then football game, then we'll get out of your hair."

I know she's speaking English, but none of the words make sense when I try to put them together. "You're coming here?" I puzzle together, finally. "Today? To visit me?"

"Yes. We'll see you in a few hours. Think about lunch places. Anyway, we'd better get on the road if we're going to be there in time for lunch."

And then my mom hangs up on me. I don't think she's ever done that, but I have a feeling she realized I'm not really up for a visit and didn't want to have that fight.

Brilliant.

With a groan, I roll out of bed and head for our tiny dorm kitchen to start cleaning up. Marcus keeps the area pretty tidy so it's always ready for one of his cooking adventures, but that doesn't mean it's up to my parents' standards.

I start with the big stuff, frantically clearing every empty beer can and bottle into the trash, then pull out the scrubber, followed by disinfectant wipes. No one else joins me until after eleven, when Jeff stumbles out of his room, scratching his belly and yawning.

"Whoa. What's happening here?"

"Where's a good place to eat lunch?" I ask him, scrubbing at the edge of the sink like it owes me money.

"Why do you want to eat lunch?"

His confused look would be hilarious if it weren't for the real-life crisis I'm actively dealing with. "I don't want to eat lunch. My parents are visiting, and they want to eat lunch."

"What, today?"

I look up from my scrubbing to give an impatient look.

"I wasn't judging or anything." He holds his hands up defensively. "I'm just trying to clarify."

"My parents are visiting today, and they want to go out for lunch. And I guess also a football game? I don't know. What I do know is that both of my parents are humans who eat human food, and I have no idea where to go for human food near Berring."

"Ah." Thankfully, he actually does look like he gets it now. "So, are we talking casual? Formal? Multiple courses? Drive-through? What do they like?"

All good and valid questions. I have no idea of the answers. I think back, trying to remember what my parents used to order from restaurants, and find that my brain has somehow become a blank page that has never once chosen a food item.

"Okay," he interrupts my panic spiral. "Let's back up a moment. Fancy or casual?"

"Definitely not fancy," I answer, glad I can be sure of one thing. "Maybe for weddings and holidays, but other than that, they're casual."

Jeff claps. "Alright. Progress. Next question. Dietary restrictions? Aside from the obvious . . ." He waves at me in a vague gesture that encompasses the whole "undead blood-sucker" thing.

"No. Nothing aside from the obvious."

"Good, we're narrowing it down. Now, we're going to drop that fast food idea I threw out. Your parents are driving too far for fast food."

The knots I've been tied up in since my mom's call loosen slightly. This is doable. Maybe I don't know the restaurants around Berring, but there are people who can help me. I set the scrubber down and sit on the couch, happy to let Jeff take over this part of the planning.

We've just narrowed it down to three places when the knock comes.

"Devon, I'm sorry for the short notice, but I just couldn't stay away any longer!" My mom says it all like one long, excited word before barreling into me and giving me a bone-crushing hug.

"Yeah, I missed you too," I admit and am a little surprised to realize just how much I mean it. I've had my heart kicked around a bit in the past few weeks, but now I'm being held and feeling that promise of "everything's going to be just fine" that my parents have always given me.

I have to clear my throat when we step apart before I can introduce Jeff. The assessing look in my mom's eyes makes me want to clarify that she shouldn't get her hopes up. Jeff and I are just roommates and nothing more. That conversation will have to wait until Jeff isn't in the room, though. It would be a little too awkward to explain to my mother that the roommate she's currently talking to isn't the roommate I'm inappropriately lusting after.

"Oh, uh. This is Jeff. Jeff, these are my parents." Yep. I can be awkward even without bringing up the lustful feelings for one of my roommates thing.

Mom doesn't mind my awkwardness, though. She drags him in for a huge hug of his own. "Jeff, it's so nice to meet you. Come to lunch with us."

Jeff shoots a questioning look my way.

"You should come," I tell him. "It'll be fun." And at least one of us can actually appreciate the food if he comes with us.

"Yeah, sure. I'd love to."

My stomach gives a warning gurgle, and I suddenly realize I was so caught up in cleaning that I haven't fed yet today. "Ummm, before we go, I need to . . ." It's not like my parents don't know what this is about. It's not like Jeff hasn't been living in the same dorm as me for weeks now. Why is it so hard to just say that I need blood? But it is. It's so goddamned hard and embarrassing and shameful to say the words. "I'll be right back," I settle on before hurrying into my room and shutting the door before anyone can question me.

I grab a blood bag from the minifridge beside my bed that doubles as an end table. It was one of those suggestions we got from the doctors soon after I was turned. Vampires can do college just fine, but it's important to always stay stocked up on blood. I'd been so burnt out on doctors and listening to doctors' advice by then that I'd barely paid attention, but I do remember a stern, grey-haired man leaning toward my hospital bed with a glare and warning me I could have permanent damage from skipping feeds. Knowing that doesn't stop the automatic gag as I take the first swallow. I force myself to keep swallowing instead of spitting it out and pray that Jeff and my parents agree on a restaurant before I get back out there because I don't want to have to think about the food I don't get to eat wherever we end up going.

MARCUS - PRESENT

My mother fidgets on the bleacher. I almost do a double take to try checking that she is, in fact, here at the football stadium with me. It is literally the last place on Earth I would expect to see her.

"Have you been making any friends?"

And if that's not a loaded question, I will use a cactus for a sex toy.

"The guys in the dorm have been friendly enough," I mumble, already knowing that's not what she had in mind.

"And your father's group?"

By "group," she means the fraternity, though I've never understood why it's so difficult for her to just call things what they are.

"I stopped by one night," I tell her. "Everyone I talked to seemed fine." And if the gods are smiling on me, she doesn't already know that the only person I really talked to at that party was Devon. She definitely doesn't need to know exactly what Devon and I got up to in addition to talking.

She heaves a put-upon sigh. The familiar guilt-trip sigh. The "why does my offspring make me suffer like this?" sigh. The sigh to remind me of everything she's given up for my sake and simultaneously ask what I've sacrificed lately.

"I suppose I could make more of an effort to get to know them," I mumble. I want to tell her that I met more of those douchebags than I ever wanted to, and I only actually met one of them. The asshole on door duty was more than enough to turn me off from the whole thing. If I had the option of making a single damn decision for myself.

Mother's eyes glisten in the stadium lights. "I hate to ask it of you, but you know how much easier it would make things if you could clear the way for later on." Maybe those are genuine tears making her eyes so shiny. Maybe she's had almost two decades to hone her manipulation skills, and right now, she's using them on me. I'll probably never know. What good would it do to know, anyway? All of our chess pieces remain in the same positions, whether we got here through love or manipulation. Maybe a bit of both.

I give a resigned nod. "I'll reach out to them again sometime." I knew from the beginning that duty would catch up to me at some point. I really thought I would have a little longer before it did, though.

Chapter Fourteen

MARCUS - PRESENT

"**M**arcus! Come sit!"

Jeff's exclamation is way too excited for comfort.

"Um. Sure. I guess I've got a minute." Translation: I couldn't come up with a better excuse on the spot. I need to work on my improvisation skills.

"I feel like I haven't seen much of you lately. What have you been up to?"

I look around in case there's an "intervention" banner hanging somewhere. I don't see one, so I look around again in case there are hidden cameras for a very weird, dorm-based reality show somewhere.

"Okay, I give up," I admit after finding no signs of shenanigans beyond my roommate being extra . . . well, extra. "What's going on?"

Jeff has a split-second conversation with the ceiling before turning his attention back to me. "Okay. I noticed that things had been a little bit tense around here lately, and I'm just trying to diffuse the tension. You know, so all of us can feel just a little more peaceful."

"Tense?" Who? Me? No way he can be talking about me, the idiot who keeps trying to hook up with the most off-limits, not a hookup option guy on campus. I'm not tense at all. "I don't know what you're talking about," I lie.

"Yeah. Tense." He raises his eyebrows like he's trying to hint at something. I give my best blank, clueless stare. "You know, ever since that party where . . . nothing happened . . . which led to you and Devon basically not speaking to each other. Tense."

I mentally run through every single curse word I've ever known, and none of them seem even remotely strong enough. So I guess he saw us together. Either that or Devon told him about it. Either way, my carelessness is officially catching up with me, and I have no idea how to respond.

I pop out of my seat and start making for the door. When in doubt: deny, avoid, and get the hell out of the situation. "I don't know what you're talking about or what you think you might know about, but it sounds like something you can worry about without my help. Besides, I've got—"

"Would you just sit down for a second and talk to me? I swear I'm not going to hurt you or . . . you know . . . out you or anything."

It would be nice if I could believe that for a second. Doesn't he realize that by having this conversation, he's threatening to do just that?

I pause with my hand on the doorknob. I'm terrified to hear what he has to say, but I'd better hear him out in case I really need to do some damage control.

"Look, I don't know what your situation is or why you've been shutting us out, but I just wanted to clear the air. Let you know that we're on your side. I'm not judging you. I would never do that. Jimmy is cool too. We just want you to be okay. Okay? You know we would never judge you, right?"

"You're right," I say through gritted teeth. "You don't know what my situation is. You don't know anything about me." With that, I sweep out into the hall and slam the door behind me.

Okay, fine. Jeff has good intentions. He doesn't want to hurt me. He claims he won't out me.

Not on purpose, I'm sure. But if he's as careless talking about this with other people as he is with me? He's probably already talked to Devon. That will be another vulnerability, I'm sure. That's the thing. Jeff doesn't have to intend harm in order to unleash a whole shitstorm over my head.

I need to head that off.

Hating it with every fiber of my being, I turn toward the vampire frat house I was at all too recently. I need to find a way to save face with my father before he realizes there's an issue.

* * *

The underground entrance just has one bored-looking vampire sitting in front of the door. They aren't too worried about outsiders coming in through this direction. I spare a thought to wondering if I count as an outsider, but I push it away. I'll always feel like an outsider with this group, even if I do manage to get them to stop seeing me that way.

"Um . . . who dares to . . ." The door guard begins his spiel before realizing who I am.

"I come as one lost from the fold who wishes to come in," I power on, not giving him a chance to collect himself. "I come as blood of your blood, to offer my strength to your cause." If rolling my eyes would do anything at all, I would be doing it so hard my eyeballs would strain. "I come as one who has forgotten the way and wishes to remember."

The door minder gapes at me like he has no idea what the correct responses are. Maybe he doesn't. How often does a legacy turn up at the door a few weeks into the semester and claim a sudden interest in getting in?

"I . . . um . . ."

I'm thinking this guy was not put on door duty as a reward for his high intelligence or stellar people skills. But feeding him his next lines might be construed as rude, so I stand there waiting for him to either remember or go find someone who does.

"Oh, yeah!" His face lights up like a little kid who just remembered he's getting pizza for dinner. "Be welcome, stranger, that we may become friends again," he intones in a completely over-the-top Serious Fraternity Business voice before waving me in.

One douchebag down. I wonder how many I'm going to have to go through to get to someone who can actually do anything to help me. I will be surprised enough to eat my own underwear if it's any less than thirty.

"What stranger enters this house?" At least this asshole remembers his lines.

I rattle off my bit as seriously as I can without being sick on his shoes.

"Be welcome, stranger, that we may become friends again." Then he breaks into a wide grin. "I heard you were coming, but I didn't really believe you'd come by here. What's up?"

Great. So I've moved up from the clueless idiot on door duty to a creepy fanboy who knows who I am in every worst possible way.

I shrug noncommittally. "Figured I should stop by and see what the deal is with this place."

"Yeah. Alright. Let me show you around."

He's already more excited about this than I can understand. Magnus Levine's son showing up at his frat house is apparently the highlight of his year. Awesome. Meanwhile, I'm just trying to grit my teeth and get through this interaction.

"So," I hunt for a topic to make him feel like I care about talking to him, "how are the numbers this year?"

Bullseye. He launches into a spiel. "Not bad. We would have liked more pledges this year so we could be a little more exclusive, but we aren't hurting for fresh blood or anything. With you around, I bet things will really pick up next year. We've got a big event this weekend. Do you think you might . . ."

"Oh. Uh, yeah, sure. I'm free this weekend." Only because I absolutely have no other options. I guess I can invite my roommates along and earn some points with them while also doing my duty as far as my father is concerned.

Chapter Fifteen

DEVON - PRESENT

This party blows already, and I just got here. At least this time, I found out the secret code before showing up and being embarrassed at the door, but the whole thing is cringy as fuck. I mean, seriously? Secret code phrases just to get through the door?

"I need a drink or seven," I tell Jeff as I grab his sleeve and start dragging him to the bar.

"Whoa! What's the rush? All of this will still be around in ten minutes."

"Yeah, but hopefully, I'll be a lot more drunk in ten minutes and therefore much less easily annoyed."

He rolls his eyes and lets me drag him to the drinks table. "And what exactly is making you need to immediately drown your sorrows? Is it more the setting? Or is it the company?"

"How about the fact that all vampires seem intent on making me embarrassed to be one of them? Is that enough reason to want to drink?" I slosh vodka into a cup and don't bother adding any mixers, for once thankful for my dead taste buds.

"Sure." Jeff shrugs, taking a little more care in mixing his own drink. "I mean, I guess you've got plenty of reasons to feel all sorts of feelings, but I can't help but think what you're actually mad about is different."

I take a huge swallow of my straight vodka, but I can't spend the next eternity gulping down liquor and avoiding conversation.

"Okay. Fine. You caught me. I'm mad about something other than being associated tangentially with a fraternity that doesn't want me around. Keen observation skills."

Jeff rolls his eyes again, the asshole. "So . . . are we actually saying the name of the other thing you're mad about tonight?"

"No," I answer almost before the question is out of his mouth.

"Come on! He invited you tonight. He told you the secret code to get in and everything. Doesn't that mean something?"

"No," I repeat, voice flat and eyes narrow. When is he going to clue in to the fact that I don't want to discuss Marcus anymore?

"But he obviously—"

"No. Look, I know you've got good intentions or whatever. I know you believe in the power of love to overcome all obstacles and all that shit." I down another gulp of vodka and pour a fresh cup of the stuff before going on. "The fact is some things were not meant to be. Some things are not going to be. I'm not at this party in some weird hope of bumping into . . . you know his name. I'm at this party because I want to drink and cut loose and remember what it was like to be alive before I got turned into a vampire. So dance with me and shut up, or go somewhere else and talk to someone other than me about it."

Jeff obligingly leads me away from the bar and toward the impromptu dance floor someone made out of some cleared space and a single, sad, probably weight-bearing coffee table.

Our movements, the music, none of it matches how I feel right now. I want to wallow at the bottom of someplace cold and dark with thousands of pounds of earth pressing down all my sadness so I can't feel it too much. I try to enjoy dancing with Jeff. I really do. Objectively, he's a good-looking guy. A catch, even, considering how hard he works to make the people around him happy. I try to enjoy checking people out with him. And while there are plenty of objectively attractive people dancing around us, I can't seem to muster any interest at all in a single one of them.

"What about her?" Jeff points to a girl in jeans and a tank top that could have been painted on her.

"Go for it," I tell him.

Jeff rolls his eyes. "I don't want to go for it. I want to know if you want to go for it."

"I don't know. I'm mostly here for the vodka. Why aren't you going for it?"

"Because I'm trying to get you to go for it," he explains like this should be obvious to everyone. "Besides, no chance is the love of my life going to be some random hookup at a frat party."

"Love of your life?"

"Yeah. The love of my life." He gets a far-off, dreamy look.

I know I'm staring instead of dancing, but I can't seem to stop. "Oh my god. You aren't talking about the RA again, are you?"

Jeff looks at me like I'm the biggest idiot in the universe. "No. We're not talking about Lacey right now, because right now, we're both looking for the girl or guy or special someone who's going to get your mind off of M—"

He shuts up when I put my hand over his mouth. "First

off, we're not saying his name. Second off, you have got to stop it with this Lacey chick. I have seen into the future between the two of you, and that way only lies pain."

Jeff grins and punches my shoulder. "That's what I'm hoping for!"

I raise my hands in surrender. "Nope. Too much information. I don't need to know what you're into. Besides, I wasn't talking about that kind of pain. I was talking about heartache and sadness and how you're going to become the guy in the dorm that the rest of us have to take out and try to cheer up. I promise, that's not going to be a good look on you."

"But there's nothing saying it has to end badly. I choose to remain hopeful." He gets the dopey, lovesick look again. "You know, she has this commanding presence that just . . ." He trails off and gives a little shudder that feels way too intimate for me to be seeing it.

Okay, not exactly the conversation I was expecting tonight, but at least the focus is off my love life.

"Fine. You are allowed to hold out hope, but I, as your close friend and roommate, am allowed to point out the flaws in your reasoning. Flaw number one, she's older than you." My only experience with someone older was disastrous. Like, assaulted in an alley and left bleeding next to a dumpster disastrous. But Jeff's situation is probably not dangerous like that. Right? I need to detach from my own experience and my own personal hangup.

"Just a few years," he says, "And it's not like she's my professor or boss or anything like that. All above board, nothing illegal or anything. Though . . . she's an RA . . . and she's so . . . in charge. Like, if I say she's mean in a sexy way, does that make any sense?"

I stare blankly at him for a moment, wondering if he's about to sprout a second head or start speaking in tongues.

"No. I can honestly say that makes no sense at all to me."

Jeff deflates a little at that, so I shake him by the shoulder. "Hey. It doesn't matter if it makes sense to me. If you say this is your dream girl, who am I to argue with you?"

He looks slightly more hopeful. "Yeah. It doesn't matter if it makes sense to everyone else. I know what I know."

"That's the spirit!" I high-five him.

He nods, the argument picking up momentum for him. "Yeah. And if I know I'm supposed to be with her, then I'm supposed to be with her. Right? If it's fate, then it's going to happen. No matter what."

His words tell one story, but his eyes are still worried.

"You want to go back to the dorm, don't you?"

"I . . ." Jeff looks around the crowded party. "You don't see anyone you want to hook up with here?"

I slap his shoulder in a manly yet comforting way. "There's definitely no one here I want to hook up with. Let's get you home."

The relief on Jeff's face almost makes me laugh, but I'm mostly overcome with my own relief that I don't have to deal with this lame party anymore. I multitask by steering Jeff toward the door while snatching the vodka bottle from the drinks table. I'm done with this party, but I'm not done with partying for the night.

* * *

I wake up with the worst hangover I've had since becoming a vampire. It doesn't help that what wakes me up is a slamming door and somebody shouting.

"Why the fuck are neither of you answering your text messages?" Marcus bellows.

Who is he shouting at? Also, why?

"Huh?" I hear Jeff groan from somewhere to my right.

"What part of 'emergency' do you not understand?"

Marcus's voice is vibrating at the exact frequency to make my skull shatter into a million shards.

"Please. Quieter," I beg him with a voice that comes out cracked and rasping. I should have had some blood last night to counteract the vodka, but planning ahead for things like that really isn't my style. Now, I'm paying the price by wishing I could be dead for real right now.

I crack my eyes open and am immediately hit by a renewed throbbing in my head and a wave of nausea.

"Emergency," Marcus says, just as loud as before. "Check your fucking messages."

Jeff and I are sprawled across the couches in our living room, surrounded by a nest of vodka bottles, beer cans, and the sad remains of several different unhealthy snack foods.

Jeff sits up with a groan and reaches for a half-empty bag of Cheetos, which he proceeds to stuff his face with. I look away because watching him eat junk food is making my nausea even worse.

"Messages?" I ask and pray Marcus doesn't shout his answer this time.

"Oh my god. I'm going to lose my shit if you don't pull it together in the next two minutes. I'm going to leave the room and give you a chance to find your phone, and by the time I come back, you'd better be reading the text conversation that you've apparently been sleeping through for the past hour."

True to his word, he turns on his heel and marches into his bedroom.

Unable to fully sit up yet, I grope on the floor beside the couch and hope my phone will magically find its way into my hand.

Chapter Sixteen

MARCUS - PRESENT

I agreed to stay in the fraternity's guest quarters—how fucking pretentious to have "guest quarters" in a frat house anyway—after the party as a show of good faith or building bridges or being under my father's control or . . . whatever. I'm only doing any of this so he'll let up on my mother. I still have every intention of drawing it out as long as possible before I actually succumb to his wishes. Not that I expect to last that long. He has too much to hold over my head for me to keep control of my own life for long.

I've just decided it's late enough in the morning that leaving won't be seen as rude and still early enough that I might sneak out without notice when I get Jimmy's message.

Jimmy: Gloria was drugged by a vampire last night. Need a dorm meeting ASAP

Me: Is she alright?

Jimmy: Alright physically but pretty shaken up. Are you at the dorm?

Me: I'll get there in less than fifteen minutes.

Me: Jeff? Devon?

The other guys don't answer, which only adds to the simmering rage Jimmy's first message brought on. If Gloria was drugged by a vampire, there's a very solid chance it was one of the fraternity members who did it. She was drugged at a party I told her about and helped her get into, and it was probably done by someone I know. Someone I'm supposed to be making nice with.

I feel sick with rage, and seeing Jeff and Devon sprawled across the couches in our living room, passed out and surrounded by empty liquor bottles and trash, does nothing to dissipate that rage.

I don't bother trying to be gentle waking them up. Thankfully, once they both see their missed messages, they kick into gear and join in my anger.

We've had just enough time to pick up some of the mess and take turns pacing around the room and cursing when Jimmy opens the door and leads Bee and Gloria inside.

I've met them both before, but I've been so wrapped up in my own life that I haven't gotten to know Bee or Gloria very well. I've spent so much time trying to avoid Devon that I haven't done much socializing at all. They both look a lot worse than the last time I saw them. Splotchy cheeks and bloodshot eyes give me a pretty good idea of how they've spent their morning, and seeing that makes my blood start to boil again. I'm going to boil over if I don't find a way to relieve some of this tension.

"Are you okay?"

"What happened?"

"How are you feeling?"

Jeff, Devon, and I all rush to speak over each other, trying to get answers from her.

"I'm fine," she tells us. An obvious lie, but no one argues with her. "Honestly, it could have been a lot worse. He didn't . . . Jimmy got me out before anything worse could happen."

"Who was it?" I practically growl the question. I try to tell myself to get control of my emotions, but they're already at a rapid boil. I know I won't be able to calm down until the heat source is removed. That's going to be a while, I'm sure of it.

Jimmy sighs. "His name is Vincent. I'd only met him once before. I knew he was a douchebag. I definitely got a shitty vibe from him, but this is way beyond what I thought he was capable of."

Shit. "You don't mean Vincent Davenport?"

Gloria nods, and angry tears well up on her lashes. "The one and only. And I'm such an idiot because I thought he was actually interested in me. Next thing I know, everything is hazy, and I can't move my body." She gives a self-deprecating laugh. "Guess I should have followed everyone's advice and only drunk what I poured for myself, huh?"

"No," I argue. "You did nothing wrong. You should be able to drink at a party without someone fucking with your drink." And also, if we're playing the blame game, it's all on me. I've known about Vincent for way too long to be at all surprised to find out he's drugging girls' drinks at parties. Afterall, he was the ringleader of my bullies at boarding school, and his father and mine are way too tight for me to trust anyone in his family.

Gloria folds in on herself, letting the couch support her as she stares off into space.

"I think," Jimmy says, then hesitates like he's waiting for someone to belittle his idea. "I think the girls should stay here so they'll be safer."

Gloria huffs and shakes her head. "That's not necessary. I'm shaken up, sure, but I can take care of myself. I need to eat something and then sleep off any drugs that are left in my system, then I need to be more careful in the future."

"But," Bee jumps in, "wouldn't you feel safer with some friends nearby? Strength in numbers, right? It might be nice to have someone to watch your back, just in case this guy isn't content to just let you get away from him."

Everyone around the room gives some kind of agreement.

I'm on board, though my brain is already supplying me with all sorts of worst-case scenarios. I'd better sort the details behind the scenes so no one else has to deal with all of the vampire politics involved. Shit, there are going to be a lot of vampire politics involved. The chances are between none and no fucking way that I keep this away from my father.

I'm deep in my own thoughts when Jimmy's voice snaps me back to reality in the most painful way possible.

"Why don't Devon and Marcus sleep together and I'll sleep on the couch? That will free up two beds for the girls to sleep on."

I shoot a panicked glance between Devon and Jimmy to decide how to play this. Devon doesn't look at me. All of his attention is on Jimmy.

"That's not an option," he says.

At least we're on the same page in that area.

"Why don't you want to share a room now? I thought you two—"

"Drop it, Jimmy," Devon cuts off whatever Jimmy was about to reveal.

Jimmy gives a confused look around the room, but thankfully everyone else seems happy to drop it and move on. While they sort out sleeping arrangements, I start planning how to manage this. Are there more victims—or almost victims—of Vincent here on campus? Are there more predators in the fraternity that need to be dealt with? Both possibilities seem all too likely. I make an excuse and disappear into my room.

* * *

"What's up?" Priscilla answers on the first ring but sounds completely casual. I can hear chatter and music in the background, so I know she's out in public and probably can't talk freely.

I put on my own fake casual voice to match hers.

"Just calling to say hi and let you know I may have stepped in something."

"Oh?"

I hear someone's voice in the background, trying to get her attention. I don't have much time, and I'd rather not risk having this story get out of hand before I can do something about it.

"Yeah. One of my brothers did something to piss me off." Pris is smart enough that I don't have to clue her in on the code I'm trying to use.

"Yeah? Do you need help mending fences?"

"I could use some advice, but it can wait until you're free to talk. Don't stop what you're doing just for me."

Code for: I don't want your friends to know anything is wrong, but I also really need your help.

Good thing she knows me so well.

"I'll call you back when I get a minute."

"Sounds good."

We both hang up without a formal goodbye. She's been acting as my older sister for a long time. If she was human, she could be my mother. But I wouldn't even think about calling my actual mother about this. I already know my mother's advice. Don't rock the boat. Don't draw attention. Be who your father wants you to be, because life will be easier that way.

* * *

"What's going on?" Pris doesn't waste time when she calls back an hour later, so I get straight to it.

"One of the vampires in our father's fraternity drugged one of my friends last night. Someone got her away safely, but we think he's probably done it before and that there are probably victims who weren't lucky enough to get away from him."

She huffs a grunt of anger over the phone. "Fuck. Do I know him?"

"You definitely know of him. I don't know if you've met. Vincent Davenport?"

"Like, of Davenport Pharmaceuticals?" she shrieks into my ear. "That Davenport?"

"Yeah, afraid so. And even worse in person than you've probably imagined."

Pris can never sit still when she's upset about something, and I can hear her agitated steps pacing from the other end of the line.

"Let me guess," she says after a few moments of pacing and muttered curses. "He's the absolute cliché of a rich, privileged, natural-born vampire and expects everyone to kiss his precious feet everywhere he goes?"

"That's pretty much him. Snobby too. And I'm sure he'll cause problems for the girl he went after last night. We just don't know what he'll do."

"I've got a few ideas of what he's capable of," she says.

Unfortunately, she knows the Vincent Davenport type all too well. One of them is why she dropped out of college as a junior and has been living her best bohemian life ever since.

"I'm really sorry, Pris. I wish I wasn't bringing up shit like this for you."

"Don't worry about it."

I let her pace and think for a while. It's not like I have any new ideas to add to the situation.

"How immediate do you think the threat is?"

"That he'll come after Gloria, you mean?"

"Yeah. Does she need protection right now?"

I think it over. "She and her roommate are going to stay with us in our dorm, at least tonight, so they'll have some protection."

"That's good," Pris confirms. "I don't think the girl or anyone connected with her should go anywhere alone until you've dealt with your vampire issue."

I nod my head, knowing that she can't see but needing to confirm for myself that I've been making the right decisions. "Okay. Yeah, that's probably best. We'll make sure they don't have to walk around alone."

"And it probably goes without saying, but no parties for the foreseeable future."

I breathe a sigh of relief at that. "I'm not ready to face any of those guys just yet anyway."

I can practically hear Priscilla's worried thoughts through the phone. "Also, I know you don't want to hear this, but you probably have to tell our father. It's going to be shitty when he finds out about it, but if you can get ahead of it . . ."

"It might help, or it might just trap me even more than I already am," I counter.

"Maybe. Something to think about. I can't tell you what to do."

All I fucking want in the world is for her to tell me what to do, as long as what she tells me to do doesn't involve telling my father.

I am so fucked right now.

"Thanks, I'll take it under advisement," I mutter.

She gives a thoughtful hum under her breath.

"What?" I ask.

"It's just . . . I know I just told you to stay away from the frat house, but what if you didn't?"

"Didn't stay away?" A new ache starts behind my left eye.

Pris sighs. "Look. I know it's probably the last thing you want to do, but if they don't realize that you're associated with this girl, you might be able to do some recon. Right? If they know you're friends with her, you're probably already cooked, but if you can go under the pretense of learning more about the fraternity . . ."

"You're right. That sounds like the last thing I want to do." I groan into my hand to muffle the sound from my roommates. "But I can't think of a better option."

"Think it over first, okay? And call me tomorrow morning with an update? If Davenport tries to escalate things, you tell me the instant it happens?"

"I promise." Right now, Priscilla is the only person that I trust absolutely with this. I hope I don't have to call her in to kick any asses before we find some more allies.

Chapter Seventeen

DEVON - PRESENT

The first thing I see when I get up the next morning is Jimmy's dick hanging out in the kitchen. The guy literally has no modesty whatsoever. Gloria is acting neither surprised nor impressed as she starts the coffee maker.

She's got a better poker face than me. The first time I caught an eyeful of Jimmy, I was too enthralled to look away. Whatever else you might say about the guy, he actually does look really good naked. But Gloria is just calmly going through the process of making a pot of coffee while completely ignoring the chubbed-up dick that keeps trying to point to her.

"I'd heard rumors about werewolves having absolutely no sense of shame or modesty," I tell Gloria, "but I never really believed them until I started living with this guy."

Jimmy's grin widens. "Don't even pretend you don't enjoy the view."

I wave my hand at Jimmy's crotch. "I've seen the view, and I'm pretty sure there's no more to see." Giving a significant head nod at Gloria, I continue. "You should keep something back if you want anyone to ever stay interested."

Thankfully, we prove that Jimmy can be shamed into putting on clothes so everyone can drink their coffee and eat the cinnamon rolls that seem to have magically appeared overnight—probably Marcus's doing—without having to stare down Jimmy's half-cocked erection.

Marcus pokes his head out about five minutes before Jimmy and Gloria said they would leave for their first class.

"Devon, you're still good with keeping an eye on Bee this morning, right?"

"Yeah," I assure him. "I don't have any classes this morning, so I'll get her to classes, and then we'll come back here for a debrief.

Marcus nods at the plan and disappears into his room again.

* * *

It turns out that Bee has the same freshman English class as me, just in the morning instead of the afternoon. The professor doesn't even seem to notice a different face in the lecture hall and seems to be at the exact same place in the syllabus for both classes. That will make life easier, if I can simply start showing up for the morning class instead of the afternoon class. And sitting next to Bee while we take notes in a companionable silence is no hardship either.

Taking her through the tunnels to get to and from class has my every nerve ending buzzing, though. If there were any way for me to take her above ground, away from any potential vampire threat, I would have.

She doesn't ask about the tunnels, though, or comment at all. She just looks around curiously the entire way there.

"They built them so vampires could get to daytime classes

safely," I offer as an explanation, wanting to apologize. Wanting to be someone else. Wanting to not be one of the monsters she needs protection from.

"Oh, yeah, that makes sense," she replies, as if she's not worried about any vampire threat whatsoever.

I keep my eyes peeled and my head on a swivel the entire time we're down there. She might not realize how dangerous vampires are, but I know all too well what can happen to someone who lets their guard down.

* * *

Jeff and his human friend Gabe are sitting on the couch when we get back.

"Any problems?" Jeff asks before we're all the way through the door.

"None at all," Bee answers. "This guy kept me safe from any lurking bad guys."

Blushing isn't really something that vampires do, but if I could, I would be blushing bright red right now.

"Thankfully, we didn't come across any bad guys this time around," I tell them.

Gabe smiles and clasps my shoulder. "It's good you were able to look out for her anyway, even if there weren't any bad guys. For all we know, you scared them all away."

Considering he's as human as can be, I'm a little surprised at how well the guy gets me.

"Yeah. We'll keep doing the protection detail until we're absolutely sure any danger has passed."

Jeff makes an "aha" face. "Actually, I'm really glad you mentioned that. Since Gabe and I can't do much on the protection detail front, we were trying to think of ways that we could help."

"Yeah?" Bee flops down on an armchair. "I'm all ears. I

would love to put all of this behind us as soon as possible, and I'm sure Gloria feels the same. It's been a long fucking day."

I don't think any of us have heard Bee curse in the short time we've known her. We all give a little synchronized jump and turn to stare at her.

"What?" She looks bewildered by our sudden attention.

I decide to drop it, and neither of the other guys seems interested in bringing it up. "You said you were thinking of ways to help?" I turn back to Jeff.

"Yeah. We were thinking, maybe if we can somehow reveal Vincent for what he really is, make sure everyone knows what kind of shit happens at that frat house, maybe that would stop him from doing it to anyone else?"

Bee sits up. "You're right. If nothing else, we need to warn anyone else away from him so he doesn't have such easy access to his victims. He's probably got other victims who we're too late to help, but maybe we can help some people."

"You realize what our problem is, though, right?" Gabe looks between us.

Jeff wilts. "I can think of a few, actually."

"Yeah, but we've got one huge problem. If we're worried about Vincent retaliating right now, we have to believe he would come after anyone trying to reveal what he's up to. We can't share one story of Vincent being awful without expecting him to come back swinging. And we can't share any stories about him without assuming he'll know exactly who to come after for them. How do we protect his victims if they do agree to come forward? I mean, we can try to put safeguards in place to ensure their anonymity, but Vincent—at the very least —will know exactly who spilled the beans."

"Shit." I scrub my fingers through my hair. "There's no way we can ask people to stand up to him when we know he'll just retaliate."

Bee taps her lips thoughtfully. "I obviously can't speak for anyone else, but I think it's worth asking around anyway. We may find there are a lot of people who have been wanting to share their stories and just couldn't find an effective way to do it. They might be willing to accept the risk. Besides, there's safety in numbers, and I have a feeling we're going to have no shortage of victims, sadly. We need to try offering them a chance to do something about this."

Jeff, Gabe, and I all nod in agreement.

"Not everyone will be willing to take a risk," Jeff says, "but if we can find a few who are, we might be able to make a move."

Jimmy and Gloria show up a few minutes later and seem cautiously excited about the skeletal plan we've sketched together.

"Are we absolutely certain we can't just lure him into an alley and rip him apart?" is Gloria's question.

Jimmy looks worried and rubs her knee in a soothing pattern.

"Only as a last resort," he tells her.

Chapter Eighteen

MARCUS - PRESENT

Spending extra time at the frat house is even worse than I imagined it would be. The guys there are either the worst kind of pretentious vampires I've ever met—case in point, Vincent, who I can't look in the eye for fear of giving away my true feelings about this whole shit show—or they're this wormlike subhuman, living in constant fear of what the more powerful vampires will do to them. I've got some protection just from who my father is, but that's the same kind of protection that had me regularly locked in closets at boarding school. It doesn't mean none of them make an effort to haze me every time I show up.

"Should we invite him down for a game?" one of the nameless vampires that I'm supposed to become brothers with asks.

He's not asking me so I do my best to ignore him. I keep my eyes trained on the TV while my senses are alert to all of the other dangers in this ridiculous, gilded living room. Or maybe it would be more accurately described as a den? No.

Man cave. There's no other word to describe the pool tables and couches and pretentious artwork paired randomly with centerfold model posters scattered around the space.

Vincent–just as vile as I remember him from boarding school–looks up with a grin. "Didn't you hear? He doesn't like our kinds of games. Marcus would never be interested in what we have in the lower level."

No. Don't react. Don't ask. He's dying to tell you. I can feel the rasp as I grind my teeth together. Good thing vampire teeth grow back like a shark's. I would be hillbilly level toothless if I couldn't regrow all the teeth I've ground down since spending more time with the brotherhood.

"Because," Vincent continues in his most condescending fuck boy voice possible, then drops into a stage whisper to catch as many ears as possible, "it's only girls in the lower levels, and he can't even get hard for them, much less play any games."

I feel a pang of sickness but school my face to stay blank. He won't get that satisfaction from me.

Vincent's smile widens even farther. I wouldn't have thought it possible, but I swear, if his grin stretches any more, it's going to actually split his head in half. "Did you know," he says in a slimy giggly voice to his neighbor and the rest of the room, "that Marcus here would rather let himself be fucked than actually stick his dick in a girl. You think I'm exaggerating, but I've seen it first hand. Isn't that right, Marcus?"

I swallow back bile and rage. He just wants the reaction and I refuse to give it to him. I'm proud of what he sees as a weakness in my character, and I absolutely don't have to justify myself to any of these fuckwads. What I need to do is add "find a way downstairs to possibly save some more of Vincent's victims" to my list of things to do here.

"His loss," another guy says, and most of the group scattered around the room gets up and follows their leader some-where else.

One of the guys left behind leans toward me with an earnest look. "Just ignore them. They're messing with you."

I roll my eyes. "Oh really? I hadn't figured that out."

"No, I mean, about the girls in the basement or whatever. There's no girls. Vincent is just trying to push your buttons. Once you've been around long enough to prove yourself, he'll calm down. You'll see. We're like any other frat on campus. No dungeons. No girls being held as prisoners. Cross my heart."

If only I could take him at his word.

He puts his hands up. "I get it. You don't have any reason to trust any of us yet. Give it some time." Then he leaves me with more questions–and suspicions–than I had before.

* * *

I can tell there's something wrong with the blood the instant it hits my tongue. That's what I get for trusting someone else with my food, I guess.

Childish snickering comes from around the corner.

Great. Of course I've got an audience for whatever I just put in my mouth.

It's not worth calling out the perpetrators, so I quietly spit my mouthful of blood in the sink and throw the wasted bag in the trash. All I can hope is that the tampering won't cause me too many issues.

Just as I think it, my stomach knots in on itself. Whatever they put in the blood, it was potent enough to cause problems with just one mouthful. But I refuse to give my tormentors the satisfaction of groaning out loud and letting them know how much pain I'm in. Keeping my jaw clamped shut, I grab onto the counter to hold myself up and use it to inch my way toward the exit.

"Is there an issue, Levine?" Vincent sneers at me from the door.

Fuck, things can't get much worse.

"Just. A Bad. Batch. Of blood," I tell him through clenched teeth. My stomach twists even tighter, and the room swims around me. Whatever he did to the blood, it's beyond the basic practical joke level of tampering. I can tell I'm in serious trouble if I don't get real blood in my system quickly to replace whatever poison I just drank.

"You have to be careful about where your drinks come from, you know," he continues in a bored voice. "You never know what someone might have put in them, am I right?"

This guy cannot be fucking serious right now.

"I'll. Keep it. In mind."

He gives a sadistic twist of his lips. "You do that. Anyway, I suppose I should let you get off to . . . whatever you were doing . . ."

I grimace in what I will swear under oath is actually a smile, then stumble past him to the tunnel entrance back to campus.

Once I'm safe, alone in the dank tunnel, I slide down the wall and double over in pain. With shaking hands, I fish a blood capsule out of my pocket, then almost curse when it slips out of my fingers and rolls across the packed dirt floor. No point in cursing. I need to save my energy.

Shaking with desperation, I scrabble for the lost capsule and barely get hold of it. It's instant relief when it explodes on my tongue. Devon was absolutely right. They are disgusting. But it sure beats dying in a vampire frat house any day of the week.

I give myself five minutes. Five minutes to lie on my back in the dirt and feel the blood flowing down my throat and doing its work to heal me. Five minutes to realize that I can't go back to the frat house until I have a better way to deal with Vincent.

Then I head back to my own dorm, probably looking like the castoffs from a cat's dinner.

* * *

I'm greeted with Jeff's horrified "What the fuck happened to you?" when I get back to my dorm, which is both comforting and lovely.

"Vampire business," I growl, stumbling into my room, where I at least know the blood hasn't been tampered with.

I would normally heat my blood bag like a civilized vampire, but I'm too desperate for its healing qualities to go through my normal rituals.

When you're near death, blood is life, and you'll take it any way you can get it.

The minifridge in my room is packed full of blood willingly given at the bank in exchange for money. I know there are humans who prefer to donate emergency blood, which is sacrosanct and only ever sent to other humans. Thankfully, there are humans willing to be paid for this service to vampires. I've never asked one in person. I suppose some of them must have realized the alternative is donating all of your life's blood at once. Most humans would prefer to donate a small amount and keep their life. It's what allows our treaties to work.

Of course, most born vampires do have a father or uncle who introduces them to live feeding pretty early on. I think I was seven when my father pressed my face down on the neck of a terrified woman and told me to drink. All while my mother looked on too, which might explain the current cold and awkward status of our relationship. My mother had the experience of living then dying, then watching her own son epitomize the type of monster that killed her.

I bite straight down on the plastic bag and let the blood flow into me and replenish my life.

"What the—" Jeff cuts off his own question as he sees what I'm up to. I don't even have the energy to tell him he should have knocked, or to get out, or explain what I'm doing. "Shit, dude, you do not look good."

I swallow the last of the blood bag and fall back on my bed. "Don't feel too good either," I tell him.

"What happened?"

I want to wave him off. Tell him it's nothing. I don't have energy for anything other than the truth, though. "Thought I had an in with the frat. I was wrong."

"An in with . . . Are you saying you tried to get in with Vincent's fraternity?" His voice jumps about an octave. "And they did something to you?"

"Yeah. Just a warning, though. I'll be okay."

Jeff paces from one side of my bedroom to the other, running his hands through his hair and muttering various combinations of curse words the whole time.

"You will be okay, or you think you'll be okay?" he finally asks.

I shrug, still sprawled across my bed and unable to move. "I got some clean blood in me. I should be fine pretty soon."

"What the fuck did he do to you?"

Sitting up is a struggle, but I get the feeling Jeff won't take me seriously until I can look him in the eye and give him a coherent explanation. "Vampires need clean blood to protect us against—" I wave my arm vaguely and hope he understands. "—you know, everything. But if someone tampers with the blood—drugs it or poisons it or lets it rot—it messes with our system. Drinking clean blood can usually heal anything, as long as we get it fast enough. Sometimes, blood capsules are enough, and in case of real emergencies, hospitals stock a supply of vampire blood because it has extra healing properties. I'll be fine, probably don't even need to go to the hospital. I don't think Vincent really meant for me to die. It was just the usual bullshit hazing vampires expect in a place like that. It was an unpleasant warning, though. I won't go back to the frat house unless I have a better plan in place."

Jeff paces some more. "We might have a better plan, if you're interested in hearing it," he tells me after a tense silence. "Come out when you're ready and we'll fill you in."

It takes another blood bag before I feel steady enough on my feet to walk out and face the others.

Chapter Nineteen

DEVON - PRESENT

Our dorm is too quiet. Jimmy and Gloria decided to take off for the weekend, which is fine by me. I think all of us were ready to get some fresh, pheromone-free air by the time they cleared out. Jimmy swore to me that he's not just taking Gloria away in an attempt to jump her bones as soon as they have some privacy, but I'm not putting money on those two not hooking up. Better that it happens away from this dorm so the rest of us don't have to hear—and probably smell and possibly see—it happen.

But now, things are too quiet. Aside from the day Marcus came back looking absolutely trashed, I've barely seen him. We're back to him sneaking out for classes like a high school student breaking curfew. And Jeff, Gabe, and Taylor have been working on a website to expose what Vincent has done, but they also have classes and lives to keep them busy.

"I guess it's just you and me for a bit," I tell Bee, trying to put a cheerful face on it.

Bee really is lovely. And nice. And sweet. And having her

around is just not the same as having Jeff or Jimmy to liven things up. And she's pretty enough, but I don't think either of us have felt even a tiny spark of attraction for each other. Nope. All of my interest is still caught up on the same closeted, unavailable, emotionally stunted vampire.

Bee thankfully doesn't notice the broodiness under my cheerful words. "I guess it is," she agrees.

We sit in silence for a few minutes. I guess we've officially reached that tipping point where we've spent too much time together and run out of new conversation topics.

"So how is Jeff's project with his friends going?" she finally asks. Thank every deity that she thought of something, because I was preparing to sit in awkward silence for the rest of freshman year.

"Pretty good, last I heard. Actually, maybe they'd be interested in coming over here to work on it. It wouldn't feel so empty in here that way."

She breathes a relieved sigh. "That's a great idea."

It only takes fifteen minutes to get Jeff to come home and round up his buddies. By the time everyone is settled in the living room and snacking, computer keys clicking away, it's actually kind of cozy here.

Marcus even pokes his head out to talk through some logistics with the guys, though the asshole studiously avoids looking at me throughout the conversation, and then sticks around to cook for everyone, which is . . . confusing. I still feel a pit open in my stomach every time I think of him. We had what I thought was amazing sex, with all of that chemistry I'd never felt with anyone else, then before I know what's happening, he slaps me with the "pretend this never happened" routine. Worse, even after he hurt me and made me feel like a gross, dirty tissue, I still miss him, even with him right there in the kitchen doing one of his miraculous stir-fries with only a hot plate and microwave. Fuck, I just want to find someone who won't make me feel utterly used and disgusting afterwards. Is that so much to ask?

"This is great, Marcus," Bee says, blowing on her noodles before taking a bite.

He looks at his shoes and mumbles something that might be an acknowledgment of the compliment but is more likely a deflection.

"I mean it," Bee says in an almost motherly voice. "I really love how you take care of us humans. It would just be nonstop pizza delivery around here if not for your cooking, so thank you."

I almost laugh at the uncomfortable look on his face. The guy cannot take a compliment.

"I'd better . . ." He doesn't even finish his sentence before dashing back to his room.

Then, I do laugh. Did I say my feelings were complicated? No. Complicated doesn't even touch it. I'm still in knots with how much I still want him and how much it hurts to want him. At least I can still laugh, though, right?

* * *

By the time Jimmy and Gloria get back, we've worked out all the kinks. Well . . . Ish. Gabe thinks it's safe enough to go live with the website to expose Vincent whenever Gloria gives the go-ahead. Marcus has spent most of his time either doing god knows what in his own room or pacing the dorm living room and muttering darkly to himself. Taylor keeps pointing out that there's no way to ensure anonymity, especially since Vincent knows exactly who his victims are.

Jeff finally breaks us out of a circular argument about keeping Vincent's victims safe by declaring a moratorium on the discussion and putting something dumb on TV. Some kind of gameshow involving shifters trying to literally sniff out their mates. Trust Jeff to put on something hopelessly romantic like that. I decide to lean back on the couch and mull over my own thoughts.

I can't say I'm much for the idea of mates. I used to be, though I wouldn't have admitted it to anyone back in high school. Honestly, the night I went out and got myself turned into a vampire, I think a part of me was hoping to find someone I was fated to be with. Someone who was made just for me. But instead, I found sharp teeth and pain and someone who was only interested in hurting me and ruining my life. I wish I was still innocent enough to believe in something like mates.

And then Jimmy and Gloria get back, and Jimmy is absolutely glowing with a smug kind of happiness that I can't figure out. Bee figures it out. She drags Gloria into Jimmy's room and shuts the door to keep the rest of us from eavesdropping.

"Looks like the girls have some stuff to talk about?" I speculate.

Marcus also figures it out before me. "Isn't it obvious that Jimmy and Gloria hooked up this weekend?"

And shit. Yes, now that he mentions it, all of the too-obvious puzzle pieces fall into place.

And, fuck, I'm fighting off a wave of jealousy because it's obvious from the look on Jimmy's face that he thinks he's found his one person, never mind that she might not think so. He believes he's found his mate, and no matter what I tell myself about naive ideals that should have disappeared with my innocence in high school, I want what he has so fucking bad it hurts.

I slide a glance toward Marcus, but he's not looking at me. I might as well not even exist for him right now. Which hurts almost as much as the jealousy tearing through me.

MARCUS - PRESENT

So Jimmy and Gloria are all coupled up and getting all lovey-dovey. Brilliant. And we've found some more stories to add to our ammunition against Vincent. Lovely. And everyone seems ready to launch our first attack against Vincent. Fucking awesome.

Except for the fact that none of them have a fucking clue what they're actually in for. Vincent poisoned me—or had me poisoned, same thing—as a warning. Somehow, I don't think he would have even been particularly put out if I hadn't survived. His message would still make it to Jimmy and the rest of them. Maybe it would have served him better if he could have dropped my desiccated corpse at Jimmy's front door. As it stands, he has to count on me to willingly deliver his message, but I'm not going to give him what he wants. I have no fucking clue how to shelter my friends from the war they're about to start, though.

Priscilla will know what to do, I decide, and she picks up on the first ring. Sometimes I wonder if she can read my mind.

"Yeah?" She doesn't waste any time.

"Some friends of mine are about to start a war against our father's fraternity, and someone tried to poison me last time I was there."

I can practically hear her eye blink over the phone. "Holy shit, Marcus!" she explodes at me. "Are you alright? Do you know who did it? And what the fuck do you mean about starting a war?"

Letting out a humorless laugh, I wait for her to calm down before I answer. "I'm fine. I had blood caps on me and clean blood back at my dorm. I'm pretty sure they didn't actually intend for me to die, though I doubt they would have been too upset if I did. As for who . . . I mean, it really could have been anyone, but I have no reason to think Davenport wasn't behind it. He could be pulling someone's strings or just asked a friend for a favor. It doesn't really help to know, does it?"

"I suppose not," she grumbles. "And the other thing?"

"Yeah. The other thing. That's what I'm really calling about. We've tracked down a few more of Davenport's victims. Enough to go public with their stories and have too much evidence to be ignored."

"And that's what they're planning on doing? Do they know what they're up against?"

"The victims at least know some of what he's capable of, and they want to do this anyway."

"Brave girls," Pris says.

"Yeah," I confirm. "If they have any idea what's coming their way and they're still standing up against him, they're definitely brave. Not everyone involved in this knows what Davenport is capable of, though. They're the ones I'm really worried about."

She sighs. Heavy. Resigned. "You're not going to like what I'm about to say."

"Better say it anyway and get it over with, then."

"You're going to need a backup plan in case they need rescuing."

I glare at the floor, at the wall, at the space between my desk and my closet. She's right, and she's also right that I don't like hearing it. "I'm going to end up having to beg him for help, aren't I?"

"It's looking more and more likely. Sorry, kid."

"Don't call me that," I answer reflexively. I'm not a kid. I don't get to be a kid, and I've never gotten to be a kid. Pretty soon, I'm going to hand over the last scraps of the childhood I had, and I won't even get to pretend anymore.

"You gonna be okay?"

"Oh, you know. As okay as I was ever going to be, I suppose."

"Let me know what happens. Let me know if there's anything I can do to help."

"Yeah. Of course. Will do." My own voice sounds faraway. I feel like I'm being pulled down a dark tunnel, away from my own body, away from my own life, and into the darkness.

* * *

Jimmy is looking after Gloria. Devon is on Bee Duty. Jeff and Gabe, because they're human and therefore less intimidating, are going to try approaching the girls we already know about and offer our help. Taylor, as the brains behind revealing Vincent's true nature, is on website duty.

Me? I've got no purpose right now except to worry ineffectually.

It doesn't take long for the shit to hit the fan.

Devon and Bee come back after their first class. No one did anything directly to her, but people were whispering just loud enough for her and Devon to hear the horrible things they were saying. Jeff and Gabe show up not long afterward, having rounded up Lydia and Kelsey, two of the girls who came forward. We were so naive to think there was any kind of safety in numbers. Vincent, or someone in his corner, at least, has leaked all the identities of the people on our website.

The dorm is crowded, and emotions are high, and I still haven't accepted that I need to face my father.

I'm still wallowing when Jimmy and Gloria get back. Apparently, Gloria was followed and harassed all the way to and from class. Everything is spiraling further out of my control.

"Shit!" Taylor shouts from his position at the computer, then, "Fucking son of a bitch!"

We all turn to him with questioning gazes, but he's

completely absorbed in whatever he's dealing with on his computer.

"Um . . . something we should know about?" Jeff asks.

Taylor looks up and blinks around at us like he has no idea where we all came from. "There have been some responses online," he explains.

As bad as things were before, I knew they could get worse. Judging by everyone else's reaction, I was the only one who realized it. Taylor keeps talking, but I hear him from a distance, through a haze. All of the names and dorms and class schedules of victims who came forward have been shared with the world, and now all of those victims are being followed and harrassed by Vincent's groupies. Or maybe his flunkies. Possibly some goons. None of the victims can even get to class safely. And I've been the worst kind of idiot for letting my friends go through with this when I knew what the outcome would be. I knew I couldn't protect them, and now I'm watching them all suffer.

Chapter Twenty

DEVON - SIX MONTHS AGO

This room is too fucking quiet. There's not even the normal beeping of monitors I keep expecting to hear in a hospital room. If there's no need for monitors, I don't understand why I'm still stuck here.

It's bullshit.

I want to get up and kick a fucking hole in the wall. Maybe tear the TV apart with my bare hands.

Instead I turn over on my other side so I can stare at a different wall for a bit. It doesn't matter. Nothing matters. I'll be stuck in this room no matter what.

There's a knock, but no pause for me to say whether I'm okay with visitors. I never get to say whether I'm okay with visitors.

"You know what time it is," the overly cheerful woman in bubblegum pink scrubs chimes at me as she rolls a cart into my space.

The only monitors they need for me now. I hold out my arm wordlessly for her. I've had a week to learn the routine.

I'm still not used to the routine, but at least I know what's expected of me now.

I barely notice the needles as she sticks them in me. I don't feel pain the same way I used to, the way I did as a human. For humans, pain is a warning of danger. For vampires, a little needle prick doesn't even register as danger. The doctors tell me I'll reach a point where my vampire senses recognize real danger, but I haven't tuned into them properly yet. Or some shit like that. Truth be told, I don't really want to tune in to any vampire senses. I want my human senses back. I want my life back.

"Looks like you're a little low still," my nurse—no, I correct myself, she's my feeding specialist—tells me without looking away from her magical mystery monitor cart. "You know what that means, right?"

I slide down in my hospital bed, hoping it swallows me up before the next part. My stomach is already trying to empty itself at the promise of what's coming my way.

"I'm going to need to push two bags for you in the next hour. So, how are we going to do this, Devon? Both bags right now or one now and one in thirty minutes?"

I don't mean to say anything, but a strangled, "no," finds its way out anyway.

She really does look sorry. That's the worst part, I think. She really feels bad about my misery, but it's not going to stop her.

"The only other option is we put you back on the drip, and that just means you'll be stuck here longer. You don't want to be stuck here forever, do you? Don't you want to be able to feed yourself?"

I'm almost crying, but I hold it together enough to sit up and hold out my hand for the bloodbag.

"That's my boy!" she says, back to her usual bounce, chirpy self.

Don't think don't think don't think, the mantra runs through my head over and over as I bring the nozzle to my lips. At least I can't smell the blood when it's in these sterile bags. When it hits my tongue, though, there's no pretending I'm trying to swallow anything other than human blood.

I manage to get half the bag down before I can't trick myself anymore and I start gagging. There's a pink, plastic basin waiting under my chin when it happens. Part of being a feeding specialist for vampires like me is anticipating when they're going to start puking up the blood you just fed them.

"There you go." Her voice is incongruously encouraging, considering she's holding a tub of my bloody vomit. "Now drink some water and try again."

I really do cry, then. Just a little. Just a few tears that drip down and mix with the mess in front of me. I don't want to drink some water and try again. I don't want to learn how to feed myself like this so I can get out of this hospital room. I just want to find a dark cave where I'll never be force fed another bag of blood.

Chapter Twenty-One

DEVON - PRESENT

There were ten victims we already knew about, but we've only managed to find and convince five of them to come back with us. And even those five extra people, plus me and Marcus and Jimmy and Jeff and Gloria and Beth and Gabe and Taylor . . . I'm losing my mind. Up to this point, my experience with vampire senses is that things are dulled from how they were when I was human. Human food has almost no taste anymore. Plants and perfumes and spices have almost no smell anymore.

But a room overflowing with living, breathing, sweating bodies? All of my senses are clanking with overload. The emotions shooting through this room, the jangling heartbeats of too many people at once, and the raised voices are enough to make me desperate to curl up like a roly-poly and hide from the world until this all passes over.

That's not an option, though. Someone has to figure out sleeping arrangements, and there's only four beds and thirteen people, and a bunch of those thirteen people don't trust the rest of the thirteen enough to sleep in the same room as them, let alone the same bed. Having been on the wrong end of a vampire assault myself, I can't blame Vincent's victims for feeling distrusting of vampires. I went through months of therapy before I was comfortable in the same room as myself.

And Jeff is acting like an absolute ass. Which is not how he usually acts, but it's not like we have a quiet room to have a private conversation so I can figure out what his issue is. Instead, we've both resorted to shouting at each other.

"Do vampires even get cold? I thought you were room temperature to begin with!"

He shouts the question like it's a normal extension of the argument we've been having. Maybe to him it is. Under normal circumstances, I would take it in stride and just remind him that it's not the most polite way of putting it. Instead of taking it in stride, it fills me with a bitter rage, though. After everything we've been going through, all the shit that I've had to go through, I thought he at least understood that there are some things you don't say out loud.

Some part of me, way off in the distance, knows that he can't understand what it's like to have your life ripped away and suddenly become something monstrous when you're still in high school. Some part of me knows he means nothing by it. He doesn't know my life, or my death, or any part of my story. But most of me, right in this moment, is just fucking furious that he's trying to weigh in on anything at all when he doesn't have the experience to warrant having a voice in the matter.

I get in his face and jab him in the chest with an angry finger. "Don't. Talk. About. Shit. You. Don't. Under. Stand."

At least he has the grace to look like he realizes he messed up. I don't think he understands how he messed up, though, and my blood is still boiling.

He backs down first, storming out of the dorm. I can't

handle the questioning looks half the room is throwing my way, so I retreat to my own room to let them sort out the sleeping arrangements without my help.

I pace beside my bed, trying to calm down. At least it's quieter here. The numerous heartbeats that I can't help but hear are muted by the walls, though I'm still hyper aware of the numerous living bodies on the other side of my door.

What would my therapist say about this situation?

I stop pacing and press my palms into my eyes in an attempt to stop at least one of the senses currently over-whelming my system. I need to calm down. I need to . . . ugh. I need to feed, I realize with a mix of relief at finding the solution and disgust at what that solution is.

With an angry grunt, I drop down on my bed and reach for the nearby fridge I use to store my blood bags.

So. Fucking. Gross.

It's been almost a year now since I was turned. You would think I would be used to this by now, but it hasn't gotten much easier since that first time when I puked every drop back up as soon as it hit my tongue.

I glare down at the bag of O positive, but it doesn't respond to my hatred or disgust or self-pity. It just sits in my hand. A promise of cold goo that's going to make me feel sick and hate myself a little more with each swallow.

And it doesn't help to know that it was willingly given. It's still human. Blood. Not made for consumption.

I run through all of the exercises my therapist gave me, then bite down on the plastic and start sucking.

It's the most horrible thing ever. It never gets better, no matter how many times I do this. It never gets any easier to circumvent my human instincts that say *wrong, wrong, wrong* while my vampire instincts try to say *food.* I manage to drink the whole thing without gagging. This time.

Hoping someone outside is figuring out solutions, I give up for the day and burrow under my covers. If I need to give up my bed to one of our guests, someone can come wake me up to tell me.

MARCUS - PRESENT

Everyone else seems content to call it a night and worry about our three still-missing girls in the morning. I can't just let it go.

Oh, and there's the little issue where we've run out of beds, so my options are to share with Devon or sleep on the floor.

No, thanks. I'll spend my not-sleeping time on something useful rather than wasting a night trying not to touch—or think about touching—Devon. It's not like I really need sleep anyway. Not in the way humans and shifters do.

Unfortunately, the girls that no one could find earlier in the day are still proving elusive. One, a human named Eileen, I finally find when I realize that her family lives in town. Even though she has a dorm on campus, which someone on the internet leaked, she has a safe house to turn to. It's past midnight when I find a friend of Stacy—a shifter we couldn't find before—at a house party. She drunkenly spills the story that Stacy has gone to live with her pack until everything calms down. I hate that we couldn't protect her. I hate that they were able to run her off like that. At least she's safe.

Which leaves one victim–a vampire named Cassie–unaccounted for. I make my way through every party I find and can't find anyone willing or able to tell me where Cassie is.

I drag myself back to the dorm at sunrise to wake everyone up and update them.

* * *

They respond about how I expected. Gabe and Taylor get to work on their laptops, trying to track down any digital traces Cassie might have left. Jimmy is too distracted by Gloria to focus on the issue at hand. Gloria is ineffectually outraged about the whole situation.

But I'm the one who should have known what was coming and done a better job of protecting everyone. I'm the one who should be feeling responsible.

Cutting through all of my self-loathing, I realize that I'm out of time. I can't put off doing the last thing I want to do any longer.

"I think we should go to the authorities," I tell everyone, and the room erupts. People are shouting and arguing and taking sides before I can even defend my statement.

It's Bee who wades into the middle of everything and gets people calmed down enough to listen and discuss rationally.

I explain into the space she creates, "I think if we let the highest-ranking vampires know what's going on, they would be interested in doing whatever it takes to minimize the damage Vincent has been doing."

None of them like it. Fuck, I don't like it. Not one bit. Jimmy agrees to go back to his wolf pack and let his pack know about the situation, though he looks like he's going to puke at the prospect of going to his leaders. Everyone else ranges from confused to resigned to worried. Every possible emotion on the spectrum is represented by someone.

* * *

I pace my dorm room and suck nervously at a blood bag as I try to work myself up to contacting my father.

Here's the thing. Once I do that, I can't undo it. If I call him up and ask for help with the Vincent situation, he'll expect something in return, and once I've agreed to his terms . . . I'm not ready for that.

The Vampiric Enclave needs to know what's going on. The highest level of power in vampire politics and society—separate from human political institutions and often working outside of human laws—is the most likely institution to be able to get Vincent and his cronies in check. The Enclave–with my father in its inner circle–is the most likely way to have Vincent wiped away and no longer a problem for any of us. I know this. Rationally, I know that I have to contact them.

In reality, I can't seem to force myself to call his number. Maybe if I had any other way of contacting the Enclave, but this is it.

My thumb hovers over the call button on my phone, trembling with the conflict raging inside me. I need to call. I need to call. I need to call.

I can't call. No matter how many times I tell myself to do it, I can't make myself.

I throw the empty blood bag across the room, missing the trash can, and sink face-first onto my bed. I'm like an animal in a trap. I know the only way out is to gnaw my own foot off, but I just can't do it.

The inactivity is getting oppressive already. I stand up with a huff and storm out of my room.

"I'm going to try searching for Cassie again," I tell the room before stomping out to make another useless circuit of every dorm and party around campus.

I know I'm not doing anything useful, but it sure beats doing nothing at all.

* * *

My stalling tactic doesn't last long at all before we're all back in the dorm, defeated.

"I think we have to tell his father," I say to myself more than anyone else. They don't know that Vincent's father and the Enclave and my father are all connected and I haven't had the guts to contact any of them.

I'm barely aware of the questions I get or the answers I give. With no other options, I march to my room and hit the call button on my phone before I have the chance to chicken out.

"Well, this is a surprise," my father answers in his smug, oily voice after a few rings. "Are you calling because you just wanted to catch up with your old man, or is there something I can do for you?"

Great. No small talk. No pretending our relationship is anything other than what it is.

"I need some help from you," I admit. The sooner I get it all out in the open, the better. Probably. Why do I feel like I'm about to die a final death, then?

His laugh is humorless. Gloating. "I knew you wouldn't last a semester before you came crawling to me for help."

"Right. So, you know the Daven—"

"No," he cuts me off. "You know that's not how this works. If you're going to come crawling to me for help, that's fine, but I need to see you crawl before I'm willing to entertain your requests."

My stomach twists. Of course, the games are already beginning.

"What do you want me to do?" I can't keep the bitterness from my voice. Don't even bother trying.

He lets out a jolly, empty laugh, like a sociopathic Santa Claus. "You know what I want, my boy! I want to see you crawling to me and admitting that you were wrong about being able to live happily with the walking blood bags. I want to see you on your knees and begging for forgiveness. I want you to come to me so we can speak face-to-face and make a deal. Is it so much to ask that a father gets to see his son in person?"

As if he has ever, in either of our lives, behaved as an actual father.

"Okay. I'll come."

"I'll send a car." I can hear his predatory grin as he says it.

Chapter Twenty-Two

MARCUS - FIVE MONTHS AGO

I clench my fists behind my back because I have to do something with my hands, and I know my father will see it as a weakness if he catches me fidgeting. If he sees a weakness, he's going to pounce on it. It's a lesson I learned the hard way almost ten years ago.

"Your mother tells me you have some kind of proposal for me?"

He says it in his bored voice. He's already decided, and the answer is no choice. I'm not willing to accept that, though. I've learned a lot of lessons from him—most of them the hard way—and one is that nothing is cut-and-dry. Nothing is absolute, and a no can be turned into a yes. You just have to find the right leverage to make it happen.

"I've been accepted into Berring, and—"

"Of course you've been accepted. Can you imagine if you'd cocked it up enough to not be accepted?"

I decide to move past the interruption without acknowledging it. "I've been accepted and am planning to pursue a business degree."

He gives me a shrewd look. "A business degree with the intention of getting involved in this business?"

"If you'll have me. I looked into it, and there are several internships within the organization, but all of them require at least one year of higher education to apply." He and I both know that interning at my father's business is the last thing I want to do. It's not like I have many options, and he also knows that.

"Well, well, well. It's good to see you finally interested in taking some ownership in the family business.

Yes, it's business, and yes, I'm technically his family, but it's not like this is some mom-and-pop organization. And it's not like I actually want to get my hands dirty with my family's blood money, but the alternative is even worse, so here I am.

"I take it you want me to make some calls to make sure the brotherhood is ready for your arrival?"

"Actually." Please let me get through this without stuttering or breaking down or anything like that. "I wanted to talk to you about living in the dorms for my first year. See how the other half lives and all that."

My father leans back in his chair. The smile on his face bodes very ill for me. If he'd lost his temper immediately, I might have had a place to start arguing from, but that smile tells me he knows what I'm up to, and he's got me exactly where he wants me.

"Is that right? You want to see 'how the other half lives.'" He makes sarcastic air quotes with his fingers. "You want to spend time with the walking blood bags. Maybe even make friends with them? Maybe make more than friends with them?" His grin looks downright evil. I am the prey in his trap. Too bad I wasn't smart enough to snatch my hand back when I had the chance.

"I just want one year to have a normal college experience. After that, I'll do what you want. Just, give me one year, okay?"

He laughs—actually laughs out loud like this is the best joke he's ever heard. "Tell you what. I'll give you your year in the dorms. I'll even give you four years in the dorms, if that's what you really want. But everything you do from your first day of college until the day you graduate is something that brings you closer to taking your proper place in our organization. You don't have to live in the fraternity house to become a brother in the fraternity. You will become a member of the fraternity, and you will accept whatever summer internship I decide to throw your way, and you will work for me with a smile on your face, because you can imagine the consequences to both you and your mother if you should . . . stray . . . from this path I've set forth. So, what do you say?"

I swallow to keep the contents of my stomach down. "I agree," I choke out, then hold out my hand for him to shake.

His grip is tight enough to break bones, though that's not much of a concern when I know I'll heal almost immediately. It's just one more way for him to remind me which of us has the power. Him. It's always been him, and it will always be him. I don't need the reminder.

"You really should have negotiated harder," he says with his hand still crushing my fingers. "That lack of a predator's instincts is the first thing we'll have to beat out of you once you join the ranks."

I grit my teeth and focus on not showing my pain. There's nothing I can say to make him stop. He's going to say whatever he wants to say no matter what I do, anyway.

"Also, don't embarrass us both by thinking you have any rights to privacy. I'll either be watching or have someone watching your every move, and we both know that there are some things in your private life that you'd rather I didn't see."

Right. Because I needed another reminder of how disgusted he was the first time he caught me with a guy.

"I promise," I grind out before extricating my hand. It's not the best deal in the world, but it's the best deal I expected to make. At least I'll have this small taste of freedom—or normal life—before I have to buckle down and start acting like an heir again.

Chapter Twenty-Three

MARCUS - PRESENT

True to his word, my father's car meets me in front of the dorm a few short minutes after I go down. The still-rational, still-calm, and detached part of my mind wonders where my father has been keeping this driver that he can be summoned to pick me up so quickly. Most of my mind is not calm, detached, or rational right now.

I don't question it when the driver heads to the airport, or when he opens my car door at the foot of a staircase leading up to a small jet. I hunch down into one of the seats and wonder if anyone will be on this flight with me. It's the type of plane where there's normally a short-skirted flight attendant offering ancient whiskey or expensive champagne, but no one offers me anything. I don't even get a friendly heads-up from the captain when it's time to take off. Suddenly, I'm airborne. It's probably for the best that no one is pretending to pamper me. I don't need someone trying to lull me into believing I'm safe or that this is supposed to be a pleasant experience. I already know if I can't come up with something my father cares about and convince him to believe I'm willing to exchange it, then I'm utterly fucked.

Another anonymous driver loads me off the plane and drops me off—like a pile of luggage with nothing worth stealing in it—at the gates of my father's manor. Not my manor. That's for damn sure. I've never lived here and barely even been here before. I grew up in one of the separate houses on the estate lands until I got shipped off to the best, most brutal vampire boarding school that money could buy. The big house has always been my father's domain. A place I visit when I need to ask him for something or he wants to have his heir seen at an event.

They put me through a security screening process at the front gate which makes airport security seem warm and cuddly, then send me through a secondary screening which I think my father must have set up especially for me, just to show me how little he cares for or trusts me.

Well, congratulations, old man. The feeling is extremely mutual.

* * *

The manor is empty and echoing once I get through the security circus my father has set up. Without any better guidance, I take my best guess and head down the main hallway. Most of the times I've been here before, it's been for some big party where I was expected to be visible in all of the right ways to make my father look good. Not exactly conducive to learning my way around this place.

"How long are you going to wander around before actually facing me?" My father's voice echoes through the hallway.

"Are you going to tell me where to go?" Okay, maybe confrontational isn't the best tone if I want him to agree to do anything for me, but I'm thoroughly fed up by now.

151

He just chuckles in response.

At the end of the hall is a heavy wooden door, intricately carved and stained dark enough the wood sucks the light out of the room. Yep, looks familiar. Like the setting for every personal dressing-down I've ever received from him.

I open the door to find him sitting at his desk and showing off every sharp vampire tooth his lips can reveal.

"I knew you would come around eventually," he says, oozing self-satisfaction and condescension in equal measure. "But before we get down to business, you know what you have to do."

I grind my own teeth together and remind myself of Cassie and all the others who are counting on me to get help from this monster in front of me.

My father clears his throat expectantly.

"I don't know what you want from me," I mutter.

"I already told you. We'll discuss your concerns after you've admitted I'm right and begged forgiveness. On your knees."

I glance up at his face to try to figure out how serious he is. Despite his endless rows of teeth in a grinning face, there's no humor in his face at all. He literally expects me to get on my knees and beg him for help. And I'm going to do it, I realize, because this is too important for me to let my pride stop me from getting help.

I manage to keep my face blank as I kneel in front of his desk.

I wouldn't have thought it was possible, but his grin widens to show even more teeth. "So, my son, you've come home. And what have you learned from your first few months of college?"

"I've learned that it's a waste of time to live with people outside of my circle, and the only important thing for me to do at college is get closer to the vampires who can further my career."

"And you almost sound like you believe it too."

Smug asshole.

"Now, let's talk terms."

I'm pretty sure I'm still in control of my face, but I can feel my teeth grinding down with the effort of keeping my thoughts to myself. "What did you have in mind?" We both know what he wants. We both know he's only making me do this in person so he can make me that much more miserable.

"Well, let's see . . ." He pretends to think about it. "There's the question of your housing situation. What was it you said when you decided to live with a dorm full of nobodies? Something about experiencing life and seeing things from other perspectives? I think we can all agree that you've achieved that objective. You'll move into the fraternity house as soon as you return to campus."

"Yes, sir," I get out through clenched teeth. If this is what it takes to protect people, it will be worth it, I remind myself.

"And I think it's time for us to start polishing your image in preparation for you to be more visible in the family business."

My stomach gives a lurch, even though I knew this was coming. "Yes, sir."

"Oh, and there's one more thing."

I dig my fingers into my knees. I'm doing this to help people, I tell myself. It's worth it if I can protect someone else. The mantra rings empty when he starts talking again.

"You know that my heir will need an heir of his own before I can publicly recognize him. I know you've had your fun playing around with your little boyfriends in the past, but it's time to grow up, don't you think?"

I squeeze my eyes shut, not sure if I'm about to shoot

death rays out of them or just cry but not willing to ruin things by doing either right now. "Yes, sir."

"I've got the number of an appropriate girl for you to call when you get back to school. Good family. Good stock for the next generation. And they know what she's getting into. Her name has been on our list for a while now."

A list. I swallow down bile at the implication. She's on a list of humans willing to bear vampire children and become vampires themselves. Just like my mother was. Just like Priscilla's mother was. I wonder how this girl ended up on that list. Did she put her own name on it? Or did someone else make that decision for her?

"What do you say, son?" The fake grin is gone from my father's face now. His voice is like dark thunderclouds. He doesn't need to disguise the danger I'm in.

"Yes, sir. I'll call her when I get back to campus."

No more "boyfriends." No more roommates, even. I'll go back to school and live in the frat house and keep my head down, and it will be worth it because I know I'm sacrificing everything for something important.

His smile comes back, even more smug and fake and threatening than before. "Alright, I believe you wanted to talk to me about what Vincent Davenport has been up to?"

* * *

DEVON - PRESENT

I shouldn't be surprised when an official-looking vampire in a suit brings a briefcase and a tablet and says everything is being taken care of. Marcus disappeared without really explaining where he was going, but the arrival of Elijah Jones, some kind of hotshot vampire lawyer, tells me that Marcus actually does know someone higher-up that he could call on for help.

But Marcus left days ago, and Elijah showed up soon after to tell us that Cassie is safe and that Vincent is in trouble for possibly stealing from his family's company, and Marcus still hasn't come back.

Not that I'm worried about him. Or thinking about him. Or remembering what it was like to be inside of him. Nope. None of those things.

We're all still staying in the dorm together since Elijah said things were still in progress. All of the girls went for some kind of testing since the company is apparently trying to build some kind of case against Vincent and need to show that the drugs he stole are still in their bloodstream. I feel shitty for admitting it, but I'm ready to have my dorm back. I'm ready for it to just be the four guys I started the year with. Which will mean the girls who have been crashing with us have found some kind of resolution, so that's a win-win in my book. I'd be lying if I tried to pretend it has nothing to do with wanting my space and privacy back, though.

"Sorry if I woke you all up, but I thought you would want to see this live if possible," Elijah says after waking us all up early on a Saturday. He doesn't even ask before bringing a video feed up on our TV screen.

None of us argue about it when we realize we're about to see Vincent put on trial.

Vincent is led into a circle of ostentatious chairs with judgmental-looking men sitting in them. And he's handcuffed.

He's trying to play it cool, but I can see his facade cracking as the trial goes on.

Do I wish they would condemn him for every single assault he's ever committed? Yes, of course. Is it still satisfying to see him convicted of all the lesser crimes they've been able to catch him at? Hell yes. He looks defeated and desperate by the time the trial comes to a close.

"Vincent Davenport Jr., we find you guilty of all charges. The punishment is one hundred years solitary containment."

Panic fills Vincent's face. I can't say I feel any pity for him at all. I feel a wriggle of satisfaction in my belly when he starts thrashing against his bonds. "No! You can't! I've learned my lesson! Please! You can't!"

But apparently they can, because I watch with equal parts horror and pleasure as he fights against his restraints before finally having some kind of muzzle fixed over his face before he's dragged away.

Someone—I don't even know who, I'm so caught up in what's happening on the screen—asks what's going to happen to Vincent.

Elijah replies, "He'll be locked in a cell and gagged so he can't speak or feed until his punishment is up."

The rest of my friends and roommates have questions that they're shouting out to Elijah right now, but I can't hear any of it. My mind is whirling, confused and detached from the rest of them.

Vincent is sentenced to a century of not drinking blood, and they expect him to survive just fine, as far as I can tell. Why the fuck am I drinking blood every day if I could survive without it for a century and be fine? Why do vampires drink blood at all if they don't need to? Is it just some kind of bull-shit tradition thing where they've always done it, so they keep on doing it? I mean, yes, I get that it can save my life if I'm about to die from sun poisoning or something, but could I go without drinking blood indefinitely if I was careful about all the other things in my life?

I barely notice when Elijah leaves and everyone else starts celebrating Vincent's downfall. I stumble to my room and wrench open my minifridge full of blood bags. Since becoming a vampire, I've tried every fucking type of blood available on the market. O, A, B, it doesn't matter. They're all disgusting. They all make me sick. I choke them down between gulps of coffee or beer or whatever I can get my hands on to dull the flavor of blood because I was certain I needed to drink blood to survive.

But Vincent was just condemned to living a century without blood.

Why the fuck am I drinking blood if I don't need it to survive?

* * *

I'm still reeling with those thoughts when the party quiets down. I don't really want to answer my door when someone knocks on it. Who would knock on my door, anyway? Everyone I care about other than my parents has been sleeping in the living room on just the other side of that door. I like to think we've gotten to know each other well enough they would just come in instead of knocking.

Though, I guess if they were worried about catching me in some awkward position, it makes some sense.

It's Marcus, though, with haunted eyes and hollow cheeks who greets me with a quick whisper and a panicked "Can I come in?"

"Um. Yeah, sure." I step out of the way, and he darts into my room and leans against the door, panting like he actually needs air in his lungs.

"Vincent's been taken care of?" he asks.

"Yeah," I confirm. "That's what the party out there was all about. He's apparently been sentenced to a century without food or speech?"

Marcus waves that off like it's exactly what he expected all along.

"Okay, good." He's talking mostly to himself, and I feel like there's no chance of me figuring out what his conversation is about.

"Was there someth—"

He cuts off my question by pulling me to him and slamming our mouths together. It should be unpleasant. I shouldn't enjoy the force of this unexpected, unasked-for kiss. I feel myself start to melt against him, then force myself back to reality and pull away from him.

"What the fuck, Marcus? You barely speak to me all this time, and suddenly, you want . . . what? For me to just pretend the last few months didn't happen?"

"Please, Devon." His face is tortured, his eyes glistening. "Please, just let me have one night. I'll never ask anything else. I just . . . I need you tonight."

Is it the manic edge to his voice or the simple fact that I've been wanting him all this time and my defenses are low right now? I thread my fingers into his hair and bring our lips together again.

Our kiss is all violence and desperation, lips and teeth and tongues seeking each other out like shipwreck survivors reaching out across cold waves, certain of death if we can't find each other and cling together. I tear at his shirt as I maneuver him toward my bed. The bed is too small for just about any activity, but lust makes me inventive. I turn him away from me and push him so he lands with his knees on the mattress.

"Hold the headboard," I order, already unzipping his pants and rolling them down his thighs.

He does it with a quiet, needy moan that shoots straight to my cock.

I kneel behind him and relish the press of his ass against my erection, the rub of his bare legs against my pants.

"Is this what you wanted?" I murmur into his ear, then leave a trail of kisses down the back of his neck, the hard edge of his shoulder blade, the divots where his hips meet his back.

"Need you," he moans into his bicep. "I just need you."

I move my kisses lower, pausing to taste each vertebra as I pass. Finally, I bite his ass cheek as a quick warning of what I'm about to do. Just a little nip, not enough to draw blood or even leave a mark.

Marcus whimpers.

"Are you sure this is okay?" I'm pretty sure he'll panic again when it's over, but at least I can try to give him an out.

"Yes. Please, Devon. I need this so bad."

Does it still count as consent if I think he'll change his mind? Fuck, I don't know. He sure seems like he wants this.

I grip his ass in both hands and spread him so I can access his hole. He muffles his own noises by biting down on his arm as I use my tongue to explore the sensitive skin. I feel a tremor go through his whole body as my tongue probes deeper, opening him up to me. I can't wait any longer to be inside of him, so I slide just one finger inside the hole I've been working to loosen up.

Vampires are never much warmer than room temperature, but being inside of him like this, I'm surrounded by what heat he has.

"More," he begs, and I add a second finger beside the first, using my tongue and saliva to ease the way.

My bedside table, which contains my lube and the still-full box of condoms, is only a few feet away, but it feels like miles. Scratch that, it might as well be in outer space.

Marcuse agrees, judging by the whimper he lets out when my fingers slide out of him and I stand up.

"Stay there. I'll be right back," I tell him and am rewarded with another whimper and a head nod of agreement.

With the lube to slick my way, I slide two fingers easily back inside and begin working them rhythmically in and out while my free hand holds him steady by gripping his hip. I quickly find an angle that makes him groan and buck his hips. Even if I never have sex again, at least I'll have this image with me for the rest of my life.

He starts to babble, letting out a stream of half words, half groans, all interspersed with "please" and "need" and "Devon" that serve to inflame my need for him even more.

My dick is sensitive, practically weeping against the inside of my pajama pants.

I can't wait any longer. With a gasp of almost pain, I pull the waistband down low enough to frame my balls and slick myself up.

"Tell me now," I say. I guess it's my turn to beg. "Tell me now if you don't want me to fuck you."

"I do want you. I need you to fuck me. Please, Devon." His words devolve into babble again.

I slide my fingers out of him so I can position my cock at his entrance. Marcus and I both shudder as I rub the dripping head up and down along his crease.

Part of me is certain I'll die again if I don't get inside him soon. I press inside of him, relishing the squeeze as I edge past his tight ring of muscle. I see sparks as he trembles around me.

I'm still trying to adjust to the sensation of being seated inside him when he starts to move his hips and fuck himself on me.

"Fuck. Marcus." I try to hold him still. "I won't last."

He mumble-babbles something that sounds like, "Good,

need you to come," and then our hips meet in a frantic rhythm, the only sounds from our skin slapping together.

Feeling the warning tingle at the base of my spine and in my balls, I reach around to grab Marcus's dick in my still-slick hand.

"Yes, fuck. I'm—" His shaft writhes in my hand as come spurts out across the bedspread. I only last a few more seconds before I find my own release, pumping it deep inside of him.

Marcus collapses on his stomach, apparently not caring about lying in a puddle of his own come, and I collapse on top of him, not quite ready to let my softening flesh slide out of him.

Chapter Twenty-Four

MARCUS - PRESENT

I'm weak. I'm too weak to accept my fate without going back for one more night with Devon. I'm too weak to leave as soon as we're finished. Instead, we toss his dirty comforter into a corner and wedge our bodies together on his too-small bed to sleep. He wraps his arms tight around me and nuzzles into the hair at my nape, and I can't help imagining a life together, just like this. Maybe with a bigger bed.

The name and phone number that have recently been entered into my phone contacts—not to mention the promises I made to my father—make that imagined life a really nice pipe dream. There's no way it can ever happen.

At three in the morning, I slip out from Devon's embrace without waking him up and sneak into my own room to pack a bag of necessities before heading over to the frat house, where all my dreams will die.

"They said you'd be coming, but why the fuck are you here this early?" a bedraggled vampire asks the instant he opens the door.

"I didn't have a reason to stay where I was. Would you just let me in?"

He waves me in and shows me to a bedroom without another word.

Despite the walls being bare and the windows uncovered, it's a nicer room than a college freshman should have any right to. I take a slow turn around the room, trying to imagine my life here, probably for the rest of my time in college. Sizzling panic crawls up my throat.

I don't want this room, or this fraternity, or the surly vampire who let me in. I don't even want my father's money, or his legacy, or any of the other shit he's dangled in front of my face my whole life as incentive to do whatever he wants. I just want to know my friends are safe and that guys like Vincent face some sort of consequences for their actions. Maybe I also want that pipe dream, imaginary future where Devon holds me and nuzzles my hair and makes me come. But if I turn my back on my father's plans, it's not only the money and the name I would lose out on. It's my place in society and protection for people I care about and knowing I have a place to sleep. All of that can go away in an instant if my father decides to snatch it from me.

Flopping down on the bare mattress, I stare at the ceiling and try to force myself to sleep. Or at least to close my eyes. My mind won't stop replaying every want that I know I'll never get, though. It's exhausting, but I still can't sleep after hours of it.

Sleep never comes, so I get to hear the house come alive with the dawn. I listen with curiosity to the movements around me. Though I've been raised my whole life to take my position here, I never did take the final step to be inducted into the brotherhood. I'm sure there are rituals and shit that I don't know about, and I don't expect a painless process to learn everything I need to.

The morning starts out normally. Birds precede the sun, which brings more birds, which are almost loud enough to cover the sounds of alarms in the rooms nearest to mine.

That's when the chanting starts.

Fucking great. There's chanting in the mornings.

And the chanting is moving closer to me down the hall.

Even fucking better. Best-case scenario, this is the beginning of the induction ceremony, and I'll get through it quickly so I can move on with my life. Somehow, I don't think it's the best-case scenario knocking on my bedroom door right now.

"Who comes before us and begs shelter?" a voice shouts from the other side of my door.

Yep. Brilliant. They're definitely here for me.

I try to remember the lines of rituals I only ever half learned to begin with.

"I would be your brother, if you allow it." I try, and probably fail, to keep any sarcasm out of my voice.

"One who comes among us and seeks to call us 'brother' must be cleansed first to show he is worthy."

Great. We've got rituals and ultimatums now.

"I . . ." Shit. What is the next line supposed to be? "I submit to the judgment of the brotherhood," I finally say.

The door opens with a bang. It figures that they would have a key to my room, I suppose. I feel kind of stupid for thinking it was worthwhile to lock it in the first place.

"He submits to the cleansing," the surly vampire who first let me into the house proclaims. Then, his lips twist in a sadistic-looking smile. "Grab him."

That's my only warning before the other guys close in on me from all sides. Panic rises in me, clawing its way from my belly to my throat. I want to scream. I want to fight them off. I want to tear at throats and eye sockets and leave a swath of bloody corpses in my wake.

I force those instincts under my control. I don't know if I

could actually take any of these guys in a fight, and the odds are even more stacked if I'm fighting all of them at once. More important, though, is the promise I made to my father. If I want his help, the protection of his name, I have to submit to whatever hazing they throw at me.

The price is worth it if it saves my friends, I remind myself over and over again as I'm dragged to the basement, shackled to the wall with heavy chains and metal cuffs around my wrists and ankles, and stripped completely naked with the help of what looks like a steak knife. I repeat the mantra some more when they light the pile of torn clothing on fire. It's when someone turns a hose of ice-cold water on me that I stop being able to put together coherent thoughts. My world narrows down to cold and misery, and I can't remember any more why any of this is happening.

Chapter Twenty-Five

DEVON - FOUR MONTHS AGO

"You've got visitors!"

Mom's voice cuts into my wallowing so I do my best to ignore it. Instead of answering, I flip through a few more random TV channels. I never watched that much TV as a human, but these days it's all I do.

A sharp gasp from a voice other than my parents draws my attention. Allie and Elliot are standing in the doorway, Elliot trying to look calm and cool, but Allie unable to hide the look of horror on her face.

"Let me guess," I drawl at her, not feeling any desire to spare her feelings in this. "You didn't think it was true?"

"I–" her throat works around some silent words before she manages to speak again. "I didn't know what it would be like. I'm just surprised."

I let out a humorless chuckle. "I didn't know what it would be like either, so we've got that in common."

Elliot lifts a backpack up to show me. "We heard you might be coming back to school soon, so we thought we'd bring some of your work that you've been missing. Maybe go over our notes with you?"

I blink away some moisture from my eyes. I haven't reached out to any of my friends since I was turned. Partly out of shame. How do you look someone in the eye when they know you got yourself killed trying to hook up with a dude at a gay club? Partly out of fear. What if I'm too much of a monster for them now? What if we have nothing in common now? But having them reach out to me gives me a sliver of hope I didn't have before.

And just when I'm going to thank them and let them help me with my month of missed schoolwork, I realize that I'm hungry. And if my feeding specialist and therapist and doctor and everyone else have taught me one thing, it's that, if I feel hungry, I don't wait to feed.

Shit.

I can't do that with my friends here. They'd run screaming from the house and never come back.

Maybe it's best if they don't come back.

I swallow and search for an out, but nothing is springing to mind. "That's really . . . thanks for coming by. I'll . . ."

Come on! Think!

My stomach lets out a loud gurgle and we all stand, frozen and awkward and staring at my abdomen.

"Are you . . ." Elliot starts.

"Oh my god," Allie gasps, her hands flying to her mouth.

And I'm so hungry that I can't even think straight to answer them. "You should probably go now," I tell them, then turn to the mini-fridge we have set up beside the TV. I don't need my therapists or doctors or feeding specialists to tell me that I need to feed. My body is already telling me.

Maybe my friends have already gotten away by the time I tear into the blood bag, or maybe they get to see me as the monster I am. Now that I've finally gotten past the stage of puking up half the blood I drink, it's easy to down two blood bags in a row. When I find my equilibrium again, my friends are gone but my mom is there, rubbing my back and blinking back tears.

I could have told her it wasn't a good idea to bring visitors over. I could have told her there were reasons I hadn't called them before.

Chapter Twenty-Six

DEVON - PRESENT

It shouldn't hurt when I wake up and Marcus is already gone. I shouldn't allow myself to be hurt by something that I knew was going to happen. Tell that to my stupid heart. For that matter, tell that to my stupid dick, which has woken up unrealistically hopeful for a repeat of last night's performance.

I will my wayward cock into submission. I am not in the right mood to jack off right now. I'm even less in the mood to jack off while trying to think of anyone other than Marcus. And there's the fact that my dorm is still full of roommates, friends of roommates, and almost strangers because we're still sorting out the aftermath of this shit with Vincent. Maybe once everyone is safely moved back into their own dorms, I'll be able to get back to my own normal life.

I put my pillow over my face and scream into it. One night with him, and I'm right back to all of those uncomfortable feelings I thought I'd moved past. But it's worse now, because now I know for sure that it's never going to happen between us.

Eager to find any other thing to think about, I get dressed so I can go out and make coffee for everyone. Jimmy has made it clear that he's comfortable walking around naked at all times —and it's not like I'm complaining about the eyeful I've gotten numerous times from him. The guy has a pretty spectacular ass. I, however, prefer to not have all my bits dangling out in the open. If nothing else, it just feels safer to wear pants whenever possible.

"Mmm. That smells amazing." Bee is the first of the girls to wake up as the coffee starts brewing. "Please say you're making enough for me to have some?"

"Don't you know by now that I always make a full pot?"

"You're a god among men," she says, wrapping her arms around me and squeezing tight enough that I'm glad I don't have to breathe.

Everyone else is still asleep, so we stand in the tiny kitchen area to drink our coffee without waking anyone.

"I take it the bedding situation isn't that comfortable if you're so desperate for caffeine in the morning?" I ask.

Bee shrugs. "Honestly, sleeping in a pile of girls on the floor has been surprisingly comfortable. Hearing Jimmy and Gloria go at it through a very thin door, though? Not super conducive to sleep."

"Oh yeah?" I have to laugh, but I try to keep it quiet. "I guess I was really out of it last night. I didn't even notice." Part of that is probably down to the fact that Marcus and I were going at it across the hall. I guess we were so wrapped up in each other—or maybe I should say I was so wrapped up in him—that I didn't hear the wolf sex happening next door.

"Yeah, well, count yourself lucky. There are some things that cannot be unheard, if you know what I mean." She gives me a dark look, and I burst out laughing.

"I'm sorry," I finally gasp out after having to set my coffee down to keep from spilling it. "I realize this isn't that funny if you're in the middle of it, but I'm far enough from the situation that I can find it hilarious."

"Yeah, yeah." She waves off my laughter like it's no big deal. "I'm probably just being jealous, anyway."

"Jealous? Of which one?" Objectively, I can appreciate both Jimmy and Gloria as physically attractive people. The thought of being stuck in a relationship with either one is not at all tempting for me, though.

"Oh, god! Not like that!" Bee rushes to correct me. "Gloria is my roommate, and our relationship is very much a sisters type thing, and Jimmy and I were raised together, so he's the closest thing I've ever had to a brother. But I can be jealous that they found each other, you know? I want what they have . . . or . . . well, definitely not exactly what they have . . ." She hides her face in her hands and lets out a hysterical laugh. "Can you just forget everything I said for the last five minutes or so? Please?"

I grin down at her. "Forget what?"

She gives me a fake scowl, then relaxes back to her same easygoing smile. "Can I ask you a super personal and inappropriate question? You don't even have to answer if it's too much. I'm just being nosey."

"Sure." I shrug. "Ask away. I can't promise to answer."

Bee bites her lip and looks nervously around the room. "So, I know, obviously, you're a vampire. But I'm so confused about a few things. Like, for example, I've seen you drinking coffee every single day since I met you, but you also drink blood, right? Do you, I don't know, feel hungry and thirsty in the same way a human does, just for blood instead of bread? Or do you still get hungry for regular food too?"

Oh, wow. I guess she's diving right in. Usually, people avoid talking about diet with vampires at all costs. I guess I have known her for a while now. And she seems to be asking from genuine curiosity, not fear or some weird, fetishy place.

"Well . . . I like coffee because it's one of a few things with a strong enough flavor that I can actually still taste it as a vampire, and the caffeine has an effect that I like too. Though, it probably makes a difference that I liked coffee even before I became a vampire."

"Oh, so you haven't always been a vampire?"

She sounds genuinely surprised, making me wonder how much she already knows about vampires. I'm guessing not much at all.

"No. I was made, not born a vampire. But, just a heads-up, most vampires don't want to be asked about that. It can be kind of a touchy subject. And if it's not a touchy subject, it's probably because the vampire in question is descended from some ancient vampiric bloodline, in which case they'll be super offended that you didn't already know who their family was . . . Let's just leave it at it's complicated, and you probably shouldn't try to talk about it with anyone you don't know really well."

She gives a thoughtful head nod. "Does that mean that you and I know each other well enough or that you don't want me to ask any more questions?"

I sip my coffee as an excuse to gather my thoughts. "I guess you and I have known each other long enough and been through some shit together. And I'd rather you ask me than some stranger who's going to get offended and rip your head off over it. As a matter of fact, maybe it's best if I act as your official vampire liaison if you have more questions."

"Well, okay then, Mr. Vampire Liaison. You said something about being able to taste coffee? Or maybe it was that you couldn't taste something else? I can't quite remember now."

"Yeah, when you become a vampire, your human senses

essentially die—I mean, all of you essentially dies as part of the change—and they're replaced by vampire senses. Vampires are predators, so all of our senses are predatory. I can hear someone's heartbeat. I can sense the vibration of someone's pulse if I'm close. I can, of course, smell blood, but I can also smell fear and any kind of arousal. But I can't see colors the same way I did as a human. A lot of the spectrum just shows up as shades of grey now. I can taste what blood type someone is before their blood actually touches my tongue, but I can't taste peanut butter anymore. So, circling back to your earlier question, no, I don't get hungry like I used to as a human. I still occasionally get this idea that suddenly my love of macaroni and cheese will return, try to eat a bunch, and end up sick and miserable for three days straight. Yes, this has happened multiple times, even though I've been a vampire for less than a year. Please don't tell anyone else about it."

Holy shit, this is the most I've talked to anyone about this, including the therapist my parents sent me to after I was turned.

"Wow. I never realized this, but I guess being a vampire kind of sucks."

I burst out laughing. "Um. Yeah. It really kind of sucks sometimes."

Chapter Twenty-Seven

MARCUS - PRESENT

Cold.

Cold and pain and loneliness.

"Imagine what you could have done if you'd started with us instead of waiting until now," the obnoxious vampire who first let me into the house sneers over me.

Icy water comes pouring over me. I try to turn, but I'm chained too tightly to a chair to look behind me.

"Now, we have to make up for lost time. You see, all of our rushes went through the cleansing process over the last few months. And none of them were associated with someone who took one of our most venerated brothers from us. There is—" He squats down in front of me and sniffs the air between us. "—so. Much. That we must cleanse from you now."

I don't bother to answer. He's settled in to torture me no matter what I say to him. Maybe he's decided that he's going to kill me before this is over. There's nothing I can do about it, and I can't seem to make myself care too much.

"Do you know the punishment doled out to Brother Vincent?" He whispers it into my ear, a deceptive caress passing by my cheek. "Do you know what they're going to do to him because of you sharing stories around? One hundred years without feeding. One hundred years of being bound and gagged and hungry. As repayment for a few whining sluts? Explain to me, how is that fair?"

I'm too cold as it is. My already sluggish blood is practically frozen solid in my veins right now. I couldn't answer him even if I wasn't choking on my hatred. I glare and hope that he'll just kill me quickly. It doesn't seem likely.

"You can't explain it to me, can you? I know that's why you're silent. We both know that Vincent's life is worth more than any of those little sluts, worth more than all of them put together, but he's imprisoned now because you . . . what . . . were trying to lash out at your daddy's organization? Is that it? You thought you could get back at your father by attacking his brotherhood? Well, I'm not afraid to tell you now, I may have to go through the motions of letting you rush because of who your father is, but if I have any say at all, you'll never survive to call yourself a brother."

He stands abruptly and walks away.

At the foot of a staircase, he turns back briefly. "Continue with the ice water until his skin is blue, then alert me to the change."

And I'm washed in cold and wet again.

* * *

I jerk back to consciousness with the same guy in my face again.

"Do you know what most of us went through to become a member of this brotherhood?" He growls at me, gripping my hair and shaking my head for emphasis. "Not just what we went through when we rushed. Most of us have been on this track since we were old enough to walk. Where were you when I was going off to the academy and working my way up through the ranks? Where were you when I was going off to summer camp and learning my place in vampire society? You don't belong with us. You'll never be a part of us."

I'd love to explain to him that the last thing I want is to have anything to do with him or his twisted brotherhood. I'd love to ask him if he had to work his way up from the very bottom and that's why he is the way he is now. I wonder if he'll kill me faster if I say that to him.

I guess I'm not quite ready to die yet because I hold my tongue.

He smirks at me. "It seems to me that you still need cleansing. The water didn't do it, so we'll have to try something stronger."

The words barely register before he flips my hand over roughly, exposing the palm, and flicks on a lighter.

Any words I thought about saying before melt away as the flame licks at my skin.

* * *

I'm hungry.

I've never gone this long without feeding. Under normal circumstances, a vampire who doesn't feed slows down and eventually enters a type of hibernation until they sense available blood. Under normal circumstances, a vampire isn't burned and beaten while also being denied blood. A healthy vampire with their system flush with fresh blood can quickly heal from all sorts of injuries. The ice water, the welts and bruises, even the burns across my skin would be no problem if

I could just drink some blood to help me heal. As it is, I've given up hope of getting through this alive.

The vampire who seems to be in charge—the same surly guy who complained about me waking him up when I first got here, a guy the others refer to as Dominic—comes in periodically to orchestrate further torture. He seems to take immense satisfaction from every broken finger or new burn he inflicts. The others don't seem to take the same sadistic delight in the process, and I often catch uncomfortable looks from them as they follow his orders.

No one shows signs of standing up to him, though. No one voices any argument when he orders my feet plunged into a bucket of ice water or barks at the guy hitting me with a Ping-Pong paddle to swing harder, harder, harder. I guess if I knew he could just as easily turn his wrath on me, I would probably just fall in line. I understand it, but understanding doesn't change my own circumstances.

I'm going to die in this basement unless someone intervenes.

I fade in and out of consciousness. I lost all sense of time back before Dominic started burning me. Has it been days? Weeks? Definitely more than hours. I'm sure of that. I'm too hungry for it to have been anything less than a few days since they tied me up down here.

I'm swimming through the black almost sleep that is my body's attempt at self-preservation when I hear voices. I want to retreat. The blackness is safer. *Just leave me alone*, I want to tell them. *Do what you have to, but don't make me be awake for it.* My brain has other ideas. It latches onto the voices and uses them to reel me back to reality, just like a fish being dragged out of the deepest water.

I gasp for air, forgetting that oxygen isn't what will save me. My dead heart thunders, trying to kick-start me back to life. *Too late. Too late*, my gut whispers, pretty sure that this is actually the end.

". . . gone far enough," one of the voices is saying. I don't recognize it, but how can I hear anything over the sound of my heart trying to pound out of my ribs?

". . . the same cleansing as every other brother . . . missed the original ceremonies . . . lost time . . ." Dominic's voice is saying. I almost don't recognize it as Dominic's voice. He's lost the sneer, the sadistic glee he normally speaks with.

"Fine. And now it's gone far enough."

I slit my eyes open and have to work to bring the room into focus. Dominic is glaring at a man in a suit. A vampire. Normally, my senses could tell me how old, maybe even whether he was turned or born as a vampire, and who turned him, if I already knew that vampire's scent. Right now, all I can tell is he's a vampire and that he's older than me.

He turns from Dominic, dismissing him without another word, and slips a blood capsule between my lips.

I groan in pain, in relief, in hope, as the blood fills my mouth and starts bringing me back from the precipice.

The man feeds me another blood capsule, then turns back to Dominic.

"Do you have any idea the shitstorm you'll face if anyone finds out about this? Didn't it occur to you that the whole fraternity is under a microscope right now, and the death of one of its most important legacies could bring everything crashing down around you?"

"If he's too weak to survive the same—"

"Don't give me that bullshit," the man cuts Dominic off mid-argument. "You knew you were pushing him too far. You let yourself be ruled by your emotions, and it's going to cost you."

Dominic glares at the man but doesn't try arguing again.

"Untie him and get him upstairs," the man orders, and, to

my amazement, Dominic does it quickly and without argument. After however long of being tortured and near death and without hope, it only takes a few minutes before I'm under the covers, lying in bed, and nursing a full blood bag.

For the first time in . . . well, how can I know how long it's been? I drift off to actual sleep, rather than restless semi-consciousness.

Chapter Twenty-Eight

DEVON - PRESENT

Everything is back to normal.

Well.

I guess normal is relative in your first year of college?

The only people staying in our dorm currently are the people I officially signed a dorm contract with. But Jimmy is staying in Bee and Gloria's dorm until he's satisfied that they're settled in and safe there, and I suspect that's going to turn quickly into either Jimmy living in their dorm while Bee lives here or Jimmy and Gloria staying here while Bee lives there. Either way, one of my roommates is definitely going to be getting laid a lot more than me. I really hope Jimmy and Gloria decide to take over her dorm so that quiet, friendly, not-loud-sex-having Bee can move in with us. I won't mind that at all.

Oh, and Marcus hasn't reappeared since our desperation fuck a week ago. Not that I expected him to suddenly be over his issues and want to be boyfriends or anything like that, but

I thought we were still going to be roommates. It's probably for the best if he doesn't come back. My heart is already halfway broken trying to keep up with his shit. Why would I need him around to break it the rest of the way?

I stare down the coffee maker as it drips out the tiniest possible amounts of coffee into the pot. Today's the day. I've decided. I'm going cold turkey. No more blood.

And the slowness of the coffeepot is already getting on my last nerve to the point that I might tear out the jugular of anyone who tries to get between me and my fix.

But vampires can survive without blood. I know this for a fact because Vincent is in a cell somewhere, surviving for a century without feeding.

No. I need to reframe my mindset on this. I'm not punishing myself by refusing to feed. This is me taking a moral stance. If I don't need to use humans for sustenance, why would I? Humans deserve to live lives outside of my depraved hunger for them. Especially since I know that I can live my life without stealing from theirs.

"Whoa," Jeff's voice breaks me out of my revery. "Did the coffee maker kill your uncle or something?"

I turn on him, already in a rage and ready for a fight.

He's just a human. He can't understand. The sensible voice in my head might as well not exist.

"I'm just waiting for the coffee to brew," I tell him, and I know it's way more caustic than he deserves, but I also know that I am not actually driving this bus right now. It's my addiction that's driving this bus. It's hunger and need and the black void inside of me that's driving this bus right now.

"Okay." He holds his hands up defensively. "My bad for thinking I could lighten the mood, I guess. I was going to do a grocery run. You want anything?"

Blood. Hot blood. Your blood. Gallons of blood. "More coffee," I tell him. "A lot more coffee and more filters too."

There. An almost appropriate, almost human response. This whole "quitting blood cold turkey" thing is going great.

"Okay." Jeff draws out the word to let me know I'm being weird without actually having to tell me I'm being weird. "I'll see what I can do."

I don't want him to do anything. I want—

Thank god there's enough coffee to fill my mug halfway. I pour myself as much coffee as I can, then stomp-slash-grumble my way back to my bed.

* * *

Three days. Three days with no blood at all. I've skipped half my classes this week because I know I'm about to lose my shit, and I'd rather lose my shit in my dorm room than at school.

Honestly, it's way too optimistic to imply that I haven't already lost my shit. A few times. I lost it all over Jeff when all he did was offer to pick up groceries. I lost it all over Jimmy when he mentioned that Gloria would probably be spending the night. Oh, and I lost it all over a barista who asked if I wanted room for cream in my coffee. Now that I think of it, probably half of my shit-losing moments have been coffee related in some way. I mean, all of them have been blood related in every way, obviously, but the coffee is there in the periphery too.

"Hey, Devon." Jimmy sounds nervous addressing me, which I guess is fair, considering I bit his head off last time he tried to talk with me. "Are you . . . okay?"

I'm about to snap that of course I'm okay, I'm perfectly fine, why the fuck is he asking if I'm okay? But I catch myself in time. And realize that I'm sitting bolt upright on the couch, staring intently at a black TV screen, and tapping my foot vigorously like I'm waiting for something important to happen.

Shit, man, keep it together.

The bad thing is this *is* me keeping it together right now.

"I'm—" I force myself to unclench all of my clenched muscles. "—I'm fine. I've been kind of trying this new diet thing, and it's been harder to stick to than I thought."

Jimmy looks comically perplexed. "Are you, like, trying to lose weight or something? Because I really don't think you have to. You really look fine."

I have to laugh. Fortunately, Jimmy doesn't realize I'm laughing at him and joins me.

"It's not that kind of diet," I tell him. "Don't worry about it, okay? It's vampire stuff. You don't have to worry about it."

"Oh. Okay then." He shrugs it off and starts to walk away, then turns back to look at me, all serious puppy eyes as only Jimmy can do them. "You would ask me if you needed any help, right? Like, if there's anything I can do, you know you can talk to me about it?"

Never in a million years, I think. *I need to do this on my own.* "Yeah. Of course. I mean, after all the stuff we just went through? Are you kidding me? I know you've got my back."

Liar, liar, liar! The voice in the back of my mind has only gotten meaner and angrier since I went off blood, and its meanness and anger seem to always be directed right at me. Awesome.

I fake a smile for Jimmy's benefit. "I promise, I'm fine," I lie through clenched teeth.

Jimmy relaxes and smiles guilelessly at me. "Alright. I'm glad to hear that."

Then he leaves the room, and I'm back to staring at the blank TV and tapping my foot again.

Surely, if Vincent can survive a century without blood and also being in prison, I can make it through the semester without blood while just being in college, right?

I make a promise to myself that today is my last day of

withdrawals. After today, everything will get easier. The withdrawals will disappear, the cravings will ease up, and before long, I will be the absolute model of the next age of vampirism, the bloodless vampire. I just have to get this one more day, and everything will get easier from there.

MARCUS - PRESENT

I wake to utter confusion but blissfully little pain. Light comes through the closed curtains but not strong enough to hurt. I'm naked but under the covers of a neatly made bed. It takes me a good few moments of staring around in confusion before I recognize it as the room I was given in the frat house.

Less than a minute after I've figured that out, a blood bag is pressed up against my lips, and I don't have any kind of stamina to refuse that if I can get it.

"Glad to see you moving around," a voice I don't recognize tells me. "I mean partly because my life is a lot harder when there are corpses to deal with, but also just because I was rooting for you to pull through."

The blood bag in my mouth keeps me from answering, but the guy feeding me doesn't seem to expect a response anyway.

"Dominic has gotten a bit rough with all of us at some point, but the way he went at you was something completely different. I guess he's got more of a complex about class than I expected."

I suck the bag dry and slump back on the bed. I can already feel the blood working its life-giving magic, but that doesn't mean I'm well enough to sit up without help. Or speak.

"I'm going to wait and make sure you keep that down before I give you another one. Are you feeling any better yet?"

I give a weak nod. I'm not on the verge of dying. Of course I'm feeling better.

"Good. Good." He gives an awkward look around the room and all but twiddles his thumbs. "So, um . . . I guess your dad was one of the big names back in the day?"

Fuck, I do not want to talk about my father right now. But

considering this guy just saved my life by feeding me blood and said he was rooting for me, I guess I should try to be friendly.

"One of the founders," I croak out through vocal cords that haven't quite bounced back from their ordeal.

"Whoa. That is . . ." I can't tell if the look on his face is more awestruck or simply trying to work his head around the math. God, I hope it's the second and not the first.

"A lot," I supply. "It's a lot."

That knocks him out of his trance. "Yeah. I mean. He must be . . ." His eyes roll to the ceiling as he calculates. "Five-hundred-some years? Can that be right?"

"Yeah. Five twenty-nine. One of the founding nine."

My helper gives a little shake of his head. "He must have some big expectations for you, huh?"

I should probably laugh at that, right? That's the kind of understatement that deserves at least a sarcastic scoff.

I don't manage it. I cut my gaze to the side so I don't have to see his expressions.

"What's your name?" I change the subject.

"Oh. Right. George. Or when my dad is trying to be, like, a little extra pretentious, it's Giorgio, but I looked it up and it just means 'farmer,' so I really don't get why he thinks it's fancier or whatever. Sorry. This is embarrassing. I mean, it's not like I'm anyone important or anything. Even my dad is kind of a nobody. I love him. Don't get me wrong. He's great. But he isn't, like, on a level with your dad or anything like that."

Now, I do laugh. "Maybe you're lucky that way."

George's nervous babbling gives over to a shy smile, and I wonder if I might be able to make some actual friends in here after all.

He clears his throat and puts his serious face back on. "How are you feeling? Ready for another bag?"

I nod my head. "Yeah, but I can hold it for myself this

time. If I'm not careful, before I know it, you'll be baby birding me, and my dignity can only withstand so much."

He grins as he hands over another blood bag.

* * *

No one is smiling in two days when Dominic stops by my room. I'm still half-asleep, sprawled across the bed and regenerating like I couldn't when I was chained to a chair and taking hourly ice baths.

"Just because your father has more power than mine shouldn't mean I have to apologize to you," he growls at me with a hateful scowl before I've fully woken up.

"Did I leave the door unlocked?" is the clever and coherent response I manage to croak out.

Dominic slaps me across my absolutely confused face. "No, you piece of shit. I have the master key."

I'm finally awake enough to have some idea of what's going on. "Oh." Awake does not equal eloquent, obviously.

"Do you understand that I'm sorry, you pathetic, waste of space, spoiled brat?" he growls into my face. "I promised I would apologize."

"Yeah, I get it. If anyone asks me, I'll be sure to tell them you apologized."

Dominic tosses me back on my bed, just to make sure I've submitted to him, and I guess I have because I just rag doll backward and lie there. I don't have the energy to deal with this guy's bullshit today.

Chapter Twenty-Nine

DEVON - PRESENT

I've never been so hungry in my life. Or death, or whatever. But it's not a stomach growling kind of hungry. I know down to my bone marrow that my body will reject any human food I try to put in it. Even coffee is out of the question right now. One whiff of the stuff this morning nearly turned me inside out. As in, my insides very nearly made a break for it and tried to get outside of my body.

Whatever. No more coffee. No big deal. It will be worth it to come out the other side without having to rely on blood.

Cold turkey. That's the way to do this.

God, I'm so hungry. And tired. The fresh blood that normally keeps my body moving has all dried up. It's by sheer force of will that I manage to stand up and walk to the door when I hear a knock.

"Is this Marcus's dorm?" the vampire I open the door to immediately asks.

Even my thoughts are moving slow, like the sludge of my drying bloodstream is holding my thoughts in place. An image of my brain cells as little army men trying to march through my brain and getting stuck in sticky mud pops into my mind, and I snort out a laugh by accident.

"Um. Are you okay?" The guy, some vampire I've never met before, looks genuinely worried.

And I realize I'm hanging on to the door handle and leaning against the doorframe and laughing at jokes no one else can hear, all while failing to answer a basic question. At least, I think it was something basic. I can't seem to pinpoint what he was asking about.

The dude snaps his fingers in front of my face. I would normally probably remind him just how rude that is, but the thought is too distant to catch.

"Um . . . dude? Are you with me here? Can you tell me if Marcus lives here or not?"

Right. Apparently, Marcus now has vampire friends who come around the dorm looking for him.

"Yeah," I answer around another fit of inappropriate laughter. "Or . . . at least . . . he did?"

"Sweet," the vampire says. "I'm George. Marcus asked me to pick up some things for him. If you'll show me where his room is?"

I stand there—correction, lean there—in the doorway as the moment stretches between us. I try and fail miserably to cover my vulnerability.

"He . . . didn't want to come himself? To his own dorm?"

The guy shrugs. "He's pretty busy getting settled in. I said I didn't mind swinging by for him. So, which room is it?"

I step back and gesture at Marcus's door. Any fight I had left in me is gone. The tiny bit of energy I'd mustered to answer the door drains out through the soles of my feet, and I barely make it back to the couch before I collapse.

Marcus is gone. Officially. And getting "settled in" some other place, whatever the hell that means. I knew he hadn't been around. I'm not an idiot. But having someone–George, I take a moment to glare in the direction of the guy who just disappeared through Marcus' door–come by to pick up his things? That's a type of permanent gone that I hadn't even considered.

My mind flashes back to the last time I saw him. The desperate look in his eyes. The way he begged me for just one night.

He knew. He must have known that he was leaving for good, and instead of telling me about it and talking with me like a mature adult, he begged me to fuck him, and then he disappeared, probably forever.

My insides cramp with hunger and anger and sadness and I don't even know what else. Marcus is gone. No, worse. Marcus left me. And he didn't even give me the chance to fight to keep him. Would I have fought for him? I don't know what I could have done, but it would have been worth a try.

"You don't look so good," the vampire tosses at me as he carries an armload of stuff from Marcus' room.

I suppose he's right, considering I'm pale and gaunt even by vampire standards and currently curled up in the fetal position on my couch.

"Just tired," I mumble. "I'll be fine."

He doesn't look convinced. "You'll drink a bit in a minute? You've got some blood handy?"

"Said I'll be fine."

Taking the hint, he shrugs and leaves me alone in the slightly emptier dorm.

* * *

MARCUS - PRESENT

I wait a full day before shuffling down to the common room of the frat house that—I guess?—is my home now.

"About time you showed up," Dominic sneers at me before I'm fully through the door.

I favor him with a dark look but don't feel any particular need to answer him with words. There are a handful of guys lounging around casually, some with blood bags in hand, others scrolling on phones like they're bored with everything. A lot of them look vaguely familiar from my recent torture sessions, but I try to move past that because I know it was Dominic directing all of that.

"Please," Dominic continues. "Come sit. Introduce yourself. We've all been dying to meet you."

Is it possible to hate this guy any more than I already do? I'm not sure. I try, absolutely, but I kind of feel used up in that department.

After I sit, Dominic spreads his sarcastic sneer around the room. "Well," he starts, "since our celebrity guest has decided to join us, maybe we should hold an impromptu meeting of the brotherhood?"

Cautious glances around the room tell me that most of the guys are not on board with whatever Dominic has planned. But he's still obviously the one in charge, so no one stands up to him.

"I'm not sure if you would have heard this, Mr. Levine, but the reason someone was alerted to your hazing experience was that you hadn't checked in with someone you promised to check in with."

I give him a blank stare. I have no fucking clue what he's talking about, but hell if I'm going to give him the satisfaction of asking him to explain.

"The human girl you were supposed to call?" he asks, like I'm the bad guy in this situation.

"Human girl?" I finally cave and ask the question he obviously wants me to ask.

His grin is sickening. He's got me right where he wants me, and we both know it.

"The human girl your illustrious father arranged to be your pet for the time being?"

My head swirls painfully, and memory floods back. Yes, before coming back here and being starved and tortured, I was at my father's house, begging for help. He agreed to help in exchange for my promise. To start begetting heirs for him. I want to run away. And be sick. I want to be sick on Dominic and then run away.

But that's not what I agreed to.

"I take it you've got her contact information?" My voice comes out a lot calmer than I feel, so I guess that's a good start.

The shithead grins as he passes me a slip of paper with some writing on it. "I suggest you get on that. We wouldn't want any more misunderstandings, would we?"

"Sure, whatever," I mutter, taking my cue to go back to my room.

My friends will be safe. That's what matters. I'm helping my friends, and Dominic missed his chance to kill me. Everything will be alright. And my friends will be safe.

I don't know whether to feel relieved or apprehensive that there's no name on the paper he gave me, just a number scrawled at a diagonal. If there was a name, it might feel too personal. I might not be able to go through with it. But with no name, I can't make any guesses. For all I know, this number is a prank. Dominic could have given me the number for a stripper instead of the girl my father wants me to talk to.

I need to call her. If I don't, someone might have to pay the price for my insubordination.

"Hello?" a nervous female voice answers after just a few seconds.

"Uh. Hi. I'm Marcus. Were you . . . I mean, did someone . . ."

"Did someone tell me you'd be calling? Yes. But they said you'd be calling like a week ago." Nerves tremble in her voice, but she's hiding it pretty well. "I guess you must have been too busy or something?"

"I guess you could say that." My voice is flat, but I'm still not one hundred percent sure this is the girl I'm supposed to contact. I'm zero percent sure I should get at all friendly with the girl I'm supposed to contact. "Do you mind telling me how much you know about this situation?"

She lets out a heavy sigh. "I don't mind, but we both know this isn't the kind of conversation to have over the phone. Where should I meet you?"

I consider, then discard the idea of having her come here. I don't want her to feel like she's going into a predator's lair. "How about the coffee shop on West Campus?"

"Sure. I'll meet you there in thirty minutes."

She hangs up immediately, and I'm left frowning at my phone. Though it hardly feels like my phone after Dominic and his goons went through it and deleted every single thing that made it personal at all. All of my contacts, all of my pictures—not that I had many of those—and all of my text messages. I wonder if they went through all of them before they clicked delete. Probably.

I think, or at least I desperately hope, there was nothing too incriminating. Not that my father doesn't already know the one thing about me that my new fraternity brothers could hold against me. That doesn't mean I want them realizing I'm gay and trying to see if they can pressure me over it.

* * *

There's only one likely candidate at the coffee shop when I get there, but I need to be sure I'm talking to the right person. I slink to a corner and call her number. The nervous-looking human in the quietest corner of the coffee shop gives a little jump, then answers her phone.

"Hello? Are you here?"

"Yeah. I didn't want to risk sitting down at the wrong table. Is that you in the blue T-shirt?"

She gives a little wave, looking around, trying to figure out where I might be. "Yeah. Blue T-shirt. You?"

I step toward her and wave, my stomach in tight knots thinking about what comes next. "White button-down in front of the plant."

She gives a shuddering sigh. "I see you."

I introduce myself as I put my phone away. Should I offer to shake her hand? Is that how this is done? I have no idea, so I stand in front of her table, shuffling my feet like a kid who's just gotten in trouble.

To my relief, she looks just as uncomfortable as I feel. "I'm Sarah. Why don't you sit down?" she finally offers.

"So, do you know who my father is?" It's absolutely the worst thing I can say, but it's literally the only thing I can think of after the silence between us stretches too long.

"Yeah." She ducks her head in a quick, nervous bob. "One of the founding members of . . . well, a lot of things, I guess. Also, the guy paying my dad's medical bills."

"Your dad's . . ." I stare blankly at her, trying to catch up, but I'm lost.

"My dad's medical bills. I figured I would get it out in the open right away so we didn't have to dance around the conversation. And so you don't have to guess at why I would do something like this. I realize I'm just a prostitute from your standpoint, but my dad is important to me, and this is the only way I could think of to help him." Her lip wobbles for an instant, and she blinks furiously. "I just thought you should know why."

I'm surprised my chin doesn't hurt from hitting the table, my jaw just dropped open so hard. "No way," I finally gurgle out around my shock and discomfort. "No. Way. You can't. We can't. You can't just throw your life away like that."

Now, she looks mutinous. No more trembling lips and wet eyes. "You don't know me well enough to tell me what I can't do. Besides, I signed a contract already, so if you aren't willing to do this, I still have to find someone who is."

I drop my face into my hands. *Calm. Zen. Focus. There has to be a way.*

"Okay," I try again once I'm not on the verge of screaming. "What kind of contract did you sign?"

She traces the woodgrain of the table and bites her lip, not even trying to meet my eyes now.

"I don't get any money until he has confirmation that we've . . . you know . . ."

"Act like I'm stupid because there are a lot of different things I 'know.' What exactly do you need to do before you get the money? And is it a lump sum sort of thing, or would they still have you on the hook later on?"

More tracing. More lip biting. I don't want to hear her answers. I'm terrified of what she's about to say. I need to know what I've gotten myself into.

"There will be an initial payment straight to the debt collectors as soon as your father has confirmation that you and I . . ." She blushes a brighter red than any vampire could ever manage. "Have had sex," she finishes with a whisper.

Well, it's only the second-worst possibility. But it's literally the second-worst possibility.

"And then you're done and we can part ways?" There's a small chance that all my father really cares about is reminding me that he's the one in charge.

"Ummm . . . there are also ongoing medical expenses . . ." She looks quickly up at me, then drops her eyes again, afraid of how I'll respond.

I'm afraid too. "And how do you pay those?"

"They said I would have to stay with you until—" She cuts off because her voice is shaking so hard.

"Until you're pregnant?"

She nods.

My hand slaps down hard on the tabletop. "No fucking way. I agreed to do what my father wanted because I thought he would at least choose someone . . . where do I even start? You're too young. You can't possibly be old enough to legally make this choice. You're too young to become a vampire. You're too young to have kids, even human kids, who won't kill you. Do you actually understand what you've agreed to do? Vampirism is basically an STD. If you have enough exposure to become pregnant from a vampire, it will kill you. It will turn you into a vampire. You don't understand what that means."

Sarah draws herself up and finally looks me right in the eye, drilling hatred straight into my skull. "Right. I'll extend my life by centuries and never get sick again. I'll be stronger than I've ever been before, and I'll save my dad from crushing debt in the process. That sure sounds like a shitty deal. Oh, and maybe you want to address the fact that you seem perfectly fine as a vampire, but you're arguing that I can't possibly want what you have? Any comment?"

I clench my fists and grind my teeth. "Okay, you're right that I'm a vampire, and I don't mind being a vampire. You're wrong that becoming a vampire is a positive for you. I don't know what it's like to truly live as a human. I've been a vampire my whole life, but all I've ever heard from vampires who were changed after being human is how hard it is. How much they miss living. How much they hate drinking blood.

My own mother can barely look me in the eye because I'm the reason she was turned. I'm not trying to keep some glorious thing from you. I'm trying to keep you from making the worst choice of your life. Why don't you get that?"

"I already signed a contract," Sarah says.

I'm trapped. I knew I was in the trap, but now that it's snapped shut, I finally understand what that means. Doing what my father wants doesn't just mean setting aside my own desires. It means giving up my morals and dragging my soul through the muck. There's no coming back from it if I destroy this girl. And I don't see any way out of doing just that.

Chapter Thirty

DEVON - PRESENT

There are three blood bags in the minifridge in Marcus's room. What used to be Marcus's room. It's not anymore because he's sending vampire friends to pick his shit up for him.

He won't even notice if I drink his blood bags. He's probably forgotten they're even here. He didn't care enough about them to have his new vampire friends get them for him.

I stare with utter hatred at the minifridge in question.

Yes, I can admit that sitting on the bare mattress where my once-hookup-slash-roommate slept and glaring my hatred at the contents of his minifridge is . . . possibly, slightly unhinged behavior.

I give in. With as much energy as I can muster, I stumble across the room and tear into the first bag.

Heaven.

If heaven exists—lol, not likely—it's got to be like the feeling of rejuvenation when I swallow the last of the blood bag and feel it hit my system. Finishing the first bag, I frantically grab for the second bag in the fridge and suck it down like I haven't had blood in . . . well, it's exactly what you would expect.

And before I know what's happening, I'm crying on the floor with a belly full of blood, three empty blood bags strewn on the floor around me.

* * *

"Whoa. You look like shit." Jeff's voice draws me out of my blood stupor. "What the fuck are you doing?"

My head lolls to the side so I can bring him into view.

He's wide-eyed, horrified, standing in the doorway and staring at me.

I think about wiping any bloody evidence off my face. Or maybe sitting up and trying to pretend I haven't been wallowing on the floor of my former hookup's's bedroom.

What's the point, though?

"Did you know Marcus moved out?" The three blood bags have only partially restored me, so my voice comes out in a harsh rasp.

Jeff steps into the room and takes a slow turn, taking in the bare mattress, the empty desk.

"I knew he hadn't been around for a few days. Did he actually tell you he's moving out?"

I shake my head, still too apathetic to even lift it off the floor. "He sent a friend of his to pick up his stuff. Doesn't want to come back and risk having to see any of us, I guess. But it sure sounded like he's expecting to be gone for good."

"Okay, let's get you up and out of this room." Jeff grabs my hand and heaves me to my feet in an impressive show of strength, considering I'm taller than him and the definition of dead weight right now. "Whatever is going on, you'll feel better talking about it on the couch than the floor."

199

He's not wrong, so I let him lead—okay, drag—me out to the common area and drop me on the couch.

"Coffee?" he asks and starts making a pot before I can answer.

On the bright side, my insides are no longer trying to eat themselves, so I think I can actually drink some coffee without wishing for death.

He comes back with two coffee mugs and sits on the coffee table, his knees brushing mine, eyeing me sternly over the lip of his mug.

"Are we finally going to admit that something is going on between you and Marcus?"

"Was," I whisper, then clear my throat, sip my coffee. "Something was going on between us, but nothing is changing about his situation, and he's never going to be able to acknowledge anything, and now he's moved out to live with his vampire friends."

Jeff blinks a few times. "I didn't realize Marcus had vampire friends."

"Old family vampires like him always have vampire friends," I tell him. "I don't know exactly who his family is, but I'd bet either his dad or grandad or someone pretty closely related to him is one of those super-old vampires who basically formed society back in the day and now expects everyone else to bow down and lick their toes."

"Is that really a thing?"

"Is what really a thing?"

Jeff huffs out an annoyed breath. "All of it. Toe licking, the fact that your dad might be old enough to have shaped society, vampires having grandads. Why don't you pick where to start, and then I can ask questions?"

"I mean, it's not like I'm really an expert. I've only been a vampire for . . ." I trail off with the realization. I've been a vampire for a year. No one in my life is rude enough to ask me about it, but I've been telling myself that it's just been a few weeks, maybe a few months, since I became a vampire. It's been a year, though. A year of blood and cravings and hating what I've become and mourning what I've lost.

"What?"

I shake off the surprise of my realization. "I just haven't been a vampire that long. And I don't really know much about these old families. But let's see what I do know. Guys like Vincent definitely come from old families. Like, his father could totally have been alive during the Revolutionary War."

Jeff lets out a low whistle.

"And you probably already knew this, but old families pretty much automatically mean old money." I scratch my head, trying to organize my thoughts into things that Jeff doesn't know already and things that might actually interest him. "I know some of these families make a big thing of, like, ensuring the family bloodline or shit like that."

"Wait," Jeff stops me, "that's one thing I'm confused about. Are you talking about a vampire turning a human, and that person carries on the family business, or . . ."

"No. I mean, born vampires. A vampire gets a woman pregnant, and the baby she has is a vampire. Like Vincent. Or like Marcus, but it seems weird to lump Vincent and Marcus together."

"But does that really mean Marcus is also from one of these creepy old vampire families? Is he, like, a secret millionaire or something?"

"I don't know about that, but, I mean, he said he was going to talk to someone about our Vincent problem, then Vincent was put in vampire jail the next day. Don't you think that means something?"

We sit in silence for a bit. I don't know what Jeff is thinking about, but I'm mulling over the timeline of Marcus leaving, Elijah Jones showing up and basically saving us all, and Marcus coming back for a goodbye fuck before disappearing again.

Jeff tilts his head and narrows his eyes, kind of like a bird examining something to decide whether it's food or not.

"You know, it kind of happened so fast I guess I didn't really even think about Marcus being the one to contact the lawyer. I mean . . . didn't Elijah make it seem like they'd been building that case for a while?"

Huh. Yeah, that's what's been niggling at the back of my mind too.

"But, I mean, Marcus said he had one more thing to try, he left, Vincent was put on trial, then Marcus came back. Those things, happening in that order, have to be connected, right? It would be too much of a coincidence otherwise, right?"

Jeff shrugs. "Maybe he added some evidence or something, but the more I think of it, the more it seems like the timeline was too tight for Marcus to be the main factor. Right?"

There's a headache starting behind my left eye, zipping across to my right eye, then throbbing to full life in my ear drums. As much as I hate the thought of it, I think I need more blood. I rub small circles above my ears, praying that it magically makes my headache and all of my Marcus-related pain go away.

"It makes sense," I admit. I'm not sure if I want it to make sense or not. If Marcus was the one who saved the day, and then he disappeared, it seems likely he had to give something up to save the day. If it's all just a coincidence, then Marcus chose to leave us—to leave me.

<h1 style="text-align:center">Chapter Thirty-One</h1>

MARCUS - PRESENT

I still haven't figured out what to do about Sarah. Meeting up with her at least got my father—and therefore Dominic—off my back temporarily. It won't last, though. If for no other reason, she's still got her family's money issues to deal with. If I had any real control over my own finances, I'd just pay off everything and never have to see her again and never have to face doing the most abhorrent, deplorable thing I can possibly imagine. I shudder just thinking about what my father is demanding. If it was just sex, whatever, I could find a way. I have absolutely no attraction toward women and pretty much zero desire to even stick my dick inside of anyone, but I could fake it long enough if I absolutely had to. But turn her into a vampire? Bring another unwanted vampire child into the world? I'm not sure which part of it disgusts me more, but I know absolutely that I can't do it. When I agreed to do it . . . well, I wasn't imagining my father would pick someone my age, that's for sure. I also didn't anticipate just how dirty the whole thing would make me feel.

No. It's not an option anymore, even if I originally thought I could do it.

I want to be back in my dorm, back in Devon's arms, letting him tell me it'll be fine. I want to put some—even just a small bit—of this burden on someone else. As it is, it's weighing me down so hard I can barely walk, barely move. I drag myself to classes, then back to my lonely room in the crowded frat house. I practically sleepwalk my way through classes and avoid the common areas of the frat house whenever possible. George comes to my room to chat, but everyone else feels too close to Dominic to be safe. And Dominic is always there, lurking in the room I have to pass through or walking down the hall right when I happen to leave my room. Always there and always ready with some threatening quip about what happens to brothers who fail to meet the brotherhood's expectations. One of these days, as soon as he sees an opportunity, I imagine, He's going to actually end me. He honestly seems a little more manic, a little more dangerous, every single time I see him.

But at least everyone else is safe, I remind myself for the tenth time in as many minutes. The fact that I saved my friends by my sacrifice is the only thing holding me together right now.

My phone is still devoid of all contacts since the brothers decided to factory reset it—thanks again, guys—but the number that pops up is one of the few that I will always remember.

"Hey, Pris."

"Where the fuck have you been?" Her ability to cut through any and all crap is one of my favorite things about her.

I roll over to my other side. That's all I've done so far today. Change positions on my bed and think of all the places I'd rather be and things I'd rather be doing. When it's obvious she's not going to let me off the hook, I start talking.

"Living at the frat house. Currently, at least. For a bit, I was here, but not exactly as a regular resident. I asked our father for a favor and have been paying it off."

"Paying it off? What the fuck did you agree to? Did you get what you needed out of him first?"

I appreciate the anger in her voice. It even perks me up for a moment, and then I remember how stuck and hopeless everything is, and I sink back into myself.

"It's not like I could avoid this forever," I mutter.

"Avoid. What."

Damn her and her ability to get at exactly what I don't want to deal with.

"I agreed to do the whole . . . you know . . . fraternity thing. And he agreed to help out with the vampire I was having issues with here."

"And?"

I bury my face in my pillow, wishing with all of my heart that I could actually suffocate myself with it right now. "He's picked this girl for me to continue the family bloodline with."

The sound of Priscilla's teeth grinding together just about causes feedback in my cell phone.

"I see. And how old is she? Did you agree to do it?"

"I didn't agree to do it," I argue, but there's no force behind my words. "I just haven't figured out how to get out of it."

A beat of silence. "How old is this girl, Marcus?"

"Too young," I groan. "Obviously, too young, but, like, way too young. Maybe not even old enough to make this decision, but apparently, she signed a contract, and her dad has some kind of huge medical debt, and even though she should be too young to make the choice to die like this, she must be old enough to legally sign a paper saying she's willing to. It's such a fucking mess, Pris." Now that I've started, I'm not sure if I can stop. Truths keep spilling out of me, tripping on each other on their way out of my mouth. "And the only reason they let me out of the basement here is because I hadn't called her, but I'm sure they'll happily put me back in the basement if I don't do what I'm supposed to, and there's no fucking way I can do what I'm supposed to because she's young and selfless and way too fucking alive for me to take that away from her. But she won't hear what I'm trying to tell her, that none of this is worth it, and keeps saying they'll just send her to som—"

"Okay," Priscilla cuts me off sharply. "I get it. Marcus, why the fuck did you agree to anything he asked for in the first place?"

I shrug, even though she obviously can't see it. "I was desperate. The same reason anyone ever gives him what he wants."

"Alright. You were desperate for his help. You agreed to something you knew you could never actually do, and he promised to help you in return. Did he already follow through on his part of it?"

"I mean . . . as far as I can know? Vincent is in prison and off blood for a century, so that has to mean our father helped me out by putting him away, right?"

Now, I can practically hear her shrugging over the phone. "Or he knew that someone else was putting him away, and he knew that you wanted that, and he took credit for it so he could get you to do what he wanted."

"But." I have to pause and think. "But it's too much of a coincidence that someone else would be planning to put Vincent away at the same time our father . . ." And I can't even finish the sentence because of course, that's exactly what he would do. Of course he already knew about my Vincent issues. Of course he already knew if someone else was building a case against Vincent. Of course he would take credit for putting Vincent in prison even if he had nothing to do with it. "Fuck! I let him play me, didn't I?"

Priscilla's sympathy rolls over me across the line. "Yeah. Probably. Does it help if I tell you there's a tiny chance he just took advantage of an opportunity and didn't plan the whole thing ahead of time?"

"No, not really."

"I didn't think so."

"So what do I do about it?"

DEVON - PRESENT

It's five in the morning, and the time has come for me to quit blood for good. Yesterday, after talking to Jeff—and yes, I can admit that at least some of this started because I needed a distraction from thinking about Marcus—I went down a research rabbit hole and found a whole community of vampires who survive on blood alternatives or without blood entirely. It can be done, and I'm going to do it. My problem before was I didn't have a plan. I just went cold turkey without thinking it through. Well, this time, I'm prepared, and I have a whole support system to back me up when it gets tough.

Here it is. Day one. I read and reread the instructions that numerous people from the Blood Free community swear by.

Wake up early and microdose enough blood to get by but a small enough amount that your body starts the weaning process. Be prepared for hunger. Remember that the hunger won't kill you.

Instead of clamping down on the nozzle of a blood bag and gagging the whole thing down as quickly as possible, I measure out a tiny cupful of blood and reseal the blood bag to use later.

"Here we go." I quietly toast myself and tip the mouthful of blood down my throat.

The internet wasn't lying about the hunger. That little bit of blood brings my appetite roaring to life.

The hunger won't kill me. The hunger won't kill me. If that fucking asshole Vincent can survive this, so can I. I want to cry with the desperation to complete my feed. Every cell in my body is screaming that it's not enough. There's not enough blood to go around to keep the rest of me functioning. *The hunger won't kill me. Sunlight can kill vampires, as can fire and beheading. Hunger just hurts, though. It doesn't actually harm.*

With a whimper, I force myself to get back in bed and try to sleep. All of the forums were very clear on the sleep aspect of this. Sleep and microdosing and willpower. That's all I need to wean myself off blood completely in one month or less.

* * *

All of my careful planning has gone to shit by ten in the morning.

I couldn't sleep. I still haven't convinced my survival instinct that this won't kill me. Each microdose of blood just makes me more hungry than I was before. I don't know what's wrong with me that this is so much harder for me than everyone else.

So I guess it's plan B earlier than I was hoping for.

I open the paper bag as slowly as I can, desperately hoping I'll get control of my hunger pains before I actually have to go this route. Everything I've read says there's no going back if I do this. There's no divine intervention, no sudden easing of my hunger, and now I have the sketchiest-looking jar of liquid ever seen in my hands. There's no legal, easy, non-sketchy way to get your hands on synthetic blood, which is bullshit because everyone I talked to said it works just fine. It's just all these old vampire families wanting to protect the status quo, keep us dependent on human blood and keep humans in their place in society. But that's okay. At least I don't have to be part of that whole fucked-up system. I'll just drink synthetic blood for the rest of my life. I'd rather just go blood-free, but I'm just a few hours into trying it, and I can already tell I'm failing. And if quitting blood is so much harder on the second try, I know it will be impossible on a third attempt.

Knocking the jar of synthetic blood against my forehead, I pray and beg and bargain with the universe for more strength.

No luck. I break the seal on the jar and swallow a mouthful before I have to think too hard about my failure.

I'll just do the synthetic stuff from now on. It will be fine. I'm the only one who has to know that I failed at this, and synthetic at least isn't part of the messed-up vampire-human ecosystem I hate being a part of.

Except that I realize the moment it hits my stomach that I've made a huge mistake. It feels wrong. So wrong, like worms crawling inside me and trying to burrow through me to get out. I drop the jar, hearing it shatter like something that's happening on someone's TV a mile away. The vile smell of the stuff permeates the room. I probably wouldn't have been able to swallow the stuff if I'd stopped to smell it first.

I wretch, trying to get it back out before it can do any more damage, but nothing comes up, and the floor is spinning under me, spinning up to meet me, and I barely notice when my face hits the broken glass of my jar of poison because all of me is in so much pain that some glass shards in my cheek don't even register.

I'm going to die now, aren't I? is the last thought to stroll through my mind before everything goes finally, blessedly black.

Chapter Thirty-Two

MARCUS - PRESENT

I don't recognize the number calling me and once again curse my lovely frat brothers, who deleted everything from my phone.

"Hello?"

"Marcus, I don't know what the fuck is going on with you, but you need to get over it and get here now. Devon won't wake up, and I don't know what happened to him, and I don't want to call a doctor and maybe make things worse, but you might know—"

"Jeff? What do you mean Devon won't wake up?" Panic is already welling up from the bottom of my intestines. I've got a handful of blood capsules and am already halfway out the door. "And where are you?" I ask belatedly.

Jeff takes a rattling breath. "At the dorm. I went in to ask him something, and I found him on the floor, and he's not responding to anything. And there's, like, broken glass and blood everywhere? I don't fucking know what happened."

His fear is obvious, pouring through the phone and dragging me faster and faster toward them. I practically fly across campus. "I'm on my way," I promise. "Just, keep trying to wake him up. I'll be there soon."

* * *

It's even worse than I imagined when I barrel through the dorm door.

Devon—usually bright and laughing and full of life—looks actually dead. His cheeks are sunken, his skin ashen. His freckles look like grey dirt smudges on a corpse's skin. But the smell is what pushes my panic over the edge. The blood Jeff told me about smells all wrong.

"Devon. Devon?" I start out quiet, but I'm screaming by the time I reach him.

Come on. Hold it together. You can't help him if you panic.

"Come on, baby. You gotta wake up for me. What the fuck were you doing?"

I have to clamp down on my fear again.

I gather him in my arms and carry him out of the foul-smelling room.

"Devon, come on. Work with me here, okay?"

No response.

Fuck, fuck, fuck! The screaming is internal. That's good. It would do even less good externally. Not that it's doing any good right now, but I sure can't stop it.

"Come on, baby. You gotta wake up so you can tell me what the fuck you did to yourself."

I'm separated out into distinct pieces, none of which have any bearing on each other. One piece of me is screaming and crying and gibbering in the corner. Another piece is chafing at Devon's hands like if I can just warm him up a little, every-thing will be okay. Yet another piece has taken in the fact that we have an audience. All of my former roommates, plus some of their friends, have gathered around to bear witness as I crumble to bits.

The competent, focused part of me shoves a blood capsule into Devon's mouth and presses his jaw up, hopefully with enough force to burst the capsule in his mouth and get the lifesaving blood into his system.

Nothing.

"Sweetheart, come on. You have to help me out here."

Devon doesn't notice or appreciate the endearment.

Think. Fucking think!

None of the obvious things are working. There really only *is* one obvious thing to do for a vampire. Give them blood, then watch them heal. But Devon won't even take the blood I'm trying to give him.

I need something stronger. I need something that his body can't just reject or ignore.

"Get me a knife," I shout at whoever might be within reach.

"A . . . what?" Jeff hesitates too long, so I turn, searching for help elsewhere.

Thank fuck, someone hands me a knife. It's a dull steak knife that one of us bought as part of a set at the nearby box store at the beginning of the year. Apparently, one of my pieces is able to hyperfocus on the minutiae of where a random piece of cutlery came from. I couldn't tell you who handed this to me, but I remember the shopping trip where one of the guys joked about buying steak knives for a dorm room where none of the residents would be eating steak.

While that part of myself is enjoying fun memories with my roommates, the competent part of me says a prayer to the darkness and stabs me in the neck.

"What the fuck, man?" comes as a distant chorus from the people around me, but I've got no time to deal with them. If this works, they won't need any explanations. If it doesn't work . . . I guess I'll have even less time to deal with them.

I pull Devon up and press his lips to my neck wound. "Come on, come on, come on," I beg him, chanting the words under my breath over and over. A mantra. A prayer.

Relief floods through me when I feel movement—the tiniest movement in the world but movement nonetheless—in the spot where Devon's lips are touching me. There's just that tiny movement and no other warning, and then his teeth sink into me deep, and I feel a thick pull as he starts to suck my blood out.

It's primal, being fed on like this, feeling my life force literally sucked away from me.

My thoughts slow, and my panic drains away along with my blood. He's drinking. He'll be fine.

Ignoring our confused—possibly horrified and disgusted —audience, I shift Devon in my arms so I don't have to hold him up. Which is good because all of my strength is swirling away, water in a drain that just got unclogged. My extremities tingle with the sensation of already slow-moving blood slowing even more and stopping before reaching my fingers and toes. My consciousness floats, calm and distant.

Was this what Devon felt when he was turned? No. I'm certain it's different. He would have been terrified, in pain, dying.

I feel . . . euphoric. Like if this is the only good thing I do with my existence, it's enough. It's enough that I could save him. It's enough to have him in my arms right now. And I know, for the rest of my time in this world, Devon is it for me. Nothing else will ever matter as much. I drop from consciousness with that conviction holding me safe, my arms holding Devon safe.

And it's enough.

Chapter Thirty-Three

DEVON - PRESENT

Sensations trickle into me without bringing the words to define them. I reach for any words at all but come up only on fragments.

Soft. That's the first word to come back to me, followed by *lips* and *sweet.* Okay, now we're making some progress. Three whole words, and I even have some idea of what they mean.

I move my lips, or maybe my lips move on their own, and feel them brushing against something smooth and soft, which makes one more word in my official vocabulary right now. The soft, smooth something vibrates beneath my lips, and I press into it, relishing the feeling.

Skin, my brain supplies, oh so helpfully. The soft, smooth something is skin, and I can feel it pulsing and vibrating against me.

Sweet. That's the taste on my tongue and on my lips.

Instinctively, I lick the skin that seems so enticing right now.

"Devon, you'll kill me," someone groans, the vibrations shooting straight from my lips to my cock.

"Hm?" I ask, still exploring this delicious patch of skin.

The voice doesn't answer, but I find myself suddenly, inexplicably on my back. Marcus presses down onto me, his eyes gazing into mine, his hip causing all sorts of the best kind of friction exactly where I want it. Now it's my turn to groan. I arch my back too, not because I mean to, just because I can't not strain for more friction.

I find Marcus's neck again, his pulse throbbing almost like he's living. I press my lips to it and prepare to bite down with my sharp teeth, but he stops me with a whimper.

"Let's go in the other room," he begs me on a gasp as my teeth graze his artery.

It turns out to be easier said than done, though. Somehow, none of my limbs seem to be working correctly, and my mind is ping-ponging all over the place. I can't figure out what's going on, only that Marcus is here, and Marcus is all that I want right now. He finally wrangles my wayward arms so one is slung over his shoulder and half leads, half carries me from the dorm living room to his bedroom.

Which is still completely bare.

I deflate a little, staring at that empty room and letting it come back to me. The way he disappeared. The way he left me after a goodbye fuck that I didn't even realize was goodbye at the time.

Maybe Marcus senses where my thoughts are heading. He maneuvers me onto the bed and kneels in front of me.

"Hey," he whispers. "We can worry about sheets and all that later. I just haven't had a chance to clean up the mess in your room yet. That's why we're in here."

"Mess?" My brain is not cooperating. Something is refusing to click into place. There's a hazy curtain in my mind that I can't look too hard or too long at before I start hurting.

Marcus's eyes tighten in some kind of pain that I can't place. "Let's not worry about it right now, okay? Can you trust me that I'll let you know what you need?"

Can I? Trust him, I mean? That's another hazy curtain that gets painful if I look too close.

He drops his forehead to my knees. "Look, Devon. I know I haven't given you a lot of reasons to trust me, but I promise you, I'm going to take care of you through this. Just, please let me take care of you, okay?"

I can't focus. I can't think about whether I trust Marcus or not, and I can't figure out why he's talking about taking care of me. So I avoid the tough questions in favor of something that seems like an easy fix. "I'm hungry," I whine.

His eyes tighten with that mysterious pain again. "You'll need to feed," he says, and he's looking me in the eyes all serious and rubbing his hands slowly up and down my thighs. I don't know much about horses, but I'm pretty sure this is how people act around horses they don't want to startle.

"Okay." I draw the word out, searching for clues about what's really going on, why he's treating me like a dangerous animal. "So, is there any blood I can have?"

"There is." And he's gone all shifty, eyes flicking to the side, then the floor, then back without actually meeting my eyes.

"But?" I press him.

His eyes finally rest on mine. "How much do you remember about what happened, Devon?"

I still can't find any clues on his face or in this creepy, bare room. "What happened when? I mean, a lot of things have happened, right?"

"Yeah, but there are a few important things that I don't think you're remembering right now, and I don't really want to be the one who brings them to your attention."

"Okay, well, now I'm even more confused and starting to

get worried, so you'd better tell me so I stop coming up with worst-case scenarios."

Slowly, carefully, his hands slide up my thighs, then down, then up again. The message is clear. *Stay calm. Stay soothed.*

I can tell the instant he makes a decision about what to tell me. Apparently, Marcus was not made to be a poker player.

"You drank something bad," he starts. "Do you remember what you drank?"

An image flashes in my mind. A paper bag. A glass jar. The floor flying up to meet my face.

"I . . . I think I had synthetic blood? But everyone I talked to said it's no big deal to do synthetic."

The muscle in his jaw clenches—once, twice—before he meets my eyes again. "And who exactly did you talk to?"

I start to answer, but he cuts me off. "No. Don't say it because I'm pretty sure I already know. The people you talked to, whoever they were, are full of shit and nearly killed you. No one has developed a synthetic blood that actually works, which is why you can't legally buy it, which is why it was fucking idiotic for you to even try getting it." He gets angrier as he talks, his voice rising, his eyes flashing. "What the fuck were you trying to do, anyway? What the fuck were you think-ing?" By the end of his rant, he can't even stay kneeling in front of me and jumps up to pace the room like a hungry predator. "Well? What the fuck were you thinking?"

And now I'm angry. Angry that he expects me to know something that goes against everything everyone told me just a few days ago. Angry that he's apparently angry at me. Angry at the fact that he left me with no warning, and now thinks he can come back and have any kind of say in my life.

"I was thinking that I was sick of drinking disgusting blood all the time, and everyone I talked to said I didn't have to anymore," I snap. "Not that it's any fucking business of yours. Don't you have important vampire shit to do some place other than here? How about you go do that." *Please don't go. Please don't leave me*, my stupid, traitor heart begs.

I shouldn't feel so gratified by the stricken look on his face. I really shouldn't.

"I don't fucking care about that other shit. I care that you could have died! Don't you get that you almost killed yourself?"

"Everyone said it would be fine!" I'm so angry now that my strength has finally returned. Enough that I can stand up on my own, at least. And shout.

"Everyone was wrong!" he shouts back.

"Well, how was I supposed to know that? Anyway, I'm fine. Look at me! I bounced back, just like I always do. No big deal."

Marcus grabs me by the shoulders, and I wonder for a moment if he's going to try shaking me until I get his point. Instead, he drops his forehead to mine and just holds us like that, his eyes closed, his fingers biting into my upper arms.

"Don't ever tell me that it's no big deal," he finally says, and his voice comes out as a harsh growl. "Never say that it's no big deal how close you came to dying."

"But . . . I don't get it. Vincent can go a century without drinking blood. There are all of these people in the blood-free community who successfully weaned themselves off blood. But I only made it a few days." My voice cracks. I try blinking the wetness from my eyes before Marcus can notice. "Why did I fail?"

And his arms are all the way around me, and the wetness in my eyes has developed into full-blown tears, and I'm crying into his shoulder. So now I'm not only a failure, but I'm also a mess, and not in a cute or a private way. I am on display, my messiness getting all over Marcus's shirt.

"You didn't fail," he whispers. "Vampires can only go long term without blood if they go into a deep sleep, basically hibernation. Vincent will be woken up in a hundred years with a blood infusion that reawakens his functions. The reason he can go that long without blood is because he'll be all but dead and not using his body for anything for the duration. And everyone on the internet claiming they don't need blood anymore is either lying, exaggerating, or selling you something. Maybe a combination of all three. Didn't anyone warn you how dangerous those blood-free assholes are? Didn't anyone warn you that there's no safe synthetic blood that anyone has developed?"

"Why would I trust the people who want me dependent on blood when they tell me I need to be dependent on blood?" I ask into his shoulder. My little meltdown has left me feeling drained again, to the point I don't know if I can stand up without help right now. Marcus must realize it because he helps me down to the mattress.

He cuddles me close to him again, and another storm of emotion shudders through me. "That stuff you drank, that supposed synthetic blood, was absolute poison to you," he continues after I'm calm again. "Usually, blood capsules would be enough to save a vampire who's been poisoned, but you were completely nonresponsive. You wouldn't swallow at all. I had to find something stronger to give you."

"What are you trying to tell me? I'm too tired to figure out whatever code you're talking in. Just say it."

He huffs out a humorless laugh. "I had to give you something stronger than human blood. All I could think of was vampire blood. It's medicinal, you know? That's how people survive the change when they become vampires. They come to the brink of death, but the vampire blood they've drunk saves them at the last moment. You were at the brink of death, so I fed you vampire blood to heal you, and it brought you back."

"But where did you find—" I stop talking when I realize.

"Yeah. My blood. I gave you my blood."

The intimacy of it makes my stomach flip. Somehow, the thought of drinking his blood is so much more personal than anything else between us. I mean, I've fucked him. I've come inside of him. That's nothing to biting his artery and drinking his blood.

I lick my lip. Bite my lip. Clear my throat. What can I say to that? What in the world is someone supposed to say to something like that?

"Did I . . . did it hurt?"

"No." He doesn't hesitate to answer. "No pain at all. Probably not at all . . ."

"Not at all what?" Where's he going with this?

"I shouldn't have brought it up."

"Well, you did. What were you going to say?"

He slumps but keeps holding me up. That's good because I'm running on fumes right now.

"It's just . . . I know it must have hurt when you were turned. Your blood was taken against your will. And your life as you knew it. But it was different between us. I wanted to give you that. It was an honor, honestly, to be the one there with you. So, no, it didn't hurt."

My throat closes up like a fist is clenched around my esophagus. He's right. When I was turned, all I could think about was the pain and what was being taken from me and how it all felt worse than I ever could have imagined. But he gave me his blood freely. He saved me.

"Okay," I manage to croak out. "I'm glad I didn't hurt you . . . like that."

He holds me, rocks me against him, without breaking the silence for a long time.

He seems hesitant when he asks, "Are you hungry?"

My body answers for me before my mouth says a word. My stomach growls so loudly there might be a jaguar actually inside of me, growling for its dinner.

"I got rid of all my blood, though," I admit.

"I don't think blood bags would do you much good anyway."

"What do you mean?" I search his face for clues, and he's staring at me with an intensity that I'm sure should mean something, but I can't figure it out.

"I'm pretty sure—I could be wrong. I mean, I've never seen it before, just heard about it—but I'm pretty sure, between the synth blood and the withdrawals and drinking vampire blood that you're blood bound now."

"Is that something vampires are supposed to know about?"

I'm pretty sure I hear something creak in his jaw as he clenches it. "Yes. It's something vampires learn about when we're young, but I guess no one would have thought to fill you in when you were turned. Blood bound is when a vampire becomes dependent on the more medicinal qualities of vampire blood. Like I said, I could be wrong, but you rejected blood capsules and accepted my blood, which I think means human blood isn't going to do it for you anymore. I think you're blood bound, and I don't know that there's any way to unbind you. You need to drink vampire blood from now on."

The room swirls, and I find myself lying down on the bare mattress with Marcus leaning over me and fussing.

* * *

MARCUS - PRESENT

I don't want to push Devon too much. He's obviously still fragile. But I also need to convince him to feed again. I'm terrified, though, that if I just press his mouth to my neck again and tell him to drink from me, he'll refuse. Then he'll starve, and I'll lose him after all.

I lower him down to the bed as gently as I can.

"I think . . . maybe I'm hungry?" He sounds lost and small and confused and so fucking young.

"Yeah, sweetheart. I think you might still be hungry. Will you drink some for me?"

Devon's eyes wander the room. His forehead creases. "But . . . didn't I get rid of all the blood? Did you say there's some blood I can have?"

Shit. He's fading fast. I need to keep him awake long enough to get him to eat, but there's no way he's staying conscious for long without feeding.

"Yeah, there's blood," I promise. "You remember what I was telling you about? How I think you're probably blood bound?"

A sleepy blink in my direction is the only confirmation I get.

"I think the blood you need is vampire blood, baby." Endearments keep slipping off my tongue, even though I know I have no right to them. I've done nothing to earn the privilege of caring for Devon like this, except that I'm the one who's here and who's doing it.

"Vampire blood? Do they sell blood bags of it?" He sounds like a lost little boy, and it breaks my heart all over again. I want nothing other than to protect this precious soul from the big bad world. I want nothing more than for him to let me.

"No, baby. They don't sell it in bags. It would lose its potency too fast. But there is some here for you to drink."

Please, please, please, let him understand now. Let him not try to fight about it.

Understanding sparks in his eyes. "You fed me your own blood before? And you want me to . . . to drink from you again?"

"I don't want to force you, but I really don't think there's another way." *There's no time*, my panic chants in the back of my head. *There's no time to save him. You're going to lose him. You're out of time.* "Please, Devon. Please, do this for me."

He shakes his head fussily. "I don't want to hurt you. Don't want you to hurt from my fuckup."

Even speaking is visibly draining the last of his energy reserves.

"Please," I beg again. "You won't hurt me, not by drinking from me. I want you to. And if you never want to see me again after, we can find some other solution, some other vampire you can get blood from. Just, please, for this once, I need you to drink from me."

Devon nods reluctantly, trepidation in his eyes.

"You don't have to drink from my neck if you don't want. It might be a little less . . ." I can't finish the sentence, can't think too hard about what he might want less of when it comes to me, so I just roll up my sleeve and hold out my forearm. An offering, a plea.

He nods again, looking less worried now, so I move on the bed until I'm leaning against the wall and have his head cradled against my thigh. I press my forearm to his lips and try to brace myself for round two of being fed on.

"I've never really done this," I admit, "but I think your inst—"

I cut off as his sharp teeth pierce my flesh with a disturbing *squelch* that I didn't notice in the panic of the first time. Again, it doesn't hurt. Not like all of the starvation and burning and bone breaking I received under Dominic's watchful eye. It's oddly powerful, this rushing feeling as my blood is sucked away from me, almost like it's immediately replaced by a tingling kind of magic in my veins. I lean back and tangle my fingers in his hair, letting myself drift as he drinks his fill, barely aware when he drops my arm and falls asleep.

* * *

Reality finds me before I'm ready.

I wake up in utter bliss for a single moment. At some point last night, I slid down on the bed, and Devon wrapped me tight in his arms, and we slept the rest of the night like that.

It feels so right, the best fit of my life. We're like two puzzle pieces who were made for each other. No, more. Maybe two pieces of wood hand-carved to form a smooth corner in a handcrafted chair. I belong here, in his arms. He belongs here, holding me tight against his chest.

Then I realize what woke me up.

"Dude, you can't just—" Jeff's angry protest is cut short by George bursting through the door.

He stares at me. Blinks twice. I should detangle myself from Devon's arms. I should sit up and try to regain . . . whatever bro-dude friendship I'd started building with him.

But I can't stand to tear myself away from Devon's embrace. My blood is in his veins now. I'm a part of him. He's a part of me. George is going to have to deal with it.

"Oh. My. Fucking. God." Each word drops from George's lips like a stone, like anger and disbelief and disappointment. "Are you fucking kidding me? This is where you've been? You disappear without a goodbye or anything, and it's because you're . . . shacking up with some boy toy or something?"

Devon is still fast asleep behind me. The only sign that he hears George shouting at all is a small whiney sound as he nuzzles his face into the hair at my nape.

"It's not like that," I tell George, though I'm not eager to try explaining what it is like. The situation is pretty fucked, no matter how I look at it.

"Oh? You're not, at this very moment, in bed with a guy who's holding you like his favorite teddy bear? You didn't leave the house without a word to anyone about where you were going? Don't you understand that your actions have consequences for other people?"

Of course I understand that. That's how I ended up being tortured in a basement, because I was trying to prevent those consequences from reaching anyone else.

"Um, guys?" Jeff steps between us. Brave man, or possibly stupid, to step between two angry vampires.

"What?" George and I ask at the same time in the same angry voice.

Jeff squares his shoulders and gulps. Maybe not so stupid. He realizes the danger he's in. "I'm guessing Devon needs to rest, and neither of you is helping with that right now. If you really have to argue, can you at least take it out of this room?"

Guilt tweaks at my stomach. He's not wrong.

"Okay, yeah."

George scowls but gives a single jerk of his head in agreement.

We head out to the living room together, where I discover there's an audience of most of the people I've met since starting school, all stuffed onto couches or open places on the floor and staring at us with wide eyes.

Fucking perfect.

"Dominic has been making life impossible for the rest of us because you left," George starts in on me once we're out in the hall together with the door shut behind us.

It's not the level of privacy I'd prefer, but at least all of my friends aren't staring at me and judging me out here.

"I'm sorry about Dominic being shitty, but I had an emergency to take care of here. I'm not going to apologize for that."

He gives an exaggerated eye roll. "Right. An emergency."

I can practically see him adding everything up in his mind and reaching the conclusion that I'm a worthless flake who drops everything just to get my dick wet.

"It's not. Like. That," I grit out.

He throws his hands up. "Whatever you say. It sure looks exactly like that."

I pinch the bridge of my nose. "Why do you even care? And why am I trying to convince you if you already think you know what's going on here?"

"I care because I thought you were coming in to change something, but you dropped it before you did anything, and I just fucking walked in on you snuggling with your boyfriend, and I'm an idiot for thinking maybe you gave a shit!"

I know my jaw is hanging slack, but I don't have the brain cells needed to fix it right now.

"I didn't come to the frat as some savior," I tell him slowly. The thoughts are coming slowly too. "My father forced me to join. He's forced me into everything I've ever done. I was just trying to help out my friends."

George turns away from me. "Don't you get that it makes it worse to know how little you care?"

"That's not what I meant. It's not that I don't care. It's that I can't care. I've got too many people already counting on me, and I've got nothing left to give."

"Fine. Whatever you need to tell yourself. I really just came to let you know that Dominic is taking advantage of your absence and making things shitty for those of us who don't have a boyfriend in the dorms to escape to. I guess I'll go back and try to deal with shit without you."

He starts to walk away, tension in every stride.

"Wait!" I grab his arm and turn him around. "I really do have to deal with things here, okay? But I also know my father is going to make me go back to the frat and . . . I probably don't deserve it, but I could use your help when that happens."

He rolls his eyes to the ceiling and looks like he's praying for strength. "You definitely don't deserve it, but I guess I don't have much choice unless I'm willing to go all in with Dominic. If you stay here with the boyfriend too long, I swear I will find some way to get revenge. Do you hear me?"

Not bothering to protest Devon's new nickname, or the label on our relationship, I give him a shove on the shoulder. "And how long counts as 'too long' in your estimation?"

"Considering I don't even know what you're doing here? Considering I have no idea what 'things' you're dealing with?"

George leaves the question hanging in the air. I have to give him something. I have to give him some reason to give me another chance.

"Devon is going through some . . . it's his story to tell, not mine, but he's dealing with some shit. Anyway, he drank something bad, and I needed to get back here to take care of him. None of his friends knew what to do."

"Okay, so you shove a blood cap down his throat and call it a day. What's the big issue?"

"The blood caps didn't work," I grind out through my teeth. "He would have died if I didn't . . ."

Realization sweeps across George's face.

"You made him feed on you, didn't you?"

I nod, knowing that nothing good can come out of this and knowing that I'm about to explain everything because otherwise it's going to fester inside of me.

"I did, and now, I'm pretty sure we're blood bound. At least, I'm pretty sure he's blood bound. I haven't asked him to try feeding off anyone else, but based on the way thinking about that makes me feel, it's not an option."

"Fuck, man." George looks like his brain just exploded in his skull. "Dominic won't be happy if you bring him back to the house."

"You think I want to bring him there? Why do you think I came here?"

George shakes his head. "It's not a question of what you want. If you really are blood bound, he has to stay with you. Everything is going to shit with Dominic running things at the house, so I really need you to come back with me. You can fuck him over, you can fuck me over, or you can face Dominic. Which one is it going to be?"

"Fuck!" I pace the hall, but there's no walking away from this. He lets me think it through without interrupting. "Okay. Let's be logical. I don't even know if Devon and I are really blood bound. Can you help me figure that out first?"

He gives a jerky nod. Vampires aren't used to being fed on, so I can understand his reluctance. The fact that he's agreeing at all shows just how desperate he is to get me back to the house.

Chapter Thirty-Four

DEVON - PRESENT

I'm only half-awake when Marcus comes into the room and kneels by the bed.

"How are you feeling?" he asks with worry in his eyes.

"I'm fine," I tell him. I don't go on to tell him that I feel like an absolute idiot. There were just so many fucking people telling me exactly what I wanted to hear. Apparently, exactly what I wanted to hear was something that could have gotten me killed. "I feel kind of weak," I admit after a few moments' reflection.

"You need to eat," he tells me, which causes a spike of annoyance, even though I know he's right. Who the fuck is he to have any opinions about me at all? But I know that's not fair. I know he's just worried about me. The same way I know my mom was worried when she finally left my dorm room on move-in day. The same way my dad was worried when he got the call I was in the hospital after a vampire attack.

"Okay. Yeah," I agree. Then I notice it's not just Marcus in the room. Taylor's hulking shape seems to take up half the space, and another guy who seems familiar, but . . . nope, every time I try to pin down who he is, the thought slithers away.

"I want you to try drinking from them." Marcus points to the two behind him without turning around. "Since we don't have any blood bags here, you know? They're the quickest blood available."

I'm sure my confusion is all over my face. Drinking from Marcus was . . . intimate. I don't think I've ever felt more connected to someone. Did he not feel that same intimacy? Does he not want me to drink from him again?

"Just try, okay?" There's that worried look again. He's not just worried because I nearly died. He's worried about me drinking from these guys. Or maybe he's worried about me not drinking from them? I can't make sense of it.

I drag myself up so I can at least face the situation instead of lying down and letting it happen. "Okay. Sure. Whatever you say."

Taylor steps forward, looking awkward and out of place. His eyes dart to Marcus, then back to me before he holds out his forearm. Am I supposed to bite into it like a drumstick? Cut him open at the vein and then suck? This all made a lot more sense when it was Marcus and me and a sense of pressing desperation to guide my actions.

Deciding I need to do something instead of sitting here and staring stupidly at my friend's arm, I take his arm in my hands and pull it toward me. I glance up—*Is this okay?* I ask with my eyes—and see what looks like encouragement. I bring my mouth closer, preparing to bite down, open him with my teeth, allow the instinctive animalistic vampire side of me to take over and feed. Centimeters away, something about the scent of his skin—or maybe it's his blood itself—turns my stomach. I push Taylor away and have to cover my mouth to keep my stomach from heaving out its contents.

"I'm sorry," I stammer. "I don't know what's wrong. I just can't."

Taylor steps back. "No need to apologize," Taylor mumbles. "If it doesn't feel right, you shouldn't force it."

That worried look on Marcus's face has wound twice as tight as before. "Try it with George too?" he asks.

The name, George, slots into place in my memories then. The guy who came to pick up Marcus's things the other day. Vampire frat boy George, who took Marcus away from me. I want to hate him, but he's stepped forward and is holding his arm out to me with an open and earnest look. Whatever else he might have done, he's on my side for this.

I take his arm and bend over it. Maybe if I do it quickly and don't think about the awkwardness of doing this with someone I just met and don't know, it will work better.

I've barely had that thought when a wave of nausea hits me so hard I have to scramble away and pant through my teeth. Something about the smell of him is just plain wrong to me. I can't define what it is; I just know it's the truth.

George looks genuinely disappointed as he steps away from me and looks to Marcus. "Well, I guess we have our answer," he says. "What do you want to do now?"

"Give us some space," Marcus tells the others, then turns back to me without checking that they leave the room.

My stomach is still rebelling against me, but it calms as soon as his hands touch me. Without words, he pulls me to him and holds me close while pressing his wrist to my lips.

Right, my senses tell me. *Yes. Finally. This is right.*

I don't have to think. There's no struggle. My teeth automatically sink into the place where his veins are closest to the surface, and life floods my mouth. One of us, maybe both of us, groans in relief and pleasure as I pull his blood into me, feeding in a way that feels like the most natural thing I've ever done.

* * *

I feel as good as new. All healed and ready to take on the world after my two days of bed rest and being taken care of by Marcus.

Marcus, on the other hand, seems to have different ideas.

"I feel fine," I grumble, packing everything I need to get back to the classes I've been slacking in or skipping entirely for a few weeks now. "My parents are paying a lot of money for me to take classes. I should probably, you know, go to those classes on occasion."

"You aren't going out there today." His response is even more grumbly than mine, and I wonder if he's been doing what he needs to to replenish all of his blood I drained. "We have more important things to deal with."

I throw my arms out. "Like what? What's more important than getting my life back on track and getting caught up in my classes? I just need to put this behind me. The sooner I can move forward, the better."

Marcus huffs and paces the room, coming to stop in front of me after his third lap. "You came as close to dying as a vampire can come without actually dying permanently. That's not shit you just put behind you. Maybe you feel like everything is sunshine and roses or whatever right now, but you can't act like nothing happened. If you do, it's going to come back to you in the worst possible ways, I guarantee."

"So, what? You want me to go to vampire therapy? I've been there. My parents signed me up before I was even out of the hospital after I was turned. It's why I'm so well-adjusted that I'm able to move on with my life now."

"Are you even listening to yourself? If you were so well-adjusted and done with therapy, why did you try to starve yourself to death and then drink poison on the recommendation of some idiots from the internet?"

I grind my teeth. "I didn't try to starve myself. I didn't try to drink poison. I took some advice from people who claimed to have successfully done exactly what I was trying to do. It wouldn't have been a big deal if it had worked, but it didn't work. That doesn't mean it has to be the big deal you're making it out to be."

"You. Almost. Died," he says slowly. "You almost died, and now you have a serious blood disorder, which will probably affect you for the rest of your life."

Right. Blood bound is what he called it. Supposedly, I messed up my system enough that the only blood I can take anymore is vampire blood. That all seems like something that requires a second opinion, though somehow, I don't think the walk-in clinic is going to be able to help me out, and I really don't have time to go looking for a doctor who specializes in blood and feeding disorders in vampires.

He sighs and pulls me in against him, wraps his arms around me, and I can't help sinking into the embrace and wrapping my own arms around his waist. Regardless of the other shit that's happened, I can't regret the fact that he's with me now. He's with me and not trying to pull away and pretend he's just my straight roommate. He's with me, and he isn't panicking after every touch and jumping back like a scared animal.

"We have to get this other stuff sorted out first," he whispers into my hair, sending a shiver of want through me.

"If I agree to that—and I'm not saying I do—what does that look like? What do you really think I need to sort out?"

"You need to talk to someone. About why you tried to quit drinking blood, I mean. Maybe you think you're well-adjusted and done with therapy, but I really think you need to go back."

"And?"

Pause. "And I can't stay here much longer, but you need to be near me to feed."

I jerk away and stare at him with narrowed eyes. "What do you mean?"

"About which part?" He matches my stare with his own slitted eyes.

"All of it. Not staying here. Needing to be near you. What are you getting at?"

He tries pulling me in again, but I step back from his touch.

"Look, it seems pretty clear that you're blood bound to me. You can't do blood caps or human blood bags anymore, and you couldn't drink from the other vampires we tried it with. You have to stay near me so you can feed and continue to heal. That's nonnegotiable. And I can't stay here because . . . I made some promises. If I don't keep them, someone else is going to suffer. Maybe someone else already has been suffering because I've been here instead of where I said I would be. Anyway, I can't stay here any longer."

"So you want to go back to that frat house?"

"I don't *want* to go back!" he explodes. "I *have* to go back! This is one thing I don't have a choice in. I tried to do what I wanted, but my father made it painfully clear that this is out of my control."

"And you want me to come with you?"

The muscle in his jaw pops in and out. "Again, this isn't a question of want. What I want is to not worry about you dying. What I need is to go back to the frat so my father can see that I'm holding up at least part of our bargain."

How can he possibly think this is a solution?

"Okay, so in this hypothetical situation where I go back to therapy and you move back to your fraternity house and I follow you there like the helpless puppy I apparently am, do your vampire friends know that I'm there in the house with you? Or are you sneaking me out on a weekly basis for therapy sessions? And at what point am I allowed to go back to my regular life where I go to classes and have friends of my own?"

He deflates onto my bed. "I don't know," he admits. "I don't know how to answer any of those questions. I just know that I have to go back there, and you need to stay with me."

I stomp to the bed and throw myself down beside him. "Well, you're going to have to come up with some answers because I'm not hiding in your bedroom for the rest of the semester like your secret mistress or something."

MARCUS - PRESENT

I can't take being in this room—specifically in this argument—any longer. I'm trying to help Devon. Hell, I'm trying to save Devon! All I want is to keep him with me so I can make sure he's safe and getting stronger and feeding as he needs to. Doesn't he feel the bond of my blood throbbing through his veins? Doesn't he feel tied irrevocably to me the way I am to him? I need to get away before I have a complete breakdown in front of him.

"I'm going to . . ." I search for any excuse.

"Go feed? So you can stop acting like a caricature of a hangry vampire?" he supplies.

I grunt a response and stomp out of the dorm. I'm pretty fucking proud of myself for not slamming any doors or cussing anyone out on my way.

The bright morning sun mocks my desire to get away and not have anyone follow. I kick the doorway as I go down into the tunnel that will safely take me away from Devon and the stifling dorm room where he won't let me take care of him the way I want to. Maybe it's early enough in the day I won't have to see any vampires down here.

And, actually, Devon wasn't far off the mark when he called me hangry. Taylor brought me a blood bag yesterday, but I haven't had nearly enough to replenish everything Devon drank from me. Feeling defeated, I make my way back to the frat house. With a little bit of luck, Dominic won't notice when I get there, and I can sneak in and feed without any issues.

Right. Because I've been so lucky in that department up until this point.

Sure enough, Dominic is waiting for me as I walk through the living room.

"Oh, wow!" he says with a level of glee that drops my

stomach into a deep, dark pit. "Look who's actually alive and kicking!"

I turn to face him. "Have you just been waiting here for me to come back, or is this a coincidence?"

"Or do I have eyes on you who told me you were headed this way?" He grins.

"Okay." I can't help but roll my eyes. "I'm not sure if that makes it better or worse. Definitely more creepy."

Anger distorts his face, making the psychopath behind his eyes all the more obvious. "Count on this. I am going to make you pay for thinking you could encroach on my territory. I'm going to make you wish I had been allowed to kill you before, in the basement. Right now, maybe you think you can come and go as you please, but you won't always have your daddy's protection, and I swear I will make you pay the moment I see a weakness."

No point telling him that "daddy's protection" has always been the most dangerous thing in my life, so I shrug him off and go up to my room without looking back.

I can't sense any tampering on the blood bags in my room, so I gratefully suck down three in quick succession. Feeding Devon has really taken it out of me. I grab a fourth to drink slower and lie down, stifling a groan.

Devon and Dominic are both right about one thing. The current situation isn't sustainable.

I dial Priscilla's number.

"Devon is blood bound," I say as soon as she answers. "To me. We're blood bound, I mean. I don't know what to do."

"Shit, Marcus! How?"

I sip some more blood and try to gather my thoughts. "I don't know. He got this idea he wanted to stop drinking blood, ended up trying some synthetic shit, which completely fucked up his system. He wouldn't drink regular blood, so I gave him some of mine, and now he can't seem to feed unless it's from me. And we had a fight because I don't know how to help him while also dealing with my—our—father, and I still don't know how to deal with our father, and—"

"Okay. Stop. You're spiraling right now, and that won't help anything. Let's set aside the new developments for a minute. Where do things stand with our father?"

My muscles start to unclench, but only slightly. "No progress. It seems obvious in hindsight that he played me, but knowing that doesn't change the situation. I still made him a promise. He still has his hooks in Sarah. I can't just walk away and ignore the consequences of my own actions."

"But even he isn't above the law," Pris points out. "Maybe the time has come to bring some of his shady shit to light."

I blink up at the ceiling. "It . . . can't possibly be that easy, can it?"

"Easy?" she asks. "There would still be repercussions. You don't get anything for free, little brother."

"Right," I say, mostly thinking out loud to myself. "There would be repercussions like . . . my mother would lose all of her status as the mother of the possible heir to an empire."

"Which she would survive just like my mother did when I was born female."

Well, she's got a point there. Female vampires are barren, so they lack any value for a man like my father, who only cares about his legacy.

"And Sarah would still be on the hook for that medical debt. I can't just leave her to figure that out on her own, can I?"

"I don't know the legalities of her money issues, but I do know it's not legal to coerce a young human into becoming a vampire for monetary gain."

Holy shit, she's right.

"This could really work, couldn't it?" I ask.

"You would almost definitely be giving up all of your own

perks of being close to the man. Have you thought about that?"

What perks? I can't think of any right now. I thought it was a perk to have someone get rid of Vincent for me, but I don't really believe he helped with that, so that perk is null and void. "I don't understand. Am I supposed to be upset at the thought of not being under his thumb and playing his games anymore?"

"Sure. Yeah. That's exactly what you should be feeling. Or, you know, the fact that you won't have access to a huge fortune, and you won't be able to use his name for clout anymore. Money and power might not seem like a big deal right now, while you still have them. They'll be a huge deal when they disappear."

"I haven't been taking anything from him, though," I try to argue, but there's a telling silence from her end of the call. "The only favor I've asked of him is this thing with Vincent, which he didn't even do. And it's not like I have any access to any of his money. I just have the allowance to pay for necess —" Yeah, now I hear it.

"Uh-huh." Pris has the good grace to not say "I told you so" out loud, but the thought definitely comes across. "So, do you really think you're ready to give up the allowance and the possibility of asking for favors? Oh, and there's that room in the frat house. Are they going to let you stay there if you send one of their founding fathers to prison? And is your tuition already paid for? If not, I'd start figuring out what you're going to do about that *before* you get yourself permanently cut off from your funds."

I knock my fist against my forehead in a steady, calming rhythm. "Fuck. Not so easy after all, I guess."

"Nope. You'll need to be sure about it before you take that step."

"I think . . ." I screw my eyes shut and try to push the

imminent panic away. "I think I have to. I don't think it's an option to keep coasting on his money and influence. Not unless I want to turn into him. It's one of those—" I wave my hand in the air, trying to grasp the right word. "—a situation where I can't keep doing the wrong thing now that I've figured out that it's wrong. What's that called?"

"It's called growing a conscience, I think. Congratulations. So what's your next step?"

In the immediate future? I need to keep making sure Devon gets the blood he needs. I need to tell George that I might be bringing a shitstorm to the fraternity's front door. I need to tell Sarah that I can't go through with things. And Pris has a point about making sure I have enough blood and shelter to survive even if I get cut off entirely. And I need to warn my mother. The list of people I need to worry about or warn or protect keeps expanding the longer I think about it.

"I have to go, Pris. Thanks for talking sense to me."

"Anytime, little bro. Go get 'em, tiger," she signs off.

DEVON - PRESENT

I'm starting to regret my decision to go back to classes today. My first class went fine, but now I'm halfway through my second and starting to feel the drag of hunger in my veins. I feel like I'm back to where I was right before my near death a few days ago. Sluggish. Delirious. Nauseous with hunger and barely aware of my surroundings.

And completely confused when I feel someone's shoulder under my armpit, lifting me up out of my seat.

"My notes," I protest.

"Later," they growl, propelling me out of the lecture hall before I know what's happening.

It's Marcus, of course, come to rescue me again. Probably

for the best since I have no idea how I would have gotten up without his help.

"Hungry," I groan, barely holding back tears. How do I keep ending up like this? Helpless and hopeless and supremely pathetic.

"Soon. Hang on," he tells me. He seems to be testing doors as he moves me down a hallway, occasionally apologizing to someone and shutting a door quickly before moving on.

After an infinite hallway of unsatisfactory doors, he hauls me through a doorway and drops me onto a chair.

There. That's more like it. Sitting is just the thing. I'll just sit here for a bit until the room stops spinning, then maybe I'll be able to head back to class and apologize to the professor and pick up my notes and—

"Come on, baby, don't do this to me again."

My wandering attention comes back to the voice in front of me.

"Marcus?" Did I know Marcus was here? When did Marcus get here? Actually, where is here? I'm sitting in a cushioned chair across from a forbiddingly heavy desk that takes up most of the space in this small office. "Where are we?"

"Ask later. Devon, drink for me."

He's holding his bared arm out toward me, but I can't figure out what I'm supposed to do with it. Something tugs at my memory but dissipates as soon as I try to focus on it. I'm so hungry. So tired. Marcus wants me to . . . Wait. When did Marcus get here? And where are we? I was in class, but this isn't a lecture hall.

"Come on, baby!" His voice is a whisper and a whine and a plea all at once.

Then he climbs on top of me, his knees resting on either side of my hips. His hands cup and caress my face, steering my gaze to his.

"Don't do this to me again, okay? You have to drink."

Right. I'm hungry. I have to drink. I nod in acquiescence.

Marcus lets out a shaky sigh, cups the back of my head, and brings my mouth to his neck.

Heaven. With my lips pressed so close to his main artery, it only takes a moment for my body to remember what it needs. I sink my teeth in and pull deeply. My hands—formerly useless lead implements at my sides—grip him close to me. I can't hold him tight enough. I can't touch enough of him.

I work my hands under his shirt as I drink and drink from him. I have just enough thoughts left to hope he can pull away before I kill him like this because there's no possible way I can pull myself away.

Every nerve in my body sparks with the feel of him. The feel of his skin under my fingers. The feel of his blood in my mouth. The feel of his weight on my legs.

"Yes," he croaks out, and the vibration of his voice against my lips shoots straight through me. "Yes, baby. Take what you need from me."

I drag my nails down the skin of his back, thrusting my suddenly hard cock against him where his weight rests on me.

"God, yes," he groans again, making my movements even more frantic. I'm desperate to connect to him in every way possible.

Now that I've fed, my strength returns. Everything sharpens into crystal clarity.

I finally manage to pull my mouth away. "I need you." My eyes bore into him, beg him to say yes.

"You sure?"

"Yes, Marcus. I *need* you."

He nods, looking just as desperate as I feel, and climbs off me.

I don't waste time. I spin him to face away from me and

tear at his fly. It's a matter of seconds before I have him bent over the desk with his pants peeled down around his thighs.

Kneeling down behind him and painfully aware that we don't have much time, I work my tongue into his hole. He cries out when I suck my first finger and then work it inside of him.

"This okay?" I ask.

"Yeah. Hurry."

I wonder if he locked the door behind us when we got here. Not that it will help if the owner of this office has a key and wants to get in.

Spurred on by desperation and my worry about getting caught, I add a second finger and open him as quickly as I can.

"Sorry this is so rushed," I say, pressing my dick against his entrance. We're both as slick as we're going to get with spit as lube.

"It's fine," he insists. "Just do it."

I push into him, just until my head is past the tight ring of his muscle, then give us both a chance to adjust. Just being this far inside of him, I feel like my entire being has been lit on fire.

"Devon, I need you too," he interrupts my thoughts. "Please. I need you to fuck me."

My hips give an involuntary jerk at the words, and we give synchronized moans of pleasure as I go a little deeper.

"Okay. Yeah. Okay. I can do that." Yes, I'm babbling. No, I can't control it. Marcus doesn't seem to care.

I start slowly sliding in until I'm balls-deep in him, buried to the hilt, actual tears pricking at my eyes.

"Fuck, Devon. That's so good."

Maybe it should be the other way. Me comforting him instead of him encouraging me while I fuck him. But he seems to know exactly what he needs. I draw myself slowly out, then glide back in with one smooth motion.

"Yes, baby. Just like that. I need you to fuck me just like that."

With his words, I start rocking rhythmically in and out, taking pleasure from his sounds of pleasure as much as from the feel of his ass, tight around me.

Then I realize, it's been a while for me. With everything that was going on, I haven't had sex—or come at all, now that I think of it—since the last time I fucked Marcus.

"Marcus, I won't last," I gasp out my admission.

"Me neither," he says, then finds my hand and wraps it around his hard, already leaking dick. He keeps his hand wrapped around mine and guides my movements as we stroke up and down his length. Once. Twice. He comes on the third stroke, his voice wrenching out of him as he catches his release in my palm. Feeling the pulse of his come in my hand and his muscles tightening around my cock is all it takes to send me over the edge. I bury my face in his neck and bite down on his shoulder. Not to feed, this time, but to hold him and claim him as mine.

After, with my body slumped over his and my cock starting to soften even though I'm still inside him, he brings my hand to his mouth and licks it clean until there isn't a trace of his come left on me.

"Come on," he whispers. "Let's go home."

I can't remember hearing a better idea in my life.

Chapter Thirty-Five

MARCUS - PRESENT

Devon's roommates—my former roommates—don't even blink when we wobble drunkenly through the living room to his bedroom. He's doing a lot better after feeding. And after everything else. Yes, I can admit it. I think we both needed the sex almost as much as he needed my blood. But neither of us is particularly steady on our feet yet.

I let him down gently onto the bed, make sure the door is properly locked behind us because the roommates might not be surprised by this development, but that doesn't mean it's any of their business, and stretch out on the bed beside him.

"So . . . I guess I should admit that you were right about me not being ready to go back to regular classes?" He gives me a beseeching look from under his eyelashes.

"I suppose . . . if we're admitting things . . . maybe I should admit that my plan of hiding you at the frat house and hoping to not get caught wasn't the . . . best plan ever."

"Oh really," he teases. "It wasn't the best ever? Was it in the running for top ten?"

I jab my thumb into his ribs. "Hush. I'm trying to do the right thing and apologize or something."

His eyes get way too big, entirely too purposefully innocent. "Apologize? But what could you possibly have to apologize for?"

This time, I try a different tactic to stop his teasing. Pulling him to me, I kiss deep into his mouth. I don't think I'll ever get tired of his taste, or the way his lips seem to fit perfectly against mine, or the way it feels like my blood was made to feed him.

When I've kissed him enough that I, at least, have forgotten that I was trying to shut him up, I drop back onto the pillow and stare at him.

"I'm pretty sure that you are the most perfect man in the world," I whisper, not wanting to break this bubble around us by raising my voice to normal speaking levels.

Devon must feel the same because he whispers back, "I'm pretty sure that's impossible. How many times have you had to save my life now because I'm such a mess that I can't even take care of myself? If I were perfect, or even remotely close to it, I would be able to save myself without needing you to do it for me."

"Hey." I sit up and glare at him, all teasing disintegrating between us. "You're not a mess, and you've been doing fine. Or, at least, as well as I would expect for a new vampire. I grew up with all of this. You're still new to dealing with it. Every new vampire slips up sometimes."

"They do?"

My heart breaks at the question, the look of confusion in his eyes.

"Yes, sweetheart. Drinking blood and avoiding sunlight aren't pastimes that come easily to people who were born human. Vampires have to learn how to do these things, then they have to practice them, and they're bound to mess up sometimes. It doesn't make you a mess."

Devon burrows his face into my shoulder. "I sure feel like a mess, though."

"Yeah, well, if it makes you feel any better, the only reason I figured out that I can't keep you like a secret mistress at the frat house is because my half sister talked sense into me. If one of us is a mess, I am absolutely positive it's me."

"Have you considered the possibility that both of us are messes?"

I stroke a hand up and down his back. "I guess I'd better hope that our brands of mess are complementary."

"Spoken like someone who's taken half a freshman chemistry class," he mutters. The tease in his voice is back now, convincing me that we're going to be okay, in spite of everything.

* * *

Time slows. Seconds tick by at the same rate as my almost nonexistent pulse. I only breathe so I can breathe in the scent of Devon all around me. I only blink so I can look at him with fresh eyes again, his unguarded face asleep and resting on the pillow beside mine. This might be heaven, the two of us together, undisturbed, nowhere to be and nothing to do.

Except we both have places to be and things to do. After hours or days or possibly an eternity of drifting between asleep and awake, occasionally shifting positions so the other one can be the little spoon, Devon wakes up hungry. I see the panic in his eyes as soon as I wake up.

"Why is it like this?" He gasps, clutching his belly like something is eating him from the inside. "Why do I feel so . . . starved?"

I don't bother explaining that the blood bound will always

feel a level of desperation to their blood cravings that the rest of us can't imagine. His system came so close to shutting down that now it will panic at the first sign of hunger, convinced it's about to be starved again.

Without words, I roll over onto him and offer him my neck, rewarded almost instantly by his teeth clamping down to open me up for him. I might not be able to feel the same craving for blood that he'll live with forever, but I've already developed a craving for this, for him, that I never would have thought possible.

The blood flowing out of me is only half of the connection, though. Desperate to complete the circuit, I fumble at the fly of his pants. Sure enough, he's hard as a rock when my greedy hands finally reach him. He groans into my neck as I slide my fist down his length.

Yes. This is right. This is what I need. But at the same time, it's not quite enough. There's some essential piece missing.

Devon finds the answer easily enough. He pulls my cock free of my clothing before I've figured out what the problem is and starts pumping both of our erections together in one hand.

It's like an electrical storm sparking through my mind. His hand tugging at our cocks and his mouth tugging at my artery is almost too much to bear.

"Fuck, baby. Fuck. I can't." Words have deserted me. My thoughts only come in fragments now. My mouth keeps babbling nonsense as he keeps working me over. Then, with one deep suck of my blood, I'm spilling my come all over his hand, his stomach, his pants. Devon doesn't complain, just strokes one more time, and then he's coming with me, moaning his release into my neck with each pulse of come and blood between us.

I collapse over him, only vaguely aware of the sticky mess gluing our bodies together. His mouth leaves the wound on my neck and finds my lips, kisses me senseless while he strokes my back.

I try to say, "I need you, Devon," but what comes out is, "I love you, Devon." His hand pauses its stroking for a moment, frozen as he processes what I just said, then continues on the same path of slow ovals from ribs to hip bones and back again. I wonder if I should try and take it back, but then I realize that I don't want to. I want this thing between us to be something other than *need*, something more than that. But he doesn't say anything back, and that's fine. Right? He's under no obligation to respond when I spring something like that on him. God, but I want him to feel it too, though.

Chapter Thirty-Six

DEVON - PRESENT

Did Marcus say he loves me? My mind is whirring. *Nope, not what I need to focus on.*

The man in question is pacing in front of our once again crowded living room couch. "It was one thing when I thought he had actually done something for me, but the more I think about it, the more I think he was just using me all along," he's explaining.

Right. There's real shit I should be paying attention to. Aside from the way his muscles flex under his clothes or the fact that he saved my life or how he tastes so. Fucking. Good. Or the fact that he told me he loves me and I didn't say anything back.

I mean, it was just a generally very intense situation, right? It probably just slipped out because of the circumstances, not because he actually meant to say it.

Jimmy chimes in, breaking my lack of concentration once again. "But if he really did help get Vincent arrested, what happens if you start defying him now?"

Marcus looks at me, even though he's answering Jimmy's question. "No matter what, if I stop doing what he wants, there will be consequences. Most of you should be fine, but . . ."

"But I'm fucked?" I ask with more cheer than I feel.

"I'll need to find a way to protect you," he amends.

"And we can help with that," Taylor adds. "I don't exactly have the family connections, but what am I good for if I can't help guard people from dangerous vampires, right?"

Jeff, ever the cheerleader, elbows him in the ribs. "You're good for more than that, and you know it."

Gabe raises his hand like we're in class.

"Yeah?" Marcus acknowledges him with a nod, and heaven help me if it doesn't make me half-hard to see him taking charge with our friends.

"I think we need to head off the legal aspects of this before we do anything else. What proof do you have of him coercing someone into becoming a vampire? And who do we take that information to?"

Marcus looks less powerful and in control than before. "If someone cares about it, word of mouth is enough for the coercion charges. If someone cares about it, we take it to the Vampiric Enclave and let them deal with the legal aspects of it." He hangs his head in defeat. "We don't really have any assurance that anyone will care about it. It's entirely possible that we let them know and they shrug it off as regular Old Family Vampire stuff. Fuck, most of the Vampiric Enclave has probably taken part in these kinds of games."

"So what happens if you tell them the truth and they ignore it?" I ask.

Marcus looks around the room before answering. "Well, for one thing, I'll be cut off from all the family money and influence. For another, I'll spend the rest of my life looking over my shoulder and waiting for retribution. Like I said, the rest of you will probably be okay, but anyone my father knows I care about . . ." He looks at me again and lets the statement speak for itself.

There it is again. He cares about me. Loves me? I can't just let him hang out to dry. "Okay, so what do we do so the Enclave can't just ignore us? What will it take to make them pay attention?"

Taylor jumps in with a solution. "From what I've seen, the higher-ups in vampire society are all about saving face. What if we convince them we can expose them but then promise not to. Do you think we would be able to control the situation?"

Marcus turns to him with the first look of hope I've seen on his face in a long time. "You really think it might work?"

Taylor shrugs. "You have more experience with them than I do."

"Yeah." He nods and grins. "I think it might actually work. Will you help?"

His grin—his hope—is infectious.

I hate to dampen the energy here, but we need to be practical. "Okay, but what does this actually mean? Who do you talk to? What do we do to make something happen here? We're not just talking hypotheticals, right? We need a game plan."

Marcus's smile loses a little of its shine, but he's still smiling. "I guess my first step is to talk to a lawyer. Someone we can trust to be on our side, obviously, and it has to be someone who understands what's going on behind the scenes. Vampire politics and all that."

Taylor grins. With a flourish, he opens his contacts and holds up a screen with Elijah's information for Marcus to read. "Let's start here," he says.

Chapter Thirty-Seven

MARCUS - PRESENT

"I am begging you. Don't do this."

My mother's face is drawn tight. I feel for her. It's not like I want to hurt her, but I can't turn back now. Sarah took my refusal in stride. She wanted my promise that I'll try to help her, which I was happy to give. The guys at the frat have been surprisingly supportive. Well, the ones George suggested I talk to. If the gods are kind to me, Dominic won't know about what I'm doing until they put him on trial. I have to hope it will work out that way. After everything he put me through—after everything he put all of the guys through, for that matter—he deserves to starve in a cell right beside Vincent.

But my mother is not on board with any of this. Maybe I should have asked Pris to talk to her. So far, nothing I've said has convinced my mother that it's worth it to upset the status quo.

"I have to do this," I retort, trying to pull away without making a scene. "I have to do what's right."

"What's right is respecting your parents and being thankful for the life they've tried to give you. What's right is accepting your place in the world. What's right is obeying your mother when she begs you not to ruin the life she's built." She steps forward and grips my sleeve in a desperate claw. "You are *ruining* my life. How can you cast me aside and destroy me so easily? I gave up my life for you. I gave up my humanity for you. Doesn't that mean anything?"

Her wild-eyed look shoots arrows through my heart. "I'm not trying to . . . cast you away," I whisper. "I know what you gave up so I could exist, but I also know that it was wrong for him to make you do that, and I know he's going to keep on doing it for as long as we let him. I can't let him. If I'm the only one who can stop him, I have to try and stop him. Can't you understand that?"

Her hand drops lifelessly from my sleeve, and her face shuts down like a rat trap. "No. I can't." She turns without a word and walks away. I wonder if I'll ever talk to her again.

* * *

The room was designed—literally centuries ago, before vampires were widely known, when they still secretly pulled the puppet strings of society without the living realizing it—to intimidate any outsiders unfortunate enough to enter. And at this moment, I am as outside as it is possible to be. Despite being born a vampire, despite being fathered by one of the most powerful vampires still walking, despite having a well-dressed vampire lawyer at my side, I've never felt less ready to face something. This is my first time stepping in front of the Enclave, and odds are it will be my last. My father is definitely going to do anything in his power to keep me from walking out at all.

"I bring a new item of business to the Enclave's attention,"

Elijah calls out in a clear, ringing voice. It carries around the room and echoes back into my skull like a hammer.

I want to go home. I want to turn around right now and forget about all of this. They never even have to know I was here. That cowardly voice rattles around and around inside my skull, so it's ringing from outside and in. But there's no turning back, no matter how desperately part of me wants to. The scene has a sense of inevitability to me. It was always too late to stop this. Even months—no, longer—even years ago.

"Aren't you a little young to come in here expecting to speak?" one of the hooded figures arranged in a circle around us calls out, mockery rippling through his voice.

"If I waited until you deemed me old enough, this item of business would balloon out of your control. I'm bringing it to your attention now so you can respond proactively."

"How magnanimous of you," a different hooded figure says with a chuckle.

My shoulders loosen the tiniest bit from hearing two voices that aren't my father's.

"And your purpose in bringing this child before us?" That's him.

My shoulders, along with my stomach and my throat, knot right back up. My father is here, watching me from beneath a hood and commenting on me to his peers.

And I might as well be nailed to the floor or cryogenically frozen in a metal tube. My body won't move while my mind races too fast to catch a single thought.

He's here. He's watching me. He's going to do everything he can to stop me, and if he can't stop me, he's going to kill me. I know it with the same certainty I know the sun will rise. I'm going to die here.

"The business at hand relates to this child," Elijah's voice rings out, even clearer than before. How has he avoided being turned into a speechless, frozen mess like me? How is he still talking or thinking? "Honorable Members of the Enclave," he addresses the ring of hoods around us, "you are all familiar with the child, Marcus Levine?"

Murmurs of assent pass around the room. My father's voice is noticeably absent again.

"And you are all aware that Marcus is considered still below the vampiric age of consent, a child, as you put it?"

My skin prickles with the venom my father is directing at me. I don't have to see his eyes to feel his glare piercing me.

A different speaker from before chimes in. "Are we to understand that his age bears relevance in the matter you wish to discuss?"

Elijah smiles smoothly, cool compared to my frozen. "Indeed, Your Honor, it does. Marcus recently made me aware that he is being coerced into making a vampire against his will." Angry mutters erupt around the room, but Elijah doesn't pause. "Moreover, after looking into the circumstances, it appears that the human in question is also below the age of consent and has agreed to become a vampire only because of a promise to alleviate her family's financial straits. Now, I am sure that, just like me, you can hardly credit a story such as this." That statement almost unfreezes a laugh out of me. Stories like this happen every day in this world. "But I researched carefully, and I fear you will be quite shocked at what I discovered."

Even knowing exactly what he's about to say, a zing of apprehension shoots through me. He walked me through the whole thing ahead of time. Several times. He said he needs me to be prepared if I'm going to play my part correctly. *Please, please, God, don't let me fuck this up.*

Everyone in this room knows what he discovered. What they're all wondering right now is which of them have gotten caught and which will get away with it.

"After a thorough investigation—and I mean I dug deep

through the records, left no stone unturned, because I wouldn't want anyone to be accused of something so serious without a preponderance of evidence—I discovered that not only is Marcus telling the truth, but this is far from an isolated incident."

"We all know that certain practices . . . were common . . . at one point," a faceless voice speaks up.

"Yes," someone else joins in. "We all know that . . . at certain points in history . . . vampires might overstep . . . all in the interest of the greater good, of course."

Elijah nods like he's taking these points into consideration. "Indeed. My generation has all heard the stories about the days when vampires made these difficult decisions from behind the scenes, from their plantation drawing rooms or masonic lodges or gentlemen's clubs. And I, like most in my generation, believed that these practices were left behind when vampire society was pulled into the light and revealed to the living." He blinks, his mask of disbelieving innocence firmly in place. "Unfortunately, my investigation uncovered multiple instances of similar situations, as recently as this year."

The mutters rise in waves around the room.

" . . . upholding traditions . . ."

" . . . a few bad apples . . ."

" . . . not my decision . . ."

Elijah lets them work themselves up, then signals that he has more to say by drawing himself up and clasping his hands in front of himself. "Once I realized the extent of this cancer in our society, I shared this information with several news networks and the Species Relations Oversight Bureau. I wanted to get a jump on the situation."

Insurance, he had called it when he explained the plan.

"Yes, Elijah, you're very clever. Congratulations." This comes from the hood in the tallest chair. "You have to realize that blackmailing the entire Enclave is no way to get what you want."

"You are correct." Elijah spreads his hands. "That's why I only shared certain information. Some of you have been relatively harmless in your activities. Others of you, I've concluded are entirely irredeemable. I'm sorry, but the world will be a better place with some of you removed from this game board. I leave it to you, Honorable Members of the Enclave, to sort it out from here. If you can save your place in society, I will take that as a sign, and I will not pursue this any further. Best of luck to you."

With that, he gives a small bow of his head and guides me out of the room by the elbow.

Chapter Thirty-Eight

MARCUS - PRESENT

Everyone in the dorm is already celebrating when Elijah guides me back through the door. And, when I say guide, I really mean he half drags, half manhandles me over the threshold and dumps me on the couch with a grunt.

"Oh shit." Jimmy sobers temporarily, looking at me with his forehead bunched. "Did it go bad?"

Elijah hurries to reassure everyone. "It went perfectly. Marcus is just . . . a little overwhelmed, I think."

I take an age to turn my head and blink at him. I'm not entirely sure how I got here. Did I ride in a car? A bus? For all I remember, we sprouted wings and flew here.

"Did . . ." I abort the question when I realize I have no idea what I'm trying to ask. I look around the living room to discover a full-blown party filling the space. Jeff and Jimmy both have cans of beer in their hands and are grinning expectantly. Devon is leaning toward me, looking quietly hopeful. Gloria and Bee seem to be clasping hands and simultaneously crossing as many fingers as they can, like they're hoping for a winning lottery ticket or something. Does that have something to do with me? The room tilts under the weight of my realization that all of these people are waiting on good news from me. Which I can't deliver.

"It's too early to tell," I croak out, and the room tilts the other way and then tilts back, and then there are black waves lapping at the edges of my vision, and then I hit the floor.

DEVON - PRESENT

Marcus's fainting spell cools the party atmosphere a little bit, but no one is willing to actually leave for fear of missing the full recap.

I sit on the couch with Marcus's head resting on my legs and revel in the fact that he's letting me slide my hands through his hair while everyone we know here at Berring looks on. He must really still be overwhelmed from whatever happened with the Enclave.

Once Marcus is settled in and doesn't seem likely to black out a second time, we all turn to Elijah.

"Well?" Taylor asks first. "What actually happened?"

Elijah gives that slick lawyer smile of his. "Exactly what I said would happen. They're going to be preoccupied with sorting through whose names have been sent to the press and who they need to cut ties with or throw under the bus to save themselves. It will be some time before they figure out that it was only Levine and our strategic five that we outed. I know I won't lose any sleep if any others accidentally out themselves, though, and I hope all of you feel the same. As for all of Marcus's other concerns . . . well, he is right to still be on guard. He could get caught in the crossfire, or someone could come after him in retaliation for upsetting the cart. His father is powerful enough to make his life hell unless and until he's imprisoned and safely in stasis."

"And what about that girl? Sarah?" This comes from a worried-looking Bee.

Elijah jerks a guilty shrug. "I'm afraid that her situation isn't what the Enclave cares about. Depending on how things shake out, Marcus might be able to help her, or the Enclave might pay her some damages—hush money, really—but it's unlikely to match the amount she was hoping for. I accepted a long time ago that you can't save everyone."

I look down at Marcus and see his eyes are still staring glassily at nothing.

"Hey," I whisper. "Are you feeling any better?"

He blinks at me a few times before his vision seems to clear. "I'm still alive," he whispers back, quiet enough that I'm sure no one else can hear. "I really thought he would kill me instead of letting me walk away, but I'm still alive."

My fingers tangle in his hair, and my voice knots in my throat.

"Yeah. We're both still alive," I confirm in a strangled voice. By a series of absolute miracles, we're both still alive.

And hungry, I suddenly realize. But there's no fucking way I'm asking him to let me feed on him after the day he's had and while all of our friends are watching. One, it would be pathetic. Two, it would be humiliating. Three, I feel dirty using him that way.

Marcus must see something in my eyes because he sits up with a jerk. "Shit. When did you last feed?"

"I'm fine," I try to soothe him, but his scowl deepens.

"Sorry, but I don't really trust when it's you saying that."

"Hey!" I squawk defensively.

And loud enough to get the attention of everyone in the room. Heads that had turned away to side conversations swivel back to us and lock in on our drama.

Marcus glares around the room in a way that would be adorable if it were someone other than me who had raised his ire. "Well?" He growls—actually growls—at everyone. "Don't you have something else to focus on?" Then, he grabs me by the hand and drags me to his bedroom.

The rest of the room apparently doesn't have anything else to focus on. We're followed by a chorus of voices ranging from encouraging whoops and catcalls to Gabe's scandalized "Are you guys fucking serious right now? With all of us right here?"

* * *

MARCUS - PRESENT

I would rather not have an audience for Devon's and my private business, but I can already see the telltale black veins pulsing wherever his skin is thinnest. At least there's a door that I can close and lock between us and our raucous friends.

Devon is already fading because of his hunger and doesn't argue at all when I lead him to my bed and sit him down on the edge.

"Stay with me just a little longer, okay, Devon?" I try to capture his gaze, though his attention keeps wandering. Fuck. I keep forgetting how ill he still is. Just a few hours without feeding, and it feels like he's right back at the crisis point where I could lose him so easily.

Thankful that I already restocked the fridge in this room, I grab a handful of blood bags and toss them on the bed beside Devon.

Devon shies away from them like they might be poison.

"Marcus, I don't think I can—" he murmurs to me.

"I know," I soothe him. "Don't worry. I won't make you try the blood bags."

His brow furrows in confusion. "Then what?"

I straddle him and quiet his question with a kiss. "Those are for me," I explain. "I need to feed before you can drink from me. Just hang on." I press another quick kiss to his lips, then tear into the first blood bag and drink it dry as fast as I can.

Devon's eyes follow the movement of my throat with each swallow. Good. I need him to focus.

I already feel rejuvenated after the first blood bag, my fingers steadier. I barely tremble as I unbutton my shirt, even though Devon's predatory gaze locks in on my every movement.

Yes. This is exactly what I need from him.

"Are you still with me, Devon?"

He nods, eyes still locked on my throat, and swallows noisily. "So . . . hungry . . ." he whispers like he's in a trance.

"And what are you going to do about that?"

"Don't want to hurt you," he whispers.

That's what I was afraid of. I stroke my fingers through his hair, needing to feel him and needing even more for him to know I'm right here for him.

"Sweetheart, you won't hurt me. I want you to do this." And because I know reason isn't leading him right now, I tear into the next blood bag and start drinking.

Come on. Take the bait.

I grind my crotch down on top of him and lean in close as I drink.

Finally, he can't stop himself anymore. Fangs sink deep into my neck where the fresh influx of blood has just started pumping, and the blood that I just took in starts to leave my body almost as fast.

Devon latches on in earnest and sucks deep from my vein with a needy groan. His hands come to life and grab me by the hips, pulling me down against himself so he can press his hardening cock against my ass.

I frantically grope for the next blood bag as soon as the current one is empty. If I'm going to keep up with his hunger, I'm going to need to keep my fridge stocked a lot fuller than usual.

Devon lets me go while I'm still finishing off my blood bag and buries his face in my neck.

"I'm so sorry. I just lost control," he gasps.

I pull away enough to look him in the eye. "Don't apologize. You did what I wanted—no, what I needed—you to do. I never want you to feel guilty about doing what you have to to survive."

"But—" His eyes cut away. "I feel so dirty, using you like that."

With my hands on either side of his face, I turn him back to look at me. "I don't feel dirty." I press a gentle kiss to his lips and feel a strange thrill at tasing my own blood on his lips. "This doesn't feel dirty, does it?" I kiss him again. "I don't feel like you're using me," I assure him between kisses. "I like being able to help you." My next kiss lands just below his earlobe and brings a sexy shudder up his spine. "I like knowing that I can save you." I tongue the same spot and am pleased by a second shudder in response. "So, with that in mind, do you still feel dirty?"

"N-no," Devon stutters when I nip at his jaw.

"Tell me how you feel."

"I feel . . ."

Maybe I'm doing too well with my tongue if I can make him lose his train of thought like this. "Tell me."

"I feel like I need you. I feel like I need to be inside of you again."

That makes me raise an eyebrow. "Use your words. What exactly do you need?"

It's my cock's turn to make itself known. The way it's pressing into my fly is painful. Hopefully, we're about to do something about it, though.

Chapter Thirty-Nine

DEVON - PRESENT

Feeding from Marcus is different from drinking from blood bags. Ever since I became a vampire, the blood has been the worst thing to deal with. It turns my stomach and makes me feel dirty to drink it. But Marcus's blood . . . it's beyond anything else I've ever tasted. The taste brings me back to life. Drinking from him satiates me in a way no blood bag ever has.

That doesn't stop the guilt from kicking in as soon as I'm done drinking. Even knowing that I need him to survive, the sense of shame at my loss of control is overwhelming.

But Marcus has an excellent way of distracting me. Somewhere between him kissing my lips and licking my neck, all thoughts of shame and guilt get shoved aside in favor of something else. I'm barely aware of it when my hands find his hips and pull him down to me. I need more. I need friction. I need his skin against mine. I need to be inside of him.

With a desperate groan, I lift him and lay him on his back, immediately getting to work to get his clothes off.

"Yes. Fuck, Devon, I need you."

Wait. *He* needs *me*? Really? I stare at him in confusion for a moment. Is it even possible that I really have something to offer him? I mean, I need him, obviously. I've now lost count of how many times he's literally saved my life. But now he's saying that he needs me?

With a feral growl, I redouble my efforts to get his clothes off. It's possible I hear something tear. It's possible a few buttons go flying and ping against the far walls. All I care about is getting him bare so I can give him what he needs.

The phrase rings in my ears. *I need you I need you I need you*, chanting on repeat as I kiss the inside of his thigh, nibble the crease at the top of his legs, nuzzle the soft hair above his dick, then lick from the base to the tip of his shaft in one wide stripe.

"Fuuuuck," he groans, and someone from outside the door gives an encouraging catcall.

Not that I need any encouragement. Someone could break down the door with a camera crew in tow and say they were sending this video to my parents, and I don't think I could stop what I'm doing. It feels absolutely vital—life or death, maybe even more so than when I was drinking from him— that I feast on Marcus in every way possible.

I have to get closer to him, be inside of him. I press his legs up and apart so I can access his hole. This doesn't seem like the time to go slow and gentle, so I slide my tongue once around the rim before delving deeper. Marcus's curses are replaced by inarticulate groans, increasing in volume as I lick deeper inside of him.

"Need . . . you . . . now," he finally gasps out when I'm already on the verge of coming in my pants.

Lightning fast, I free my aching cock from my pants and press it to his entrance.

"Is this okay?" I ask. It might kill me to pull away if he tells me to, but at least I still have enough working brain cells to get his consent.

"Yes, baby. Please. I need you to fuck me."

No sooner are the words out of his mouth than I'm sliding inside.

The tightness of his muscle closing around me, the slickness of his hole from me eating him, is almost too much. Now it's my turn to lose my capacity for speech.

Once I'm all the way inside of him, Marcus takes my face in his hands and looks me in the eye, just like he did before.

"No guilt, right?" he whispers, and I shake my head. "No feeling dirty?" I shake my head again. If I could speak right now, I'd tell him that dirty and guilty are the last things I feel when I'm inside of him.

That's when it hits me. Having my teeth inside of him is exactly the same as having my cock inside of him, as long as he consents to it. They both feel equally necessary to me, and they should feel equally right too.

"Feels too good," I try to tell him, but fuck, thinking in words his hard right now. "Not dirty. Good."

He seems to catch my meaning and drags my face down for a kiss.

Just like when I feed from him, instinct takes over, and I start rocking my hips forward in rhythm with some unheard but well-known song. He responds with a gasp, wrapping his legs tight around my waist and joining my movements with his own hips.

"Fuck. Marcus. I can't last," I warn him.

He nods his understanding and takes my hand to wrap around his erection. "Like this," he tells me, moving my hand up and down his shaft at the speed he wants, and fuck if that isn't one of the hottest things I've ever experienced.

Is it three seconds or an eternity that I hang on, holding back my impending orgasm by the skin of my teeth? Either way, it slams through me with a bellow as soon as he spurts his release into the space between us. I rock into him one last time, loving the feeling of slick when his hole is full from me coming inside of him, then let myself collapse on top of him, not caring about the mess gluing our bodies together.

Chapter Forty

MARCUS - PRESENT

"I come bearing gifts!" Pris crows at me the moment I open the door.

I respond with intelligence and grace by staring at her with my mouth slack.

Pris rolls her eyes and pushes past me. "Oh, come on! It's not that weird that I'm here!"

I scratch the back of my head and try to figure out the best way to answer. "I mean . . ."

"Oh, shut up." She punches me for emphasis. "Are you going to take my gifts or not?"

I straighten up with renewed interest. "Wait, there are actual gifts?" Most of the gifts I've received in my life were bought by some high-paid assistant and chosen for the express purpose of reminding me who I was expected to be.

Pris shrugs nonchalantly. "Okay, maybe not gifts as other people would see them, but I think you'll appreciate them."

"Oh?" I cock an eyebrow at her. She knows me better than most people, so she probably knows what I'll appreciate.

She digs two handfuls of stuff from her giant purse and holds them up with a proud grin. "Ta-da!"

I look back and forth between several blood bags in one hand and what appears to be a bunch of pamphlets in the other.

"Um, Pris?"

Her smile doesn't falter at my lack of faith in her. "No matter how things shake out with our father, you're probably going to need some help making sure you don't run out of blood," she explains, pressing the blood bags into my hands. "I wanted to make sure you're eating enough, so I brought these just in case." She fans out the pamphlets and waves them at me like some cheap magician at a carnival. "These are just in case the fallout lasts longer than expected with the Enclave."

I take the fanned pamphlets in confusion.

Blood Banks in Your Area, one reads. Another has *Where to Feed* across the front in red.

"What is this?"

Pris makes herself at home, grabbing a beer from the little fridge by the TV and plopping down on the couch with a sigh. "It's times like this that I miss college," she says with a grin and sips the beer she just stole from me.

I wave the pamphlets in her direction. "Come on, Pris. What's this actually about?"

"I'm trying to help you out." She rolls her eyes expressively, so very put upon by my lack of intelligence. "Look, it seems likely you won't be able to afford blood for a while here, but the last thing the government wants is a bunch of starving vampires turning to live humans to feed because they can't buy blood, so there are some government assistance programs available in case you need them."

I look more closely at the pamphlets. Sure enough, they each list places to go for blood, emphasizing that "bagged is better."

"What does 'bagged is better' mean?" I ask.

"You've never heard that?" Pris looks surprised. "They came up with that slogan a few months after the invention of the plastic blood bag. The higher-ups try to play it as bagged blood has been specially sterilized or whatever, but what it comes down to is it's a lot safer for the donors to have their blood taken in a sterile environment where output is carefully monitored, compared to the bad old days when vampires kept blood slaves around to feed on twenty-four-seven."

I shake my head to clear it. "I never thought much about where my blood was coming from," I admit.

"And now you know," she replies breezily.

Jeff comes in then, focused on his phone. "Hey, I think we may be starting to see . . ." He trails off when he realizes there's someone else in the room.

Pris's eyes light up. "Is this him?"

I can't help but roll my eyes. "Now I get why you're actually here. Not to bring me blood or pamphlets or even to catch up. You were hoping to meet Devon and, knowing you, torture him."

"Well?" She gives a significant tilt of her head toward Jeff.

"Jeff, this is my half sister, Priscilla. Pris, this is my roommate Jeff."

Jeff looks confused. I can practically see his thought process and say a silent prayer that he reaches the logical conclusion without opening his mouth.

No such luck. "So, if you're half siblings, does that mean you're also dealing with Magnus Levine fallout?"

I put my face in my hands and groan. "You can't ask people shit like that, man. What's wrong with you?"

He blinks back and forth between Pris and me. "I don't get it. What did I say?"

Pris stands up and ruffles his hair like he's a cute, dumb dog. "Don't worry about it. Marcus just gets overly sensitive about these things. And you should probably be aware that in the vampire community, it's considered rude to ask personal questions, especially about family and someone's background as a vampire. If someone has a blood lineage they want you to know about, you can trust they'll find a way to bring it up. If they don't bring it up first, assume it's not something they want to talk about."

"Oh." Jeff has the decency to blush and shut his damn mouth.

"But since you obviously didn't know better, I'll let you off the hook. Yes, Magnus is also my father. He turned my mother about fifty years ago as part of his ongoing quest to produce an heir to his empire, but sadly for him, he produced me. It took thirty more years before he got the son he wanted." She punches me playfully on the arm, and I glower at her. I've never before wanted to harm her, but this situation is bringing up some new feelings.

Meanwhile, Jeff is back to looking curious. "Why did he want a son so bad? Girls can't . . . inherit . . . or . . ."

"Female vampires are barren," she explains, completely matter-of-fact, like I'm not dying of embarrassment beside her. "I could never pass on the bloodline and am therefore entirely useless in the eyes of my father. But before you feel too sorry for me, remember the great things that Marcus here has gained by being the presumptive heir." She turns to me with a grin and starts ticking points off on her fingers. "Growing up under constant supervision but without any love whatsoever. Being sent to boarding school and being told that failure may lead to being disowned or possibly dismembered. Having any potential relationship prospects either chased away or bought off before the second date. I think I'm okay with my lot in life."

Jeff looks at me aghast. "That's really what growing up was like for you?"

I rub my hand through my hair and wish I were anywhere other than having this conversation right now.

"You know what?" Jeff continues. "Actually, that makes a lot of sense. Like, for real, that explains a lot about"—he waves his hands in the space in front of me—"your whole vibe."

"Awesome," I growl, trying to convey that the word is a threat, not a compliment. "Anyway, you were saying something when you came in. There's some sort of news?"

"Oh, yeah! Shit, I can't believe I almost forgot." He pulls his laptop out of his backpack and opens up several news sites.

Pris and I lean over his shoulders and start reading headlines.

"Oh, shit," Pris and I say in unison as the first headline comes up.

Prominent Businessman Imprisoned on Multiple Felony Charges

Our father's face takes up half the page. Of course, they used one of his professional photos, not a regular mug shot, but he still practically burns a hole through my skin with the force of his glare.

Business magnate and well-known political figure Magnus Levine was arrested yesterday by a special forces unit of vampires. He was taken from his own home in the early hours of the morning of the twenty-third. A spokesperson from the Levine family stated earlier today that Magnus had been taken into custody to be tried in a vampiric court. They declined further comment. Charges have not been made public, but an anonymous source listed the following charges . . .

I stumble back from Jeff and the couch and the headline.

"Is this really happening?" I hear myself ask, but the rest of the world is too distant to hear anyone's answer.

Chapter Forty-One

DEVON - PRESENT

"Marcus? Marcus, are you with me?"

Yes, my voice is panicked and shrill. No, I can't control it.

"Marcus, baby, come on! Wake up for me?"

This man is the only way I've been able to feed for a week now. More importantly, he's the man who implied that maybe he loves me, and I'm not letting that go.

"Oh, hey." He blinks up at me like I haven't been trying to shake him awake for half an hour now. "Did you hear about my father? Apparently, he's been arrested."

My whole body slumps in relief. "Yeah, love. I heard. How are you feeling about it?"

Marcus rocks his head side to side. Maybe confused. I don't know.

"I'm feeling . . . like I don't know how I'm supposed to feel. Do you know? How I'm supposed to feel?"

I trace his eyebrows, his cheekbones, his lips with my

fingers. "My therapist told me that I'm allowed to feel whatever I feel. I think that's pretty good advice right now."

I bite down on my lower lip, praying that's the right thing to say to him.

"What if I don't know what to feel?" Marcus finally asks.

"That's okay too," I promise him. "Whatever you feel, I'm here for you, alright?"

He blinks at me with a clarity I haven't seen since before the news came through. "Yeah. I think I'm alright. As long as you're here with me, I'm alright."

To say my heart soars is a huge understatement. My heart takes flight and sings with a full chorus of heavenly beings.

"Yes. I'm here with you. I'm not going anywhere."

Marcus nods and closes his eyes in relief. I think he's about to go to sleep—or possibly pass the fuck out again and scare the shit out of me—but instead, he tugs me toward him and gathers me in his arms, holding me close against his chest, completely ignorant of the roomful of people watching us.

His half sister, who I've only just met, gives a long whistle. "Well," she says, "I wasn't sure what to make of it when he said he'd found someone, but I guess he really did find someone."

I snuggle in closer to Marcus's chest. Maybe I'm not used to having an audience like this, but it sure as fuck isn't going to stop me from getting as close as I can to the man holding me. The man who's saved me time and time again. The man I am fucking head over heels in love with.

* * *

We spend the next two days watching the headlines roll in. Magnus Levine arrested and magically disappeared into the secrecy of the vampiric courts. Elijah says that even he can't find out further information on what's being done with him. And several other prominent vampires have been publicly arrested and stripped of their power and assets. Apparently, this thing of coercing young human women into having vampire babies has been a widespread practice in these ancient vampire families for centuries. It wasn't explicitly outlawed until a few decades ago.

It's crazy to me. For someone like Marcus's father—who was around when it was legal to own slaves, a man who kept his own blood slaves—to finally have to face consequences after all this time? And all it took was Marcus putting himself on the line. To say that I'm proud of what he's done would be an understatement.

Over the course of these two days, there's pretty much been a nonstop party in our dorm. It's gone through phases, sure. No one can party for two days straight without slowing down at some point. But there hasn't been a lot of privacy or quiet time to process things. I want nothing more than to kick everyone out and sit Marcus down for a real talk. A "what do we actually mean to each other?" talk. A "where do you see this heading?" talk. But those aren't the types of questions you can ask when there are between ten and thirty people all shoved into one dorm and slamming beers to celebrate your boyfriend's father's arrest.

I'm not sure what the right situation for these kinds of discussions is, but it's definitely not mid-dorm rager.

"Holy shit! I think we've got another one!" Gabe shouts over the crowd and holds up his hand to grab everyone's attention. "It says here, twenty-seven women have come forward about receiving bribes or kickbacks in exchange for agreeing to give birth to vampiric children when they were below the age of consent." He looks around the room with a mix of outrage and disgust. "Twenty-seven women. And some of them have named vampires who hadn't previously been named. I bet there's a few folks scrambling right now trying to cover their tracks."

Even after two days, none of us have figured out the correct response when something new comes to light. On the one hand, it means more predators are getting what they deserve. It means Marcus, and others like him, can breathe a little easier. It means maybe he doesn't have to watch his back so carefully, and maybe he's one step closer to having access to some of his own money again since every one of Magnus's accounts is currently frozen solid. But news like this also confirms twenty-seven people who essentially lost their lives playing Magnus's game. Twenty-seven more women who lost everything because the vampires in charge had the power to take everything from them. The system has been rotting from the inside for two hundred years now, and these latest twenty-seven people are just one small part of the symptom.

Marcus squeezes my hand in his. "Hey, let's try to keep looking at the positives, okay?"

I nod and squeeze his hand back. Positives. Like, the fact that I'm here with him, and he was able to get out of perpetuating this rotten system.

George chooses that moment to come in, searching with wild eyes until he picks Marcus out of the crowd.

"You need to get back to the house right away," he says.

I squeeze Marcus's hand again. "Still finding positives, right?" I whisper before letting him go to face whatever this new complication is.

Chapter Forty-Two

MARCUS - PRESENT

My anxiety spikes at seeing George in my dorm again. I close my eyes and take a moment to remind myself that my father can't reach me. Whatever else is going on, I'm going to be okay.

"You need to get back to the house right now," he shouts into my ear over the party happening all around me.

"I can't be the guy who deals with Dominic anymore," I argue with him. "I found my way out, okay? I can't go back."

George grabs my arm. "That's just it! We don't have to face Dominic anymore! But I sure as hell am not going to try and take his place, so I need you to come with me."

I rub my ear, certain I misheard something. "What did you just say?"

"Dominic got taken in." He rolls his eyes to show how dense I'm being. "The brotherhood needs someone to take over leadership, or it's just going to be fucking Lord of the Flies until they all destroy themselves. Come on!"

"What are you talking about? Who's taking over leadership."

He raises his eyebrows at Devon, a plea to get at least one of us to understand. "You. You absolute idiot. You're the only one who hasn't been touched by the shit. And the guys respect you for how you handled the basement."

"But," I sputter, "no one actually wants me leading them. Why don't you do it?"

George steps back and gestures at himself like he's revealing something obvious. "I'm not their leader. I've been the guy who stands in the corner and does his best to avoid getting involved for two years. You're the guy who actually stood up to Dominic, and most of the guys realize that you're the reason we're free from him now. Come on, Marcus!"

I turn to Devon, helpless and hoping for support.

He stands tall and looks George in the eye. "And what if I come with him?"

Not what I was expecting. Not at all how I was expecting Devon to respond.

George looks him earnestly in the eye. "Look. I won't lie and claim that no one will have an issue. Some guys will have a problem with you being male. Some guys will have a problem with you being made instead of born a vampire. Some guys will have a problem with you not coming from a recognized bloodline. But everything is turned upside down right now. I think they'll get over it in favor of having some stability. Even Dominic's biggest supporters realize they need some kind of stabilizing influence right now." He turns back to me. "Look, I get that it's a big choice for you, but the rest of us are desperate for someone to take over *now*. If you think about it too long, you lose the opportunity."

He's damn right it's a big choice. A choice I never really expected—or wanted—to have. I turn back to Devon and try to read his mind. I'm not willing to sacrifice him to help George.

Devon surprises me by sliding his hand into mine. "It sounds like they need you like I need you. Are you really going to turn your back on that?"

"You think I should do this?" I search his eyes, but instead of finding answers, I find trust. My heart gives an extra, unnecessary *thub-dub* at the sight of that trust. As fucked-up as my family is, as fucked-up as my childhood was, he still has trust in me. "Are you sure?"

Devon nods, gives my fingers a squeeze. "I think you have to do this."

* * *

The house is in quiet chaos when we get there. Vampiric faces look even paler than usual, with uniform dark circles under everyone's eyes. Everyone is gathered in a huge meeting room, crowded to the edges because no one seems to want their back to anyone else. Glances shift nervously from side to side, trying to suss out enemies and allies, constantly searching for the next threat.

Our arrival is met with long moments of intensifying silence. No one wants the full attention of the group. No one wants to be put forward as a potential decision maker, knowing all too well that the decision maker is also going to be the problem solver and the first to be sacrificed if it all goes to shit again.

"You have got to be joking," a guy that I remember as one of Dominic's lackeys finally breaks the silence. "Who the fuck is that guy?" He points at Devon, whose fingers are still intertwined with mine.

George steps to the center of the room, already making

calming gestures. "Look, I know we're all a little shaken right—"

"You're fucking right we're shaken," the other guy steps forward. Steven? Stellan? Strider? I feel confident his name starts with *S* but can't remember beyond that. "We've lost two leaders within the brotherhood in a short period, and now you're coming in with this stranger? Not even a born vampire! You have to be fucking playing some sort of a prank here. There is no way you're serious with this shit."

George grits his teeth to respond, but I know it's my turn.

"The reason I'm here is because you fucked everything up while you were in charge."

All of the chaos that was tamped down just under the surface of all those silent, assessing looks boils over across the room. Suddenly, vampires who were sitting in silence are striding to the center of the room and shouting over the rising noise. Guys that I thought were friendly with each other are in each other's faces now. We're a few angry words away from the first punch being thrown.

Okay, maybe my approach wasn't the best idea in the world. Part of me wants to slip out the way I came in and let them tear each other apart.

But there's George, standing in the center of the room and waving his arms, trying to restore order and shooting me death glares whenever there's a gap in the crowd. Shit. I hate that I just let him down like this.

Shattering glass whips everyone's attention to one side of the room, where Devon is standing on a table and holding a vase above his head, ready to break in case the first one isn't enough.

"I know I don't have the money or the bloodlines or whatever to command your respect, but just listen for a minute," he shouts over the mass of vampires. "At this point, after everything that's happened, you can either adapt or die. You all know it's not possible for you to go back to how things were here. The only way your fraternity has a chance of surviving is if you show that you can change and get away from all the mess that people like Vincent and Dominic made. Marcus has enough distance from the mess that he might be able to help show the world you guys are cleaning it up, and he has the credentials that everyone here could theoretically follow his leadership."

My heart swells a little more with each word. I'm so proud of his bravery, standing up and talking to these people who hate him, and his clearheadedness, actually speaking reason when I was ready to start a fight.

I stand next to Devon's table and look up at him with all of the love I can show on my face. "Devon is right. I'm sorry for the way I came in here ready to argue instead of listen. He's saying what I should have said before. Look, this whole organization my father started . . . well, it was kind of fucked from the beginning." I hold up my hands and quickly shout, "Hear me out!" Before the brawl can resume. "My father is a fucked-up man who has never done anything that didn't serve him in some way, and this fraternity has some of that baked in. But that doesn't mean there's no use for an organization for vampires on campus, and it doesn't mean that this fraternity is irredeemable. Devon is right, though, that we need to show the world we're willing to clean up our mess. No more allowing psychopaths to lead based on the importance of their bloodline. No more turning a blind eye to rapists just because they come from a wealthy family. And if we're not willing to clean it up, we honestly might as well burn it down because it's just going to get worse if we do nothing."

Devon's hand, still holding the vase, sags until it's hanging by his side. The look on his face has my knees shaking. He's looking at me like I'm the only guy in the room, like I just finished a lifesaving surgery, like maybe he loves me in at least part of the way that I love him.

"Who thinks they can follow Marcus?" George asks into the silence following my speech. Tension leeches out of the bodies around me. Shoulders slump, and fists unclench. There's no rousing cheer, but there are grunts and mutters of assent all around the room. Even the first man who spoke—Strickland? Sunny?—cracks his neck and then gives a jerky nod. "Okay, then let's get some rest and come up with a real plan tomorrow."

No one even questions it when I help Devon down from the table and lead him up to my room.

Chapter Forty-Three

DEVON - PRESENT

I wake up to kisses and the weight of Marcus's body stretched out over me.

"Good morning, lover," he whispers into my neck as his lips trail down, down, and down some more. He pauses long enough to hike my shirt up so he can nip at my lower abdomen, making me shiver.

"I could get used to waking up like this," I admit, lifting my hips so he can drag my boxer briefs down and free my quickly hardening cock.

"Oh yeah?" He kisses the side of my shaft so light I can barely feel it. "You might be able to allow this?" He punctuates each word with a feathering kiss.

I groan, my hips twitching uncontrollably. "Marcus, you're killing me."

"But I thought you said you could get used to this," He kisses up the other side, from root to tip, never giving the pressure I need.

"I said—" I have to pause and collect my thoughts when

he flicks at the tip of my dick with the tip of his tongue. "I could get used to *waking up* like this. But now I'm—" All of my words are lost as he swallows my entire shaft with no warning. Every thought I've ever had is lost to the slick suction of his mouth.

"Now you're what?" he asks with a grin after releasing me with a pop.

Done playing games, I drag him up and roll over on top of him. "Now I'm going to fuck you so you can't think straight," I warn him in a husky whisper.

And about then is when I realize that he's already completely naked.

"When did you . . ."

"About a minute before I woke you up." His grin is back, by far the widest I've ever seen him smile. "What were you saying about fuck—" I shut him up with a forceful kiss.

A desperate kiss.

The only thing more desperate than my tongue trying to claim his mouth is my hand trying to claim his dick. I wrap one hand around both of us and give a couple of hard jerks before admitting defeat. "Lube? Where's the lube?" I gasp into his mouth.

He hands me the bottle before I even finish asking. Fucker must have had it ready, just waiting for me to ask.

I pour an indiscriminate amount into my palm and start working our erections again.

A stream of half-coherent babbling falls from his lips. "Fuck, that's it. So perfect. You're so good for me . . ." reaches my ears.

Encouraged, I work my slick palm down, rolling his balls for a moment before sliding a finger against the puckered skin of his asshole.

"Yes, Devon. Fuck. I need it, love."

Maybe I don't want to shut him up, after all. I kiss his

neck, just behind his jaw, so he can keep up his litany of adoration, and slide my finger inside of him. My plan pays off. The speed of his words doubles while his coherence disappears. Now, it's just broken curse words interspersed with gasps and the occasional L-word. That last one I'm going to count as an accident until he says it to me straight on, without any distractions or extenuating circumstances. But it's still nice to hear it, even if he doesn't realize what he's saying.

The head of my cock keeps dragging along his stomach and the hair of his happy trail, and fuck, I can't wait any longer.

"Marcus, I—"

"I'm ready," he sounds as desperate as I am. "Please, fuck me," he begs.

I don't need more invitation than that. Besides, I'm going to burst if I don't get inside of him right fucking now. I press his leg up higher, hooking his calf over my arm to spread him out as far as possible and say a silent prayer of thanks as I position my head at his entrance.

I have to pause as soon as I slide in because I'm so overcome with the absolute rightness of it. The way we fit together, the way he gasps my name, the way fireworks explode behind my eyes, like all of this was preordained or something.

"Marcus," I whisper, and this time it's a reverent whisper, rather than a desperate one, and fuck, I'm pretty sure there are tears gathering on my eyelashes.

"Yes, love?"

"I love you," I tell him, then slide all the way inside of him, feeling a missing piece of my heart click into place and make me whole.

"I love you too, Devon. I want to love you, and keep you safe, and let you fuck me every day. Is that okay?"

"Yeah." I start to move in him, slow strokes, then picking up speed. "Yeah. That's okay with me."

No way I can last much longer, I fist his cock and slide my hand up and down in time to my thrusts until he's moaning loud enough to probably wake the whole house up. They'll have to get used to it. I plan on doing this every morning from now on.

With a shouted "Fuck!" he stripes both of our chests with his release, and then I'm following, falling, tumbling after him, filling him with my own come, burying my face in his neck as I moan out my orgasm.

Yeah, I think as I drift through the haze of the aftermath. *This is definitely okay with me.*

Epilogue

MARCUS - NINE MONTHS LATER

"So I guess this is really it." Jeff looks completely lost in the mostly empty room. "You guys are really moving out for good."

Devon claps him on the back with a grin. "First of all, we're all moving out. Didn't you hear that it's the end of the year? Second of all, you know as well as anyone that we've been basically living at the frat house for the past few months anyway, so it's not like anything is going to change."

"Yeah, but . . ." Jeff scratches his head and looks sad as well as lost. "It's never going to be the same again. We're never going to be able to do freshman year again."

"Thank fuck," Gloria chimes in with an eye roll. "Goodbye and fucking good riddance to this whole year and everything that came with it."

Jimmy looks like the words break him a little bit. "Really? Everything?"

"Fine." She brushes a quick kiss on his lips. "Not good

riddance to *everything*. Most things, though, I'm happy to leave in the rearview."

Devon gives me a hungry look that almost has me reaching down to adjust myself right there in front of everyone. "Yeah. There are a few things I'm happy to have come across this year."

Jeff rolls his eyes and blows out an annoyed breath. "How nice for all of you. Some of us didn't magically find our soul mate on the first day of school."

"Technically," I point out, "we all met before school started." But I'm not arguing against the soul mate thing. I never really believed they existed until Devon turned my world upside down.

"Take heart, Jeff," Bee calls in a singsong. "You're still in the best company. The rest of us are still as single as can be."

"I suppose. I just can't believe that this is actually coming to an end, you know? Even with all of the drama, and dealing with vampire politics, and facing down evil frat boys, we had some good times in this dorm. And it's all changing today."

"It's not changing that much," I argue. "You're all welcome at the house anytime, and half of you are moving in together next semester, aren't you?" I look at Jimmy for confirmation, certain he and Gloria are about to take that step.

Gloria answers for him. "Well, you're half-right. Bee and I are moving into a house off campus together, so that will stay the same."

"Oh? I thought you two"—Devon indicates Jimmy—"were officially attached at the groin these days."

Jimmy scowls. "Gloria doesn't trust me to not get her pregnant if we share a house," he mutters.

She gives him a look that speaks volumes, though I'm not sure if I'm translating it correctly.

"But I still say it's a terrible idea for the two of you to live off campus without any kind of protection."

"Well . . ."

Both girls seem to be avoiding his eyes.

"Well what?"

"Well," Bee says, "we actually will have some protection."

Jimmy narrows his eyes. "How? Who?"

"Taylor's moving in with them," Jeff supplies. "You didn't know that?"

"What?" Jimmy's disbelieving look bounces back and forth between the two girls. "You're fucking kidding me! You're living with a vampire over my dead body!" He realizes what he just said and has the decency to look ashamed. "Um. No offense?"

Devon and I look at each other. "I mean. Some offense," Devon says. "What's wrong with them living with a vampire? And Taylor? He's probably the nicest guy I've ever met."

Jimmy looks around the room for support but finds none. "Oh, come on. After everything that's happened this year, I'm supposed to trust a vampire to keep the two most important women in my life safe?"

"And this is why we didn't tell you about it," Bee brushes past him. "Let's all grab a box and finish moving this last load out, shall we?"

Devon and I stay behind as everyone else clears the last odds and ends from the dorm, Jimmy still grumbling and Jeff still bemoaning all of the changes ahead.

I catch Devon's hand and pull him toward me. "Hey. I love you," I tell him.

"I love you too. You were, hands down, the best thing to happen to me this year."

"You were the best thing to happen to me this lifetime," I say, then pull him in for a kiss before he can try to one-up me.

I'm glad we're through everything this year threw at us, but I honestly can't say I would change a moment of it.

* * *

Want to stay in touch? If you sign up here, you'll get the extra spicy short story Bound, a Berring College story featuring George, a vampire, and Neil, the human who's been pining for him since freshman year. I'll send you weekly(ish) updates about what I'm reading and writing, when new books are coming out, and what my cat has been up to lately.

Thank you! Thank you a thousand, no, a billion times, for reading this book. One of my fears each time I sit down to write is, "is anyone ever going to actually read this? Is it even worth writing it if no one is going to read it?" Which is, of course, incredibly unhelpful negative thinking. So I sit, and hope, and maybe even pray (if I'm in the right mindset) that someone—anyone—will pick up this book and actually read it and maybe even like it a little. This is the purpose of books, to be read, but also their downfall, since it will literally be impossible to read them all in one lifetime. That you would spend some of your limited time reading my book is truly touching to me.

Acknowledgments

It's an impossible task, to properly thank everyone who contributes to a book's creation. There are so many people who contribute in huge and tiny ways, and without all of those contributions, the book never makes it to the shelves.

I know, as a fact, that I will forget someone. Please accept my apologies in advance. Know that, even if your name doesn't make it in here, you are very much in my heart and my mind.

First, of course, my family. I sometimes write about horrible, toxic parents and siblings and pseudo-family members, and I want to make it very (very very very) clear that not of these toxic people are even remotely close to the real people I keep close in my real life. I am so grateful for parents who have always loved me as I am and never made me believe I needed to change or earn their love in any way. I hope everyone has someone to love them and support them unconditionally like my parents do for me. I love you both so much and I will never have enough words to tell you.

Speaking of family, my brother, who has pretty much been my partner in crime since I could walk (maybe before?) and my sister in law, who keeps him and all of us on the straight and narrow. Keep up the good fight, Alex, even when the rest of us are wild monkeys fighting against you every step of the way.

And I can't very well talk about family without talking about the Ks. Amy, maybe you remember that camp song about the two plants that grow together, and one is flowery and beautiful and one is all thorns. Well, you know which one I am, and I'm so thankful to have been able to grow up with all of the beauty and love you bring to this world.

Sean, just keep reminding me to go to bed at a reasonable time. And make the coffee. Even if you do nothing else, I would love you for those two things alone.

The whole Greek-Irish crew, who else would have welcomed me in after I made a fool of myself at our first meeting? Thank you for trying to keep me safe around bodies of water.

Big shoutout to my Between the Covers friends for keeping me sane-ish on a daily basis amidst chaos.

And to the North Texas Romance Writers, who are a large part of how I managed to publish anything at all.

Oh, and Sandra, editor extraordinaire. Thank you for all of the things you made better. I'm sorry about all the things I couldn't make better. Please, don't give up on me.

Kayla grew up in the mountains of New Mexico, where she fell in love with snow, small towns, and the idea of the redeeming power of love. Now, she lives in a big city in Texas and tries to spread the good word about romance novels wherever she goes. Kayla writes steamy romance stories about shifters, vampires, aliens, and sometimes even humans. She lives with her partner and cat, and enjoys running, playing ukulele, and watching her partner play video games.

If you want to receive a FREE bonus epilogue of Wolf Bound, if you would like monthly updates on my life and my writing, or if you want to be the first to read snippets of upcoming releases, you can find my newsletter here https://kaylabrook sauthor.com/!

I would love to hear from you, whether you want to ask questions about the books, talk about your pets, or let me know something you wish you could see in a book. Feel free to email me with any of that and more at kayla@kaylabrook sauthor.com. I hope to hear from you!

Also by Kayla Brooks

Bear Mountain Men

Saved by My Three Bears

Bear Mountain Men 1

Mated to My Three Bears

Bear Mountain Men 2 (coming 2025)

Berring College

Bound

A Berring College Short Story

Wolf Bound

Berring College 1

Blood Bound

Berring College 2

Earth Bound

Berring College 3 (coming 2025)

Keep reading for a preview of Saved By My Three Bears, available in ebook everywhere!

Saved By My Three Bears

Keep reading for a preview of the first Bear Mountain Men book, Saved By My Three Bears.

* * *

AURELIA

I am so cold. So hungry. So close to dying for good. And I can't even care anymore.

This was my coven's goal when they kicked me out. They knew I had nowhere to go and no one to turn to. They were comfortable knowing I wouldn't be their problem much longer. Vampires can be cruel that way.

I stumble through the snow. It's almost certainly too late to make any difference, but if I can just find shelter from the sun, I might be able to go into a deep sleep until I sense an opportunity to feed again. More likely I'll go into a deep sleep and slip away and never wake up. A bitter laugh rattles out of me at the thought. Slipping away in my sleep would be preferable to feeling it as the sun burns me away, at least. Besides, my family could at least get what they want. Someone should get some happiness out of this, shouldn't they?

Another bitter laugh makes me stumble and fall on my hands and knees. It's just little scrapes, but every drop of blood I lose right now brings me closer to death.

I resettle my thin sweater around me, trying to hide as much of myself as possible from the blasting sun, which is reflecting every fucking place from the knee high snow and leaving no safe places in this whole damned mountain.

I'm going to die here. I know it now, more than I knew it before. I feel the inevitability of it in my bones.

Taking the last chance that I have, I find the largest snow covered pine tree I can and burrow under its branches. I doubt it will be enough to save me, but the pain of the sun beating against me lessens immediately. Better to freeze than to burn, I think before settling into the pseudo hibernation that can keep a vampire alive almost indefinitely. The only possible way to survive this is to get fresh blood in my system.

* * *

BERNARD

I'm out on the edge of our territory when I catch the scent. I'd be able to track it easier in my bear form, but I came out here to check fences and make sure there are no hunters crossing our territory lines. Harder to do that as a bear, and a pain in the ass to switch back and forth, even if I had brought a change of clothes. No, my backpack has the essentials for fixing fences and signs, plus a canteen with water and a few granola bars in case I get hungry while I'm out here.

But that scent–faint as it is–calls to me in a way I can't ignore. My bear is already claiming it, chanting *mine, mine, mine,* before I'm even sure what I'm going towards. I am going there, whatever it is. Barrett and Bryce would probably both tell me to wait, maybe even go back and get one of them for backup. I go by my gut, though, and usually leave the thinking to them. My gut is pressing me forward, away from the big house and beyond the bits of wire that mark this part of the mountain as ours.

I find her half buried in snow beneath a pine tree. And it is a "her." My bear gives an annoying, satisfied kind of *I told you so* rumble at that. He isn't so happy when we realize that she's so cold she must be walking the edge between life and death.

"Hang on," I tell her as I dig her out and start to chafe her limbs in an attempt to get some blood flowing in her body. I don't know if she can hear me or if she's too far gone, but I have to try. "Hang on a little longer. I'm going to save you, just hang on."

I wish I'd taken one of the others with me today. They would both know what to do. What do I know about helping a girl who may be dying in the forest? I've never even seen a girl close up before. I've seen girls on TV, but not in real life. Not close enough to touch them.

I take a desperate look around the forest, but there's no one out here to help me. It's down to me.

Gathering her up as carefully as I can in my arms–gods, she's so tiny and light, like the baby birds I used to try to rescue before Barrett convinced me it's not a good idea–I start the trek back to our nearest cabin. It's just a little hunting stand, but it will give her shelter. Maybe I'll be able to warm her up there.

"Please," I barely hear her whisper. "Please."

"I'm going to help you," I promise. "Just don't die, okay? I'm going to help you."

It's agonizing, carrying her through the snow when I'm not even sure if she's still breathing. The only sign I have that she's not dead is her scent. She doesn't smell like bear–and that gives me a twitchy kind of feeling between my shoulder blades, I can tell you. She doesn't smell like death either, so I think there must be some hope. If she does die, I guess I have to dig a grave out here for her on my own.

I'm not sure the best thing to help her when I get her to the tiny cabin. It's really just four walls, a roof, a bed, and a wood burning stove. It's just for emergencies, in case one of us gets caught out here in a blizzard. Or if our work out here isn't finished and we need to camp out to get an early start. It's made for bears, though, not humans. Bears don't need heat and shelter the way this girl does.

I slide her into the sleeping bag that's unrolled on the little cot in the corner and start setting the fire. My hands are shaking so much with fear over her that I break three matches just trying to get a spark.

"Please."

The rattling voice draws me instantly to her side.

"What do you need? I'm lighting a fire to get you warm, but you have to hang on a little longer."

"Need . . . feed . . ."

"Food? I've got gran–"

"Feed," she insists, emphasizing the word and lifting her lip to reveal a long, sharp canine.

Shit. Not human. Vampire. She doesn't need granola bars. What she needs is blood, and the only blood in this cabin is in my body.

"Please," she begs again. "Feed."

I've never met a vampire in real life, just like I've never been close enough to touch a woman before. How do I know she won't drink me dry and leave me for dead? How much of my blood does she need?

No way in hell am I letting her die, though. My bear takes up its chant again. *Mine, mine, mine, mine.*

I look around frantically for a solution. Digging my

canteen out of my pack, I empty the water into the kettle. No use wasting it, right? Then I take out my multipurpose tool and don't let myself think too hard about it before slicing a neat cut across my wrist. Not deep enough that I'll be in any real danger. Shallow and careful about the tendons. I'll heal as soon as I shift, but it doesn't look like I'll get a chance to do that too soon.

Carefully, I angle my wrist over the mouth of the canteen so my blood drips into it. Is it enough? I have no idea how much she actually needs, but I have to try. Is it just my imagination that her nostrils twitched when I cut myself?

Cradling her head in my bloodied hand, I hold the canteen up to her lips and send up a prayer that this works. I can't look away as she swallows the little bit of blood I can offer, then laps at the lingering drops around the edge. The thought of me—well, part of me, my blood—being inside her has me hypnotized. I never want this to end. I want this close feeling, like I'm a part of her, like I'm necessary for her survival, to stretch forever.

"Do you need more?" I ask, but she's already fallen into a boneless, deathlike sleep.

Find the rest of Aurelia's story wherever you buy your ebooks!